PENGUIN BOOKS

GOOD FOR NOTHING

GOOD FOR NOTHING

MARIAM ANSAR

PENGUIN BOOKS

PENGUIN BOOKS

UK | USA | Canada | Ireland | Australia
India | New Zealand | South Africa

Penguin Books is part of the Penguin Random House group of companies
whose addresses can be found at global.penguinrandomhouse.com.

www.penguin.co.uk   www.puffin.co.uk   www.ladybird.co.uk

First published 2023

001

Text copyright © Mariam Ansar, 2023

The moral right of the author has been asserted

The editor and publisher gratefully acknowledge permission to reproduce
copyright material in this book.

Quotation from 'A Coworker Asks Me if I Am Sad' copyright © Brenna Twohy, 2019.
Originally published in *Swallowtail*, reprinted by permission of Button Poetry.

Quotation from 'TheBlackScholar Interviews: James Baldwin' copyright © The Black World
Foundation, reprinted by permission of Taylor & Francis Ltd, http://www.tandfonline.com
on behalf of The Black World Foundation.

Set in 10.75/15.5 pt Adobe Caslon Pro
Typeset by Jouve (UK), Milton Keynes
Printed and bound in Great Britain by Clays Ltd, Elcograf S.p.A.

The authorized representative in the EEA is Penguin Random House Ireland,
Morrison Chambers, 32 Nassau Street, Dublin D02 YH68

A CIP catalogue record for this book is available from the British Library

ISBN: 978-0-241-52207-3

All correspondence to:
Penguin Books
Penguin Random House Children's
One Embassy Gardens, 8 Viaduct Gardens, London SW11 7BW

With love for my family, Bradford, and my students – past, present, and future

'*Grief is not a feeling but a neighbourhood. This is where I come from. Everyone I love still lives here.*'
— excerpt from 'A Coworker Asks Me If I Am Sad, Still' by Brenna Twohy

'*If I love you, I have to make you conscious of the things you don't see.*'
— James Baldwin, from 'TheBlackScholar Interviews: James Baldwin'

PROLOGUE

The boy in the supermarket moves slowly between the aisles. It is early on a Saturday morning, and the reflected glass of the automatic doors shows the candyfloss pink sky above Friesly. A very sweet colour.

But the boy already knows the view like the back of his hand.

The tall, winding spire of the old cathedral, the red-brick buildings where people sleep and eat and live. The chimneys that curl with plumes of smoke on cool days like this one. And the statue of the old man with the thick beard, the wide-brimmed hat, the pigeons that continually coo at his feet. That's Sir William Barker, of course. The boy wrote an essay about him and his factories for school once. Then there are the glinting shutters of the not-yet-open Asian clothing shops. Beside them, the ramshackle barber's where Jafari Williams stands with his bad back and cuts hair. And the launderette with the peeling sign.

The sleeping cats on strips of corrugated cardboard the homeless also nap on. The skipping ropes left in the middle of the road. The green of the faraway moors.

Everything is quiet in the mornings. Not echoing with

the *rat-a-tat* of screeching wheels and fast cars, scores to settle, drug dealers, and people dying amid the deals. Everything is bathed in a rosy glow. It makes Friesly feel less like a throbbing wound and more like a heartbeat. Steady. Alive. So the boy keeps his back to the view. In the sixteen years of his life he's memorized it all. It's written on the inside of his eyelids.

He doesn't realize that one of his socks is falling lower and lower on his ankle though.

Well, the boy had made sure to tuck both of those socks inside the ends of his grey joggers when he'd woken up, slipped his sliders on, and anticipated his mum's wishes. It didn't matter to him that those socks were still wet with *wudhu* from the morning prayer. He'd headed to Mahmood's Foods – the large international supermarket out by Sir William Barker's statue – for the cereal and breakfast biscuits he knew his family loved.

But now, in the dull glow of the supermarket lights, one sock dips down his right ankle. It itches at the bone. And there is a yawn itching at the corners of the boy's mouth. He stretches it open, wide as a mile, before dashing a large box of sugary cereal into his basket. *Oh yeah*, he thinks, picking up the custard-flavoured biscuits his mum's always going on about. And then a pack of chocolate straws for his sister, some *halal* rashers for his brother. *Can't forget those.*

He makes his way past the meat counter, laden with lamb chops and mince out front, and an aisle that smells like chopped chillies in airtight packages. The boy smiles a *salaam* to the uncle at the till. He readjusts a jacket which is large and puffy for the slanty January sunlight.

'Keep the change, Uncs,' he says.

Old Qasim Mahmood doesn't stop thumbing his well-used prayer beads, the silver hairs in his beard catching in the shop's glow. He grunts a response.

The boy picks up the carrier bag full of shopping he walked down two cobbled streets for. It's pale and white, see-through and flimsy like chicken skin. It barely weighs anything for him. But the boy still exaggerates a groan as he brings it down off the loading part of the till.

The way home requires no map. Just muscle memory. The steep, winding streets, the hedges bare and dry in the winter months. He's smiling on the short walk, one of those *halal* rashers already between his teeth, a still-rosy sky up ahead. He texts his mum that he's got the goods.

What would you do without me? whooshes to her text inbox.

'Oi. What do you think you're doing out here?' whooshes into his ears.

The boy falters, teeth hitting fleshy tongue instead of rasher meat. The taste of blood floods his mouth as he faces the police officers standing in front of him. They stare Zayd Ali up and down. They repeat their question.

'You heard us. Don't act stupid. What do you think you're doing out here?'

TWO AND A HALF YEARS LATER

PART ONE: STRANGERS

featuring:

a newspaper article – an accident – a stone woman – Barker Summer Festival – spray paint – a video game – a broken washing machine – a leather wallet – the police – a running route – a barber – a piggy bank – three troublemakers – a napkin rose – the first haiku – PC Chris – aloo gobi sandwiches – jalebi – a field of grief – ice cream – a wedding portrait – a playground – an old kiss – and a homeless man

CHAPTER 1
AMIR

There's a newspaper stand outside Mahmood's Foods that's all rusted metal and creaky wire. It gets warm in the sticky heat. It's right beside the saggy cardboard boxes full of fruit, the little plastic bags you can stick the fruit in, and the bottles of cola-smelling carbonated fizzy drinks that have been there for so long they taste like supermarket dust. I learnt that the hard way.

Anyway, the important headlines for the day always get put on display on that stand. They're kept behind this dark criss-cross mesh thing that stops the newspapers from flying away in the dull breeze, and the headlines are written so big you can't miss reading them. Not that I'm into reading and books and that.

I just remember that once, a few years back, when I was thirteen, the newspaper stand had this headline on it in massive letters:

FATAL TRAFFIC ACCIDENT LEAVES LOCAL BOY, 16, DEAD

With my brother Zayd's name in the article. The local boy.

3

Even now, I don't like remembering the details of what happened to him. In my opinion, Zayd was the best brother in the world. A nice guy. Proper smart, sick at *FIFA*, and the worst singer ever. He could've gone to uni. Not for singing obviously. The guy used to try and make everything sound like Elvis after this one time when we were all going into town, and we were looking for a normal radio station in my mum's car, and he accidentally put the oldies one on, and this weird hound dog song started blaring out. We all burst out laughing. He always found excuses to make his lip go weird and go *ah-ha-huh* after that. It was so stupid. So funny.

Still, the article said there was an unnamed eyewitness who'd seen the whole thing. How Zayd died.

There was an actual person who saw the entire traffic accident. The police in their uniforms.

Zayd running into the busy street because they were after him.

The bright headlights of the Express Deliveries van with the angel's wings painted on the side. White like the snow we'd hurled at each other in the winter months, me with gloves on, him with none, just cackling like a maniac.

The lights and wings becoming blurred as the van's heavy wheels ran over his body.

Zayd's carrier bag full of biscuits and sugary cereal scattered over the tarmac. Along with one outstretched arm, a hand holding on to nothing. And his blood.

The unnamed eyewitness said it wasn't true what the police were saying. That they'd gone after Zayd, chased him down, because he was dealing drugs and transporting them beyond

Friesly. To Lowbridge, to Bramracken, to Hent, and everywhere around us. The unnamed eyewitness said it was a case of mistaken identity, that he hadn't been the one they were looking for, and Zayd must've been scared, and that was why he ran. Not because he was a drug dealer or a criminal or anything. He was just scared. He had been scared.

But there weren't any clues in the newspaper for who the unnamed eyewitness was.

There was just the name of the lady who wrote the article.

Zakiya Bhatti. *A journalist with an eye for injustice*, the little biography about her said. No picture or anything. Just that line.

Back then, I asked Qasim Mahmood – the old guy who owns Mahmood's Foods – to give us the newspaper. I didn't have any money to buy it. I just needed it. I was a kid, and I needed to show it to my mum, who kept crying at our kitchen table, and to my uncle Nadeem, who kept patting her shoulder and looking off into the distance, like he couldn't stand seeing her cry at all.

Fiza, my sister, was too young to know what the newspaper article meant.

She was nine, just tall enough to reach my waist.

I don't remember if she even realized Zayd was dead or not. She just kept trudging around the empty silence of our house, asking us if we wanted to watch *Gladiator*, that old movie with Russell Crowe, for the hundredth time. Looking back, Zayd probably shouldn't have shown her it so young. But us lot were always climbing trees, making swords out of branches, fighting together in the colosseum that was our back garden.

Qasim Mahmood gave me that newspaper. He didn't say anything when he passed it to me. He didn't even look at me properly. I thought it was like my uncle and my mum all over again. I don't think people like looking at other people when they're crying.

'Ma,' I remember I called out when I got home. She was sitting on the sofa, with Fiza curled up asleep next to her, the both of them facing a blank TV screen. No *Gladiator* on. No nothing.

'Ma, look.' I shoved the newspaper in her face. 'Look, this says Zayd wasn't doing anything wrong –'

She kept staring at the blank screen.

'It says someone saw he wasn't doing anything wrong.'

She moved the newspaper away from her face.

'Look –'

She moved the newspaper away again.

'Look –'

There were tear stains on her cheeks. Like when rain goes down a window sill and later on you can still see where it dripped down.

'Amir,' she said, and I saw the corners of her lips turn down and go wobbly, 'I'm tired today. Too tired to read. Will you make us a cup of tea? You always make the best tea.'

I went into the kitchen and opened the cupboard for teabags. Sugar. A dash of fridge-cold milk. I left Mum's mug on the table because I knew her hands got too shaky to hold it when she started crying. She took my hand when I passed by though, and sat me down, and she held me by her side until my cheeks were dry and the rest of me warm with sleep. Her tea stayed untouched. Warm for a bit. Then cold.

I waited for a long time after that.

I waited for her to stop being too tired to read the newspaper article I kept at the bottom of my underwear drawer in mine and Zayd's room. I thought Fiza would be old enough one day, and we could find out who the unnamed eyewitness was together, and then everyone would stop muttering all these lies about our brother.

'He deserved it,' people said behind our backs. And with their eyes when they looked at us joking around the shops in town, and with their mouths when me and Fiza were late out of school because of detention. 'He was guilty. Good for nothing. A criminal, a thug. Otherwise he wouldn't have run away in the first place.'

I checked the newspaper stand outside Mahmood's Foods for more articles by Zakiya Bhatti every day. Three hundred and sixty-five days a year.

When it was hot out. When it was cold out. When the Asian clothing shops got new stock and threw away the old weird-wigged mannequins in last season's *choori dar*. When Wash 'n' Wear's creaky old painted sign peeled an extra layer off in the heat. When my mates got us rotisserie chicken from inside Mahmood's Foods and we ate it together, trying to avoid oily stains on our school ties and blazers, licking our fingers by the pavement, laughing at nothing.

I shivered in my parka in January, looking at the newspaper stuck behind the criss-cross frame.

I felt cooler in my basketball shorts in June, squinting at headlines across the tarmac. I looked up Zakiya Bhatti's name online, too. Tried to find a phone number or something. But nothing came up except a press profile with an email address. I messaged it a lot. I never got a reply.

Eventually my mum didn't cry at the kitchen table any more. She stopped letting her tea go cold. But she found new reasons to be tired. Stuff that was as hard as our dad leaving us for a *gori* and a new family, but never harder than Zayd dying.

Fiza caught up, as well. She knew Zayd was dead.

But it was still just me checking the newspaper stand outside Mahmood's Foods for Zakiya Bhatti's name. Finding nothing.

'Oi.'

'Oi, what? Fiza, I'm older than you, it's my sixteenth birthday in, like, a month. You can't talk to me like that.'

I could practically hear her rolling her eyes on the phone. 'Can you chill out please? Stop acting like you're the boss of me.' And then, in response to me saying nothing: '*Fine.*' Fiza made her voice even girlier than it already was. 'Amir *paapu* . . .'

I swear I cringed so bad at her calling me that sappy brotherly nickname I missed a goal in *FIFA*. And then my mates' cackling was so loud in my headset it didn't even matter that I wasn't wearing it properly.

'Look, Fiza –' my grip on my phone got tighter, my fingers struggling over the cracked screen – 'just tell me what you want already. Unless it's something for Uzair. Then I don't care.'

I really hated our cousin. He lived next door. He was older than us, always did *salaam* to our mum, and always had different car fresheners in his pockets. Mint, pine tree, sandalwood ... Old-man smells. He was always trying to get me to go for a drive with him in his banged-up car as well, get desserts from Long Road out by the river. Always acting like he was driving a Lamborghini Gallardo or something. *Kasmey*, he was a proper beg.

'What the hell, Amir,' Fiza moaned down my ear. 'You're so mean to him. At least he's helping out at Nishaan right now! Unlike some people ...'

I knew she was pacing up and down in the back room where we stocked the frozen samosas and pakoras, waving her hands about as she told me off. My almost-teenage sister, the perfect little madam, doing the first extra waiting shifts of the summer at our mum's restaurant for fun. I would've had to do those waiting shifts at Nishaan too, but I'd just done my GCSEs, so I was allowed to chill out for two weeks before it was back to being just like her and stupid Uzair and his little brothers. Everyone was always running between packed-out tables, taking a billion orders for parathas, five types of *salan*, samosa chaat, paninis, wraps, burgers, chips, and don't forget the mint sauce.

'Alright, listen.' I imagined Fiza cocking her hip. 'Mum's saying can you take the bins out? She forgot it's bin day tomorrow.'

'Fine.'

'Also, can you shower? I bet the living room stinks of boy sweat.'

It was my turn to roll my eyes. 'Oh yeah?' I said. 'I bet you lot stink of *salan.*'

I hung up before she could shout at me. Because Fiza probably did stink! Everyone who even took one step in Nishaan ended up reeking of garlic and onions and a really good curry. It was the curse of having a great chef like our Mohamed.

I told my mates I had to go after that. I'd already embarrassed Manchester United that game, barely even gotten us any goals. They were all shouting at me to stay on, but the bins were looking a bit rank outside, and the living room did smell a bit disgusting in the jammy afternoon heat, and my mum would definitely kill me if I left it like that.

Lace curtains letting no breeze in. A plate of cut-up apples going brown on the table.

So I held my breath and took the bins out. I swatted away bare flies by the outside kerb. I got some shade though. That was because of the overgrown hedges our right and left neighbours still hadn't cut. Nearly all of them were sitting outside anyway, enjoying the hot weather, listening to whatever random Bollywood song the ice-cream man had for his van that week, or to the crunch of worn tyres that meant the fruit-and-veg guy was coming round. Bare green chillies, potatoes, tomatoes, garlic bulbs for only a quid. The old aunties had been doing the same thing every day for weeks, ever since school broke up for GCSEs. They sat on the warm stone walls, fanning their faces with their dupattas, watching their kids as they played cricket using old crates for stumps, talking about everyone and everything while peeling potatoes or chopping ladies' fingers for *pindiya.*

Including us lot always being late putting our bins out. But that was better than some of the other stuff they said about us Ali kids.

I watched this lanky kid tell his little brother to 'run man, what are you doing, start running', when he hit the ball proper far. The little brother got so confused, hearing that. Like he'd somehow forgotten the rules for cricket. Then he started running, a split second too late, with this big toothy grin, all bright on his face, and the lanky one started cheering, with the same toothy grin, their cricket bats dragging loudly behind them.

I started smiling, too. Just watching them, from the shade. Just seeing them together. Until I wasn't any more. Smiling, I mean. I went back inside after that.

'. . . He may have passed away in 1819,' the TV blared as I opened all the living-room windows and started spraying air freshener everywhere, 'but Sir William Barker's legacy of helping to end child exploitation in millwork is part of Friesly's history. The Barker Summer Festival will return in August, but you can discover more details about the man himself in a new series, starting tonight at nine p.m . . .'

I don't know what it was about hearing that same name we always got taught about in school, and seeing those film shots of Sir William Barker's bearded stone statue in the middle of town, but it really pissed me off. It was all we ever heard about: Friesly, the birthplace of Sir William Barker. Friesly, the small town in West Yorkshire where the old mills that little kids used to work in still stand, and where there's a little train station that random old people like to come and take photos of.

That's north Friesly of course. Us lot, we're south Friesly.

And sure, there's nice streets for shopping here. Bits of green fields and too-steep hills that make for good leg workouts. Architecture for days. You can't hate a place like this unless you love it, too. Because there are also druggy gangs running the streets in south Friesly. People getting stabbed on street corners, turning everywhere we walk red. Addicts and crackheads stooping to knock on windows of stopped cars at traffic lights for change. Kids dying in traffic accidents because the police scared them so bad – and killed them.

Anyway, I don't get it. I never have. Why some people get to be remembered so long after they've died, with a statue and a big song and dance every few minutes and some people don't. Not in the same way. Not at all.

My mum and sister were all chatter at dinnertime that night:

'Amir –' Fiza's elbows were on the table again, crashing into her plate of lamb biryani – 'you should've seen this guy eat all these gulab jamun today. Innit, ma? He was worse than Amir! He kept going even when I thought he was about to stop!'

'Well,' I said, 'some of us are growing boys, not shrimpy little gets like you.'

'Who you calling a shrimp, you stupid cheeseburger?'

I burst out laughing. 'Cheeseburger? Who taught you that one, your best mate Juveria?'

Mum sighed when we started aiming kicks at each other: 'Wouldn't it be nice to eat some lamb *biryani* with my kids in peace?' she moaned to the heavens. 'I think so! I think it would be nice!'

We helped her clear the table afterwards though. We wiped everything down, turned the TV on, and the kettle. I showered. Fiza shouted at me for not cleaning the shower afterwards. I shouted at her for thinking it was fine to shout at me in the first place. But I reread the newspaper article again, halfway through taking out a new pair of boxers.

I thought of my brother, and the angel's wings on that van, and the carrier bag spilling the groceries out on the side of the road.

Downstairs, the TV was playing that advertisement about Sir William Barker again.

The next day, I took the spray paint cans we were supposed to be saving for fixing the paint job on Uzair's banged-up car out of our garage. I thought that the bus shelter opposite the statue of Sir William Barker looked like a good spot for Zayd's name. With the sun warming it up on the other side, stopping it from getting cold.

CHAPTER 2
EMAN

'I'm telling you –' Farida aunty crossed her arms over her long black jilbab, her back as curved as her long hooked nose – 'if the mosque committee gave us more money then maybe we'd be able to drum up more publicity for these community projects you keep bringing up. Hmm, Maariyah? Don't you think? I've heard these days they're putting more money into hosting *halal* speed-dating events than into fundraising for the homeless. *Astaghfirullah*, like speed-dating can even be *halal*.'

'I don't know, Farida.' Balqis aunty winked at me from across the freshly mopped chequerboard floor in Wash 'n' Wear. 'Maybe if you'd tried it earlier, you wouldn't be single at sixty-four.'

Steam seemed to rise from Farida aunty's flared nostrils. 'What did you just say, Balqis?'

My nani looked hurriedly at me. Old Maariyah Malik was immediately desperate to hush her best friends' squabbling, their swearing in multilingual tongues. But two pairs of bony fists and a billion insults about 'overgrown moustaches' and 'looking like a donkey' were already flying in the middle of the launderette.

Nani was really good at distracting Farida aunty and Balqis aunty though – in those days, always with a reference to the benefits of charity work, a phone tree, gathering donations for the homeless.

She had a tiny stub of a pencil in her hand, and her big Nokia phone nestled between her shoulder and her cheek.

'*Acha meri gal sunno!*' her crackly voice bellowed. 'Listen to what I have to say! Are we telling people to donate their unwanted things to make the mosque look better? No! We're doing it because we know the homeless need blankets and food and the things we take for granted!'

The list of necessities, along with who would supply them, that she was always writing down on the back of an old receipt was simple and clear:

So-and-so was down to drop off toothpaste.

Her cousin had a few jumpers she no longer wore.

His brother-in-law was sure there were a few dented cans of tuna he no longer needed at his takeaway on the outskirts of town.

And deodorant.

Dried mango slices and pruney-looking raisins for snacking on.

Shoelaces and hair ties. Soap. Leave-in shampoo.

These things always needed to be chased up though. These people had to be prodded into remembering their capacity for goodness. And Nani never minded doing the prodding. Even when it was the kindred spirits she'd gathered by her side since childhood that she had to prod.

'Take it back!' Farida aunty yelled now, about that comment regarding her dating history.

'Why?!' Balqis aunty said. 'I just spoke the truth!'

'Yes, and God loves the truth!' Nani agreed, her Nokia still nestled under her ear, the eyes behind her large googly glasses squinting at a number she'd written down just yesterday. 'God loves when we are kind to our brothers and sisters in Islam, too! So why don't we apologize, hmm? All of us! It'll be fun!'

I had a different idea of fun though.

I just ried to focus on the game I was playing on my phone. The intricacies of *Ball*, Level 27, always making my eyes go funny with concentration.

But I couldn't help the smile taking over my face listening to all of this.

And I could tell that Nani was trying to stifle the laughter coming out from under her command of our Mirpuri language, too.

Even if she was trying to act all busy and solemn and serious. I could always tell when she was close to cracking. Her smile always turned her eyes into little crescent moons.

'And you call yourself a Muslim,' Farida aunty huffed at Balqis aunty. Then she busied herself with tugging her black *dupatta* tighter around her head. 'Exposing other people's flaws like this, laughing at other people's flaws like this . . .'

Her grimace was already disappearing though. Farida aunty's rage disappeared completely when Balqis aunty started pulling at her arms, when Nani searched for a non-existent dimple in her gaunt cheek.

'Don't you know, Farida?' My grandma cackled, her head thrown back to reveal the silver of her plaited hair. 'You should by now. We only love to tease.'

This was a usual weekday in the summer holidays for me. The aunties' arguments in Wash 'n' Wear, the rasp of my nani's language, the sunlight drifting in through the overhead windows, the dry street dirt that mingled with a fresh laundry-powder breeze . . .

It was all as much of a constant as the bright sounds and twinkly lights of *Ball*, leaving squiggles and shapes on the backs of my eyelids.

As the sound of my mum's car, crunching into the gravel of our driveway when she was finished with her evening nursing shifts at Friesly General Infirmary.

As the coloured-in GCSE revision posters for science and maths still hanging on the rough wallpapered walls of the bedroom I shared with Nani.

Beside the drawings and doodles of my favourite video game characters, of course. Sonic, Mario and Tails. Tails, who Nani especially loved for looking like a particularly happy cat she'd had in the village of her youth. '*Mano*,' she sometimes hummed fondly at that sketch while standing by our big dresser, rubbing half of the strong-smelling green tub of Vaseline into her wrinkled skin.

'Ah!' I yelped, watching my phone screen light up with another level defeated. Level 28, winking and blinking and disappearing in front of me. 'Ah!' My trainers tapped a rhythm against the chequerboard floor. 'I did it!' I looked for Nani's eyes. 'I did it!'

I'd never gotten that far in *Ball* before. People on the forums online said even getting past Level 20 was impressive.

'Well done!' Nani beamed at the sight of my giggling face.

She offered me a thumbs-up that felt as warm as the gold wedding bangles on her wrist. And even though there was all this distance between us – the silhouette of the squabbling aunties, and the sound of customers on the weathered stoop beneath the peeling Wash 'n' Wear sign – I gave her a thumbs-up back.

Pretty soon all the usual faces were dragging their bin bags full of washing from the flats south of the river and Nani and the aunties were ready to greet them. Smiles for the tired nods, small talk for the change in coppers. A helping hand for the stained pushchairs, aching backs, sleepless eyes, hungry happy kids.

Azrah Bhatti aunty was there, too. But she was a lot richer than our regulars. She lived north of the river. That was where the water ran clear, the pavements were swept regularly, blossom trees dropped their pretty pink petals, and the buses always came on time.

'Don't forget, Eman,' Nani said as she grinned in the face of a gummy little toddler, 'washing machine number twelve is your responsibility.'

'Hmm?' My thumbs were flying over Level 28. Soon to be Level 29. 'Um, *jee*, Nani.'

Her walking stick sounded far away in seconds, her mouth already grumbling in response to whatever Azrah aunty was saying about her apparently very expensive clothes and our apparently very rough handling of them.

Washing machine number twelve was a running joke to all of us inside the launderette anyway. We'd heard so many warnings about it, ever since Nani had decided to take over Wash 'n' Wear's maintenance at a Friesly South council meeting, and the aunties decided to follow along, and I had to anyway – as my grandma's only granddaughter.

Old washing machine number twelve is prone to errors, the old stories went. Old washing machine number twelve is completely beyond repair.

We only used it if we really needed to.

On hot days and in heatwaves, like the one we were stuck in that summer. All these sweaty sweltering months, with no breeze rustling the drying leaves outside, and busy worker bees resting lazily on the warm stone walls, dehydrated and dying on the kerbs. Mouths swallowing air that was as dry as our breaths. Wash 'n' Wear got really busy at those times. Everyone came in with double loads as they didn't have to spend money on the dryers. They could just hang their delicates up on the twisted washing lines they propped up with broomsticks in their gardens or on the latches outside their tower block flat windows.

Still, you could only put a little bit of laundry detergent inside machine number twelve. Just enough of the Brand New Day one, so it wouldn't bubble over completely and drip foam all over the floor.

I think I was only putting in a little bit when the sign for Level 29 came up.

I mean, I dropped the detergent, I was so happy. I danced a bit, waggling my arms and legs around, almost skidding on the quickly spreading cream spill. But I recovered quickly. No one saw.

I thought the amount of Brand New Day I'd put in was fine.

I dropped a tissue on the spill.

And I figured I hadn't cracked my head open on the floor, and that was the more important thing. Or, at least, that's what Nani would've said was the most important thing.

'Maariyah, you promise you'll be careful, won't you?' Azrah aunty said distantly, in her usual busybody tone. 'With our wedding clothes? They're imported from my mother-in-law's favourite *bazaar* in Karachi. They won't be in shops here until at least next year . . .'

I knew Nani hated that tone as well. Nani thought Azrah aunty didn't really need the washing machines in Wash 'n' Wear. Nani often said that people like Azrah aunty took up space that other people needed more than they did.

'We have seven weddings to attend this summer – including that really big one at Nishaan – and dozens of stains on these newly imported fabrics, and not a single one of them properly washed. Not just my fabrics either, Maariyah.' She looked behind herself at the silhouettes of her tired waiting daughters. 'I think we're really in need of some help.'

'M-hmm,' Balqis aunty said cynically, looking Azrah aunty's silky *dupatta* – and the poorly dyed yellow hair poking out from under it – up and down. 'I think you really need some help, too.'

Nani ignored this comment, promising to do her best for the woman. Behind Balqis aunty's snickering, Farida aunty shook her head in disappointment. Then all the grown-ups started talking about the inconvenience of a terrible stain, and embroidery that needed a 'soft touch', and these fabrics needing to only be washed in lukewarm water so they wouldn't shrink and be ruined when they were sewn into suits.

Nani glanced at me from behind her googly glasses as she steered Azrah aunty towards the bench in the middle of Wash 'n' Wear. It was only for a split second. But I knew what the warm brown glow of her eyes meant.

It was the same way she used to look at me when I didn't want to go to primary school some mornings, after the first time I was tripped up from behind – knocked right in the fleshy back of my knee – for being a little slow to answer my name on the register.

'For being new to this town that knows everyone and everything inside it by heart,' Nani had said about the bullying. 'For being different to the rest of the kids.'

Mum had sighed extra hard after hearing about the burning sensation in my face, the bruises on my legs. The seconds that felt like hours as I stood alone, surrounded by bodies that were too busy with playground games to ask if I wanted to join in.

Nani said it was only a matter of time before the kids at school would get used to me. She said one day no one would be able to tell the difference between a family like ours and a family native to Friesly. Even if all a family like ours knew was rejection and the road that led us away from the punches my dad used to throw at my mum.

'You shouldn't promise her things like that,' I once heard

Mum say after an evening shift at the hospital, when the dryness of my throat had beckoned me to come down for a glass of water.

Nani had shifted her bad leg, making the leather sofa stretch. 'Your husband promised bigger things to you, didn't he?' I watched her shadow stretch out as she touched a healing bruise by my mum's hairline. Heard the wince of pain.

'He promised them to all of us. And we still believed them. I want Eman to have a hope that serves her better than that *soorna* – that pig – did.'

I decided to trust my grandma. I kept going back to school. I believed in the warmth of her brown eyes, her shining belief that there was something in me – in all of us Malik women – that someone could like some day.

So when she glanced at me in the Wash 'n' Wear that day, I was happy to go and speak to Azrah aunty's daughters, Noor and Juveria. Juveria was really little, after all. Eleven years old, and wandering around the launderette, weaving around people counting their change and laughing at the skid marks on a stranger's dirty undies. And Noor was in my form at school. She was fifteen like me. It would have been rude to let her stand behind her mum, on her phone, all alone and silent. Especially because we were friends.

Well, Noor's best friend was this girl with sparkly eyes and a lip-glossed grin called Tahmina Begum. But Noor and Tahmina would always wave at me – big-armed and giggling to themselves – when they saw me playing games on my phone in the corridor, fist-pumping the air in silent victory.

I put my phone in the back pocket of my jeans as I approached Noor in the launderette. I tried to calm the nervous flutter of my heart. 'Hi,' I said.

The raised fingers of her thumbs stood poised over her phone screen.

'Oh!' I exclaimed. My voice got all thick and jumpy when I was excited. 'Do you play games on your phone, too? Have you got *Ball*? I know everyone says that it's really hard, but –'

Noor's eyes were dark and coated with mascara. She looked me up and down. 'No,' she said, laughing. 'I don't play games on my phone.'

'R-right.' I laughed too. 'You must be texting or something.'

'Yeah.' She didn't look up from her phone this time. 'Or something.'

I cleared my throat, stuck for what to say next. She looked so pretty, leaning by the wall, her bracelets dangling all delicately on her wrists. I fidgeted with the plastic bands on mine.

'Were you talking about *Ball*?' Juveria piped up from behind us, all missing teeth and a too-long fringe. 'I play that! What level are you on?'

I glanced at Noor. I tried really hard not to sound too proud of myself. 'Twenty-nine.'

Juveria's eyes got even wider. 'No way.'

She started clinging to my arm, dragging down my hoodie sleeve as I fought to get my phone back out of my pocket. It was hard not to smile at her mouth turning into a perfect circle when she saw my phone screen.

'*Baji*,' Juveria said slowly, calling me sister because she'd definitely forgotten my name – even if she did come to ours for mosque-house with Nani every weekday. 'That's sick!'

I beamed at Juveria. Noor rolled her eyes in front of us. I stopped beaming. I rolled my eyes too.

'I guess,' I said. Noor had her arms crossed over her chest. I folded mine the same way. 'If you're eleven.'

Noor laughed again. This time, it was a real throw-your-head-back laugh, her pretty eyes dancing as she did. That didn't seem to bother Juveria, though. She just shrugged and started racing around Wash 'n' Wear with the energy of someone Nani would've described as a *janglee* – a wild person.

'Hey, you wanna see something actually cool, Ehsan?' Noor said.

She said it so confidently I almost forgot that wasn't my name. Noor shoved her phone in my face.

'Check it out. I literally got in so much trouble for this. My mum took my phone off me for, like, a whole day. She said I shouldn't put my face up on the internet, but come on. Everyone puts their face on their profiles. What does she want me to have anyway? One of those weird cartoon animal icons?'

The cartoon monkey icon I used for everything flashed loudly inside my head. I didn't use it because I thought it was cool or anything. I didn't put my face online because I didn't want the government stealing my data. It was the same reason I covered my webcam with sticky tape and only searched about the Illuminati in a secret browser.

'Don't I look cool?' Noor waved her phone even closer to my face. 'You can say it, y'know. I look cool.'

A filtered photo of her revealed red lip gloss and a very proud pout on her lips, as she perched on a window sill that looked bigger than any window sill in my house. I wondered what was more dangerous – the government's eyes on mine, or a gaze as beautiful as Noor's easily was.

'You do,' I said. 'You look really cool.'

Noor smiled. Just this quick, cat-like thing. I thought about telling her my name was Eman and not Ehsan while I had her attention, but she was back to typing on her phone in seconds.

Then her mum was calling her over – Juveria squabbling and kicking, but tucked firmly under her shoulder – and Azrah aunty started bidding everyone a goodbye that carried the threat of not messing up her and her daughters' future partywear.

'See you soon!' Nani smiled as she waved them off over the cobbles. 'Give my *salaam* to the rest of your family!'

'You lazy rich people,' Balqis aunty muttered through gritted teeth as she waved, too. 'You should focus more on fixing your own washing machine instead of coming over here and taking advantage of these ones! They're not really for you!'

'Now, Balqis,' Nani said, scolding her once the Bhattis were all the way around the cobbled corner. 'You know they can't use it right now, not after little Juveria shoved all of that toilet paper in there and proved how smart she is, clogging both toilets in their house and the washing machine in one day . . .'

'How could I forget?' Balqis aunty grumbled. 'They're undiscovered geniuses, aren't they, those Bhatti girls?'

'Noor's predicted to get all Level nines in her GCSEs, after all,' Zainab aunty said, mimicking Azrah aunty's usual speech. Everyone in town knew that one already. 'She's going to be famous some day, just like her journalist cousin.'

That was what Noor and Tahmina and our friends on our lunch table always talked about. Growing up. Getting rich. Getting to be on TV. I could understand it though. They were beautiful. Beautiful people want everyone to know about their beauty.

'*Challo*, Eman.' Balqis aunty turned to me, jolting me out of my thoughts. 'Let's hope you do just as well. Results Day isn't so far away. It'll be August before you know it.'

Suddenly I remembered all the exam papers I'd struggled to finish. The sunlit chequerboard floor of the launderette and the distinct smell of the soapy-clean Brand New Day laundry detergent turned into the peeling paint and the stifling sweaty warmth of my school's exam hall in an instant.

'Oh, Eman never has anything to worry about!' Nani's warm hand rested on my shoulder again. Her smile turned her eyes into crescent moons again. 'Except trying her best, of course.'

Machine number twelve jerked unsteadily behind us. It wailed and wept as it spun its cycle. Thick white bubbles dripped ceaselessly from the tray compartment.

'Yes,' Farida aunty said unhelpfully. She pointed directly at the foam. 'And that.'

*

Only a little bit of laundry detergent. You should only put a little bit of the Brand New Day laundry detergent inside machine number twelve. Just enough, so it wouldn't bubble over.

After all, old washing machine number twelve is prone to errors. Old washing machine number twelve is completely beyond repair.

I thought I'd done that right, followed all of the instructions, the ones that had been drummed inside my head ever since that very first Friesly South council meeting.

But there I was, standing in this sea of whiteness, my trainers slipping and sliding all over the place, as Farida aunty yelled at me for not knowing what 'a little' really was, and I couldn't remember exactly how much I'd put in.

'It was a cupful! No, wait! Half a cup ... Or was it really a cupful ...?' My fingers tapped confusedly at my bottom lip. 'Oh, but then I cleared another level in *Ball*, didn't I? And Noor came in, and I went to say hi, and I spilled some beforehand, and ...'

'Eman, you should really know better by now!' The aunties roared their varying protests in a little leather-loafer-wearing circle.

'It was an easy mistake!' Nani got in between them. 'You can't blame her, the machine is broken anyway!' She glared at all of the aunties in turn, daring them to say anything else. And then, in her heavy accented English, to our customers:

'Sorry, everybody! Mistake! Tomorrow will be better! Don't worry, tomorrow we'll be back to normal!'

Our regulars started grumbling and groaning as they pocketed their change, making their palms smell like pennies.

My stomach dropped to the floor seeing nearly all of them rush outside, where the cobbles were dry, and sunlit, and nothing smelled quite so strongly of soap.

Their pushchairs, trundling frustratedly over the moss-covered floor.

Little kids with their morning's breakfast still stuck on their chins, trailing after them.

'I'm sorry,' I said, knowing the launderette would have to shut early because of me. 'I'm really, really sorry, Nani.'

I could feel the panic climbing up my throat, the blood rushing hurriedly around my body.

Deep in the darkness of my childhood, voices as angry as the colour red yelled in the night. I sat on my bed, hearing the thunder of my parents' voices, and fists meeting fleshy skin. I cried silent tears as the volume got louder, and not even Nani's hands over my ears could block out the sounds of another argument.

My grandma shoved her handbag inside my soapy, sodden arms. Her cracked leather wallet, her phone, her stub of a pencil.

'We'll deal with this. Why don't you go to Mahmood's Foods? Buy yourself a treat, hmm? For doing so well in your game, hmm? Level twenty-nine, you said! Wow!'

I felt my face flood with heat, eyes prickling with tears.

'Go.' Nani smiled at me. Gave me a little nudge. 'Go.'

There was a real strength to the way she urged me on my way to Mahmood's Foods. A real sweetness to how she looked at me, whispered wisely, and let go of my sleeve. So there was nothing tethering me to her any more. Except for the pull my nani seemed to find with almost everyone. Something about her gaze and wit and wisdom, soothing us all in an instant.

'It's OK,' she'd insisted, wiping my face with her *dupatta*. 'Don't worry, Eman. It's just a mistake. Nothing to worry about. Silly little mistake, hmm?'

'Nothing wrong with you. You're prone to errors. But you're not completely beyond repair.'

I didn't know if I believed her. And I still felt guilty when I stood in the air con Qasim Mahmood had installed everywhere in the supermarket, no weird leaking washing machine in sight, barely any people at all.

My eyes boring holes into a fashion magazine that offered up a free tube of red lip gloss. The skin beneath my eyelashes rubbed raw from crying. My hijab a little messy around my face.

It was always intimidating shopping in Mahmood's Foods anyway. Nani and the aunties had told me lots of times that Qasim uncle had once been one of the wiriest kickboxers in the world, an almost-gold medallist, a fierce southpaw. So he wasn't the kind of old man to cross. His white beard and pale hazel eyes weren't a sign of weakness.

Neither was the big wall of banned customers he was always adding to at the front of the supermarket. Photograph upon photograph of unruly faces, of kicked-out adults, and kids I crossed paths with at school every day.

Still, I would take the bored nod he gave my awkward *salaam* over a leaky, foamy washing machine any day.

Gosh, I was so stupid. How could I not have noticed how much detergent I was putting in?

Qasim uncle scanned the Mars bars and Crunchies I'd put on the conveyor belt in silence. He shoved the fashion magazine with the free red lip gloss I'd been mindlessly staring at on the conveyor belt, too.

'Just buy it,' he grumbled, his fingers so quick over his prayer beads. 'I know how much you want it. And I can't sell it now anyway. Other people will be able to feel your eyes on it.'

That didn't make any sense to me. But I knew better than to argue. I bought the magazine, even though Balqis aunty would've sucked in her teeth and called Qasim uncle a cheating *kutha* – a cheating dog – for doing that, and Nani and Farida aunty would've pretended not to agree.

But that red lip gloss had looked nice on Noor. Everything looked nice on Noor, and Tahmina, and the girls they hung around with.

So I peeled the little plastic tube away from the magazine. And I tried it on my lips on the walk back to the launderette. I thought I could just wipe it off if I didn't like it. Definitely before I got back to Wash 'n' Wear and Nani and the aunties saw it.

And when I put it on – slowly, my hands shaking as I looked into a shop window – I thought it didn't look too bad. Not at all. I couldn't pout like Noor. No. And if I smiled everyone could see the two slightly large front teeth I always thought made me look all weird. But the lip gloss didn't look too bad if I kept my mouth shut, if I didn't fuss too much with the dark of my hijab.

'Oi!' A boy's voice interrupted my moment of vanity, making me jump out of my skin. 'Eman! Eman Malik!'

Amir Ali, who went to my school, was standing on the other side of the road with a girl called Kemi Adebayo.

She waved me over. 'You're in our form, right? Eman!'

'Yeah, you got that shout-out in Rewards Assembly for being good at art!'

'Over here!'

I looked around, I was so surprised.

I didn't know they were friends. Kemi, with her two fluffy buns and perfect flicked-up eyeliner, who always took every PE lesson so seriously. And Amir, with the smirk and the shameless eyes, who held the record for getting the most detentions.

I didn't know they knew my name either.

Honestly, I started thinking maybe there was another Eman Malik among the humming flies, the glinting high-street shopfronts. But there was no one else Kemi and Amir could've been waving at from the shade of a tired bus shelter.

Her in her running shorts. Him in the dark logo-bearing cap he always wore for deliveries.

The bike that I'd seen Amir sometimes use to get food around for his family's restaurant lay near his slightly scuffed Nikes. It was white, with spinning wheels. It looked like it must've been propped up, warm, by the already-warm bus-shelter glass, and had fallen down in some mysterious rush.

I mean, it was mysterious until I saw the metal spray paint cans keeping Kemi and Amir company. They knocked against their ankles as they kept calling my name, louder than the strangely silent roads around us, the light wind teasing at the weeds growing between the pavement slabs.

Kemi and Amir took turns glancing at the arrivals and departures board behind them as well. It was like there was something way more interesting on it than when the next bus was coming in from all the usual neighbouring stops: Lowbridge, Chealme's Way, Burnside, Yeamwood, Allingley, Bramracken, Hent.

My stomach jumped around as I walked over to them. My palms slick with sweat. A name I sort of recognized dripped blue spray paint down the streaky glass. ZAYD ALI, in sharp, spiky handwriting, bright as the boiling metal of the shelter.

'Kemi thinks I should've wrote it neater,' Amir said. He had this way of talking that was really, really quick. And a voice that was as rough as a cough. 'What do you think? I mean, it's not like I wanted her opinion in the first place. She just gave it. But –'

'Well, I was just saying.' Kemi chewed a stick of bubblegum beside him. She fussed a bit with her edges. Patted them down on her forehead. 'You know how it is. When things look proper, the police don't do anything about them. You know, if they look like they're supposed to be there –'

'Alright, so, what? I should've written it in handwriting? I should've made the Y all fancy?'

Kemi rolled her eyes. She was taller than Amir. She took the spray paint can he was shaking and looped over the Y like we'd all been taught to do in primary school.

'There. It looks better now, don't you think?'

There was a moment of silence as Amir inspected her handiwork. Hand on his jaw, expert-style.

'Nah, it looks shit. Forget it. Forget you lot, it looks shit.'

'Amir, it's fine! Innit, Eman? It looks fine! Nice, even.'

I nodded. I couldn't believe they were both talking to me. 'Yeah. Yeah, it looks really good.'

'See?' Kemi grinned at Amir. She handed me the spray paint. 'Eman'll fix it even more if you want. She's good at art.'

I smiled at her. Kemi felt like the sun. Our year's golden girl.

'Nah.' Amir shook his head just as I pressed down on the nozzle. 'It doesn't matter. Leave it.'

But a hiss of blue paint came out and decorated the pavement anyway, right by my shoes, their canvas material a bit splattered, as Kemi asked Amir if he was really sure, and a part of me wondered if they wanted my opinion on that too, and Amir started nodding yeah, yeah, *kasmey*, yeah.

All the while, a police car was creeping around the corner. Its lights flashing, wailing dully in the daylight, its lazy shape completely unmistakable.

Suddenly we were all yelling and swearing and starting to leg it, fast as we could, out of the way like bugs.

But that police car's wheels kept pace with my running, with my sweating face. I could practically feel the grin forming over that officer's mouth. The light in her carefully watching eyes. Even though I was doing my best not to look at her. Even though I was only focusing on the heavy thump of my own footsteps, Kemi and Amir's slightly faraway figures, the smack of my laces against the kerb, the lump in my throat.

'Oh come on,' the officer yelled through the cracked-open window. 'There's no need to run, is there?'

I was so scared. But I only had to look at the spray paint on Kemi and Amir, and on my own palms, to know she was right. We were already caught.

CHAPTER 3
KEMI

It wasn't supposed to be like this. Not for me.

Ask anyone, I'm not the kind of person to get stopped by the police in the first week of the summer holidays. I mean, stopped because I was doing something wrong.

I know that the police love to stop us even if we're doing everything right, even if we're perfect, and more than perfect, so maybe it's just me being naive.

But growing up, when I heard warnings from my uncle Jafari and his loyal Clean Cutz customers about Black people getting stopped for walking weird or laughing too loudly, I always imagined someone else getting stopped. Jafari himself. Or his gang of buddies. Chris and Fady and that lot. Not me. Not me, with my good manners, my excellent report cards, my quick tongue, and how good I am at styling everyone's hair. Even better than Uncle Jafari's magic fingers, his big collection of clippers and razors.

'Kemi,' the old man used to joke every time I went on a morning run. 'Kemi, don't go too fast or they'll ask you what you're running from!'

And I'd make sure to get really close to the barber's shop

stoop, drag my scuffed Reeboks in circles around his lazy lanky figure: 'I know how to answer, don't worry.' Tongue lolling out of my mouth, nudging his bony hip with mine. 'I'm running away from you!'

Uncle Jafari always pretended to fall off the stoop, then caught himself. He'd laugh into his rolled-up cigarette. He'd click his fingers faster than a match catching flame.

Still, I was about as serious about rule-breaking as Uncle Jafari was about being my actual uncle. As in, not at all. He's not Yoruba like me and my family. Not Nigerian. There's no blood relation. Just an old familial friendship, worn-in like the soles of all his flip-flops, his strong ashy musk, his gold chains and his backstrapped zoots.

I mean, I do my homework on time.

I'm the only person in my entire family to have returned all of my library books with no fines. I've never even accidentally stolen a pen from school. I think I just forgot that getting caught with a can of spray paint has consequences. I lost my head. In the moment and all that.

Hey, the voice inside me had said while I stretched out my calf muscles at a zebra crossing, *that's Amir Ali over there, isn't it? He looks like he's about to spell something wrong on that bit of glass.* My toes had tingled with the sensation of a new destination. *I should probably go and help him stop spelling it wrong.*

I forgot that's how graffiti happens. In my case, with the need to correct a classmate's grammar.

I guess that's why my mum and my sister Ada always groan when I say some things, and tell me to think harder, to start acting my age and not my shoe size. It happens sometimes. All

36

of the common sense I've gathered gets bunched up together in my brain and none of it can breathe and I just don't have the time to untangle it, comb through it, make it make sense.

To be fair, my mum and my sister Ada aren't rich in time either. When we were little, all Ada did was sit up in our flat on school nights and translate the government documents that got given to us so that our family could have some extra cash to go around.

'This is boring,' I used to moan, my feet not touching the floor next to her. 'And why are we having toast for dinner again? We just did all the shopping at the supermarket. Why did we have to leave it there? Ma, what does it mean if your card gets rejected?'

Back then, Ada and Mum would just ignore my chattering. Their tired eyes rimmed with purple. They'd try and distract me. They'd ask me to go and check if the telephone in the hallway – a regular pale office phone with big clicky buttons – was working or if we needed a new one.

It took me years to realize that dialling nonsense numbers, waiting for a dial tone, and talking and talking and talking for hours on end about what I'd done in school that day to absolutely no one on the other end was their way of keeping me busy.

Well, years went by and one winter evening Ada asked me to chuck that regular pale office phone in the bin.

She'd held up the chewed-up end of the connecting wire after dinner. 'It's done for, see?'

I'd glared at her. 'Ada, you told me that wire only looks like that because it makes your voice louder to other people!'

A cringe creased her ear to her shoulder. 'Well, you're stupid for believing that. And anyway, even if that was true, it's not like you'd need it!'

These days, Mum works really hard at the flower shop in town, cutting and pruning spiky stalks and large-petalled flowers for funerals and birthdays and special events. She's the number one lady everyone asks for when they step past the bouquets of roses resting in cooled water outside Say It With Flowers. Ada wouldn't have got into one of the best universities in the country for politics, philosophy and some other subject that I can't remember right now if she hadn't always worked really hard as well.

Long hours with the lamp on when I was trying to sleep in the bed we shared.

Her throwing a pillow in my face because I'd stared at her and asked her if she'd even blinked while reading for the past hour.

And I wouldn't be the fastest long-distance runner in my school, breaking my own record for cross-country repeatedly, if I wasn't such a hard worker as well.

Effort. That's what our school's most important value is: a vigorous or determined attempt to achieve.

We had an assembly all about it a week before we broke up for GCSEs, an entire speech about the distances we could go if we just kept pushing, just kept on with our efforts. There was a slide show featuring all the hard workers in our year: all of us predicted to get good exam results, company sponsorships, college placements, trips to celebrate sports excellence with the

Running Right residential in France, internships at the steel mill in Lowbridge . . . Me, I was there thinking I didn't need the reminder about effort being important. It came naturally to me. It may as well have been my middle name. Oluwakemi 'Effort' Adebayo.

Then I realized Jasmin Gill's school portrait was on the slide show for the Running Right residential. So was Michael Taylor's. Mine, too. With our stiff white collars, our dark jumpers, our blazers and our perfectly knotted ties. The three of us hooted at the back of the school hall, chucking our hands in a circle and wiggling our fingers in glee.

The letter detailing the amount of cash needed to go on that trip stopped the smile on my face though. But not on Jasmin's or Michael's.

Way back in Year Seven, I'd picked my best friends for the richness of their hearts, the quick fizz of their jokes. I forgot they were rich in ways I wasn't, too.

'Wait,' Jasmin had said during break time on the last day of term, interrupting the game of hangman we'd been playing in my planner with a toss of her long dark hair. 'Aren't you going to bring your residential letter in? Kemi, it's the last day to do it.'

Michael was leaning back on his chair beside us scratching at his head, wondering why his hangman guesses on just consonants weren't working out for him. Then he'd realized what Jasmin had just said.

'Kemi!' He shook my shoulders with his hands, clown-like, goofy. He made his voice reverberate on my name. 'Kemi, you have to come with us!'

Their signed letters of permission were slotted neatly into their planners, alongside two thick brown envelopes. I tried not to picture the ease with which they'd gathered the sort of cash my family sweated over, and borrowed, and cried over. Our £20 and £10 notes always so soft and torn with touching. Not crisp. Never crisp and lying flat when they were bundled up and sealed in a similar envelope labelled 'for the landlord'.

'My mum said I'm already talented enough.' I'd shrugged Michael's hands off my shoulders. 'I don't need extra training when I have better timings and better grades than everyone in the school already.'

He was still looking at me, one blond eyebrow cocked in concentration. Jasmin was too.

'Well,' Michael relented finally, 'no one can say you're not confident, huh?' Then his hands were on my shoulders again. 'Eh, champ! The people's champ, our champion!'

I laughed, trying to shrug him off. I didn't want him or Jasmin to think the tears in my eyes were from anything but laughing too hard.

But Jasmin refused to let it go.

'Kemi, are you seriously not going?'

I didn't say anything. I used my pen to draw on my hangman drawing. Two crossed-out eyes. Dead meat. Dead before anyone even tried to save it.

'Well,' she said awkwardly, 'we'll text you every day, Kemi. We'll do you a favour and tell you everything we learn.'

I smiled tightly. 'Just race me when you get back, OK? Then we'll see whether that residential did you any favours.'

Michael and Jasmin said it was a deal. We fist-bumped to confirm it. Then they nudged one another, started asking about what type of water bottle to bring, which trainers didn't bring out blisters, what running shorts, vests, deodorant . . .

That hangman with all its letters empty loomed in front of me. E F F _ _ _. I scribbled all over it. Black scratches. Ink all over the blanks. Circles and loops of deep dark rejection.

The feeling reminded me of a warm hand gripping on to mine when I'd done the same scribbling thing as a child, mid-reception homework about halving fractions which I just hadn't understood.

'Don't make a mistake into a mess!' My late dad's voice had always sounded so warm. A lion's rumble in a lion's throat. Eyes as bright as the sun. *'Now how do you expect to fix a mistake when you're insisting on making it into a mess?'*

On my walk home I decided to solve it. My money problem. My missing out on the Running Right residential in France.

'Huh.' On the morning I got in trouble with the police, Ada stared at the inside of the big pink piggy bank I'd won in a primary school raffle with me. Her fingers coaxing gently at my curls. The ends sticky with coconut oil. 'Maybe you should've waited a few years.'

I put the thick university economics book that I'd used to smash the porcelain to the side of Ada's study desk that was engraved with little etchings of 'Ada + Nathan 4EVA'. My fingers sang a heavy metallic tune as I counted the coppers and silver coins from past birthdays, past errands, past Christmases.

'Six pounds seventy?' I said. The stack of pennies mocked me. 'Not even a full seven pounds?'

Ada picked up the biggest shard of thick pink porcelain and turned it upside down. Both of us craned our necks upward, hoping for an extra fiver or tenner or hundred-pound note to come drifting out of the air.

Ada sighed. 'All those meals for you getting older, all those cards from Aunty Sunbo and Aunty Ifeoma. For six pounds seventy. But hey –' she tucked a stray curl behind my ear – 'wasn't there a pair of new Reeboks in the charity shop window for five pounds? Pink ones? With the cool Velcro straps –'

I groaned as I pressed my palms into my eyes. 'Ada, we're past the point of new Reeboks from bloody Barnardo's!'

'OK, so tell me what you want me to say. Tell me what you need.'

'Five hundred pounds for the Running Right residential in France. And a time machine.'

Ada laughed.

I tried again, made my eyes wide and woeful: 'And better luck than what we've got.'

She stood up from where she'd been perching on the edge of our bed frame. Slowly, and without a word, Ada wound her arms around the tight scribble of my body. I sighed. We stayed like that for a little while. I was reminded of her always standing behind me on the bus to school, her limbs long enough to protect me from the crush of bustling passengers.

'Kemi, you know Dad'll be proud of you whether you make it to the Olympics one day or not, right?'

I bit my bottom lip. Outside our block the sky was a clear shade of blue. A group of birds flew calmly over our heads. Their wings stretched out, delicate and swooping low, then high, then low, then high, in tandem. Larger wings cradling smaller ones closer to them.

'I guess,' I said into the criss-cross of Ada's arms.

The smell of Mum's special eggs drifted down the hallway, the spices as rich and heady as her voice shouting down the phone to our grandparents in Nigeria.

That sound was usually the cue for me and Ada to shuffle awkwardly in the kitchen and fill the crackly line with stories about our achievements that Mum had already greatly exaggerated. Though Ada's didn't need any exaggeration. My sister said she'd save me a good fork as she headed towards the compliments she definitely deserved.

Me, I took my time in the corridor. I stopped by the framed photograph of my dad's smiling face. Kissed the tips of my fingers. Stretched them to his cheek.

'I'll do something about this, Dad,' I promised him. 'Don't you worry.'

Of course, that was before my skin got stained with spray paint.

Before I found myself sat in a police station office. Still with no money. Still with no luck.

'Listen,' Amir Ali said in the stuffy expanse of the police station office. He looked exactly the same as he had back in our old reception class. Only taller. Sharper. With a razor slit in one of his eyebrows. 'Listen, none of us have to say anything. They can't force us. We don't have to explain anything at all . . .'

But then he suddenly stopped talking. No rough-as-a-cough rasp in the air. He leaned really close to this girl, Eman Malik. The same one who'd been new in town in primary school, who always got tripped up because she walked so slowly, spoke so slowly, could never quite keep up. Not with our easy-Friesly speed.

'What?' Eman's eyebrows creased in confusion. I think because Amir was really close to her face. Like, kissing distance. 'W-what is it?'

'Did you bang your mouth or something? It looks bare red.'

I rolled my eyes. There wasn't a lot of space for the three of us on the sofa in the office. It moved every time we moved.

So I could feel Eman backing into me, terrified, arms and legs scrambling like they'd just been in contact with a spider. I wasn't afraid of spiders though. I reached over her lap and shoved Amir away.

'It's called lip gloss, you weirdo. Don't you know what lip gloss is?'

Amir looked at me. And then at Eman. And then at me. 'I know what it is!' The tips of his ears tinged pink. 'I was just – I just thought . . . Who was talking to you, anyway?'

I know Amir didn't really mean it when he aimed a kick at my Reeboks – with their dusty white shoelaces, not pale pink Velcro – but I had to try and kick him back. I really did.

The sofa kept moving as he yelled at me and I yelled back, and Eman tried wiping her lip gloss off her mouth, all crammed and quiet in the middle. Then the officer who'd chased us after our graffitiing – the one whose full name was PC Katie Phillips – came back in, with a full line of people behind her.

They weren't a series of criminals meant to scare us. No tattooed prison inmates, or dealers with deceptively casual smiles and the faint smell of marijuana on their tongues. But this identity parade featured its own sense of terror. It was as familiar as a pile of clothes left on a chair in daylight, and as striking as the horror that pile became when the sun went down.

My sister shook her head as she entered PC Phillips' office, her box braids hanging low over her face. Disappointment curled her bottom lip. The sight of her curled lip made mine get all dry and chapped in an instant.

Amir's cousin Uzair came in next, glaring at Amir. I would've paid more attention to how fit he was – whether he was playing football with the local neighbourhood gang or standing in a police station glaring at Amir – if I hadn't been so worried about him thinking I was a bad kid now.

Finally, a little old lady with massive glasses and an equally large walking stick brought up the rear. She was probably Eman's grandma. I obviously couldn't ask her. No, all I could do was stare at her stick and wonder if it stung as badly as my mum's sandal did on particularly short-tempered days.

PC Phillips paced the floor in front of us. Her hands stayed behind her back the whole time. The blonde of her short hair lifted a bit as her clunky boots hit a regimental rhythm. Heel-toe, heel-toe. Heavy as my heartbeat. Heel-toe, heel-toe.

'Vandalism,' she eventually barked in a tone as forceful as spitting. 'Right in the middle of our town. Graffiti, all over the bus-shelter glass.'

She took advantage of the silence that followed. 'People look at that every day, y'know!'

'Yeah,' Amir muttered at the other end of the sofa. 'That was kind of the point.'

Uzair sighed, running a large hand down his very pretty face. But it didn't seem like PC Phillips had heard Amir.

'Look,' she continued, 'I know all three of you are old enough to understand how disrespectful your actions were. And I'm here to tell you we won't stand for it. In fact, we're doing our best to tackle this kind of anti-social behaviour before it develops into criminal offences. So, congratulations – all three of you will be joining our summer volunteering programme. Go and tell your friends. As of now, you're officially part of our Pursue, Prevent, Protect and Prepare strategy.'

I sat open-mouthed, shocked.

'We are?'

Ada gritted her teeth, her eyes desperate for me to agree with the constable. 'You are,' she affirmed.

And then, just for PC Phillips' sake, she tossed her braids off her shoulder and a strange university-affected accent left her mouth.

'It'll be good for them, won't it?' she articulated. 'Good kids take up this kind of community work because they understand they're helping others.' My sister eyed me deliberately. 'They won't develop a bad reputation in the community. Or get into more trouble as they get older.'

PC Phillips didn't seem aware of the weirdness of the accent, of the strange puckered-mouth sound that made Ada sound oddly refined. And distant.

'Exactly, Miss Ade-Ad-Adeb—'

'Adebayo,' Ada finished stiffly.

A dull silence followed, punctuated only by the electric fans, whirring against the thick inside heat. Thanks to me, it only lasted for two seconds.

'But I only stopped my morning run to give Amir some friendly advice!' I said. 'That's not fair! How was I supposed to know this would happen?'

'Maybe someone should've given you some friendly advice about it,' Amir said, low enough for only me and Eman to hear him.

I swear on my life, if Eman hadn't been sat in between us, I would've knocked his stupid Nishaan cap right off his head.

'Settle down,' PC Phillips said. 'I'm not finished yet.' And then to me: 'And you need to watch your tone. Hasn't your sister already emphasized how much of a privilege it is to help your community like this?'

My Reeboks tapped impatiently on the carpet. I sighed. Then I crossed my arms over my chest.

I mean, I knew that Ada was looking out for me – there was something about the way she was staring at me that said as much.

Me and her knew enough about racism and the Stephen Lawrence case to be wary of brushes with the law. I think she knew we were all in sort of an impossible situation and the only way out was to just go along with it. For now, at least.

So that was how me and two other kids from my school ended up spending the rest of our summer washing the bus board with soap-filled buckets and sponges, picking up litter in Fowley Park, and delivering police leaflets through every letter box in Friesly as part of the 'Volunteering4Friesly' scheme, designed to stamp out the threat of organized crime.

As the heat in her office grew from all the bodies stood inside it, PC Phillips said it again: good kids did stuff like volunteering because they chose to.

Friesly Metropolitan Police were all about improving the community and putting it first.

That was how they stopped kids turning out bad. No scratched seeds, no rotten apples like the drug dealers on the roads, the crackheads lurking on the street corners, the invisible thieves, the money launderers, the counterfeit crooks ... A programme like this was reformative.

'Deep down, you three are good kids, aren't you?' PC Phillips said as she handed informational sheets to us all. 'Even if you made a bad choice with that graffiti.'

It was clear that rejecting the informational sheets would've meant owning up to being rotten apples – and having everyone else in the community agree.

'Think about it.' She gestured out of the window to a boiling kerb with a single figure shuffling along in the distance. That guy that everyone called Danny *Dangar*. 'You don't want to turn out like him, do you? Old Danyal got in trouble with the police when he was around your age. And look at him now. An addict. And homeless.'

There was some more awkward shuffling on the sofa. All of us watched the old man pause and stare up at the sky, tracking some imaginary sound, fingers searching around in his ears, before he looked down, readjusted his carrier bags, and carried on walking again.

'I am sure he has his own story to tell, PC Phallow,' Eman's grandma said in thickly accented English, smiling despite her serious words and the newness of her voice.

PC Phillips' head whipped around quickly. 'Phillips.'

Eman's grandma's eyes narrowed behind her glasses. 'Phil-ling . . . ?'

'Phillips.'

'Phillips –'

'Yes!'

'–es. Phillipses.'

PC Phillips' eye began to twitch. 'Never mind.' She sighed, missing the exaggerated wink that Eman's grandma gave to all of us on the sofa.

Ada tried to cover up her smirk. Me too. I suddenly doubted whether the old lady's stick really was used for the same purpose as my mum's sandal.

But anyway, back to Danny *Dangar*. Eman's grandma was right.

There were definitely real truths behind the half-ones that said that guy didn't mind silently wandering the streets for money, that ex-convict who shivered a lot – even if it was boiling hot out there – his carrier bags always in his hands, his awkward bowed legs the reason for his nickname. *Dangar*. Jasmin said that meant pack mule or donkey. Because that's what he looked like. A service animal, straining under the weight of its burden.

He probably did have a real name though. A real story. Even if I didn't actually know it, and he never actually spoke a full sentence. I mean, beyond the same word, over and over again. 'Please,' to anyone he saw seeing him. 'Please,' for money, or food, with his eyes all big and wide, his shoulders shaking, the bathroom slippers he wore as shoes trudging hard against the concrete. They were always a bit too big for his feet.

None of us were in a position to argue with PC Phillips though. Not when her lip was lifting in that proud way I was beginning to recognize was usual for her.

'I expect to see these three right here at eight sharp on Monday morning,' she said to Ada, Uzair and Eman's grandma. 'This programme will do them a world of good.'

CHAPTER 4
AMIR

It was the sort of morning that turned everything blue. Pale curtains closed shut, along with the lace netting that Fiza sometimes stuck her head in to be a ghost. A fly buzzing somewhere, desperate to get out. And a gloom everywhere around the streets.

You can just feel it sometimes, what the world outside the window will look like.

And it's always a better decision to stay in bed.

Pull the duvet right up to your neck.

Keep the warm in.

Still, that morning there were footsteps going up and down the carpet in my bedroom, dodging the collapsed line of my trainer collection, the ratty ends of my school bag, the bashed-in football rolling out of my laundry basket ... A boy swaggered inside the cocoon, humming a little tune to himself as he checked his phone from where it was charging right next to my head. The glow of the screen too much. Too bright.

My throat always felt so scratchy in the morning. 'Turn it off,' I said.

The boy kept pacing. He had this energy about him. Even from under the duvet, I could tell he was doing his usual thing of tapping his fingers and sniffing his nose for no reason and itching his leg. Humming as well. Nothing in particular. Just a series of high notes and low notes for his own entertainment.

'Oi, it's the morning,' I told him. 'Go do your stupid singing outside. I'm trying to sleep.'

The boy leaned close to my duvet, speaking to my yawning face. 'The birds sound good today, Amir. Angels, innit.' He tapped at my duvet with his fingers. 'Go and wash up for *Fajr*, you bum.'

I realized I hadn't heard his voice in so long.

My heart lifted in my chest.

I tore off the duvet.

The dream broke like egg yolk.

The real morning was orange. Like a sauna, with the burning dawn stretching out across the hills, the dirty river, the tower blocks and Sir William Barker's stone face. Fiza didn't knock before she came running into my room.

'Hurry up if you want a shower. Mum says the boiler's gone weird in our house and Uncle Nadeem's.' She sniffed the musty air, stared at a bowl of cereal I'd forgotten to take down. 'Maybe be quick about it as well. It smells like *ulti* in here.'

I threw a pair of balled-up socks at her. I couldn't be bothered to tell her she was the one that smelled like sick. Fiza shut the door with a shriek.

*

The steam drifting across the landing – with the cool smell of what might have been my expensive mint and cucumber shower gel – had me hammering on the bathroom door. No matter who was in there.

'Oi, hurry up!'

Fiza's laughter travelled from where she sat talking on our mum's phone in our mum's room. 'Amir's having a toilet emergency!'

'Shush, you,' I said, without even looking back in the direction of her voice. 'Oi! Why are you taking ten years for?! Zayd, I swear down, I'm gonna shove my foot –'

The door clicked open. 'Sorry!' It unleashed more steam and a boy in a towel. 'Hang on a minute . . . Sorry, Amir.'

Uzair's face was warm from washing, redder than his usual brown, his hair damp and hanging closer to his eyes than my brother's ever had. And his nose. It wasn't as big. It wasn't as hawk-like.

'Your mum said I could get in before you since you like sleeping in sometimes.' Uzair threw my shower gel into my hands. 'This is nice though!' He sniffed his own armpits. 'So fresh, where'd you get it?'

I barged his shoulder with my own. 'Who said you could use it?'

The door closed shut on his smiling face. And the soft of my palms ached as I held on to the edge of the sink. Breathing in. Breathing out. The mirror was steamed over. I saw no reflection in there. And there were three toothbrushes in the pot, not four.

Me, Fiza, Mum.

I counted them again.

Me, Fiza, Mum.

And again. Me, Fiza, Mum.

The only good thing about Uzair Ali being my cousin is that he's nineteen years old. A certified adult. He helps his dad sell gold in a jeweller's shop neither of them own on the right side of town. Part-time yet though. Unlike his dad.

But everyone thinks he's a certified adult just because he's tall and his long fingers are used to weighing wedding bangles and dainty earrings, and tapping prices into a flat calculator, and charming his customers into an extra plated ring or two. His days are crammed with wedding talk, riches and commissions him and his dad always joke about. Like the rest of us even know what they're talking about.

I mean, Uzair used to only talk about cars and stripped-back engines. He used to die if me, Fiza or his brothers even breathed on his banged-up little Ford Fiesta resting in our garage for space reasons.

'Look!' He once jumped out of the wardrobe he'd chosen as his spot for a cousinly game of hide-and-seek, his perfect hair a little sticky-uppy for once. 'I'm not trying to be harsh, but can you all avoid the car as a hiding spot please? She's fragile.'

I'd stopped holding my breath under a sheet we used to keep the greenhouse dry when it rained. Made a face no one could see. 'She?'

'It!' Uzair's voice climbed up a few octaves. 'I said "it", didn't I? It's fragile. The car is fragile. It needs more work –'

A series of metallic groans came from beneath the car. Laughter that sounded suspiciously like Mikaeel and Shuaib. 'No, Uzair. You said "she". What's her name? Car-la? No, wait! Ca-ristmas!' They couldn't talk without exploding into giggles, without chanting 'Jingle Bells' beneath the car's creaking framework, and I couldn't help joining in.

Uzair sounded like he wanted the ground to swallow him up whole, shushing us so hard his throat got raspy by the end of it. That was how Fiza found us all in seconds. She didn't even have to pull on the garage light. One arm on her waist and one eyebrow cocked, she itched at a scratch in her leggings, smoothed over her dress, and then asked us to at least try and make it hard next time.

After that, Uzair came over to Nishaan to help out on Buy One Get One Free weekends. He used to fry samosas and talk about engineering courses the whole time. He said he wanted to know about different types of gears, clutch pedals and engines, and about the difference between a van and a rocket, a road and outer space . . . He said he'd checked out the student finance website and was looking at universities close to home just in case Uncle Nadeem needed extra help taking Mikaeel and Shuaib to school, which was his way of supporting his mum – our aunty Ayesha – with her dialysis appointments at Friesly General Infirmary.

She missed a lot of those. She couldn't help having such a busy family and such weak kidneys.

'Have you done your engineering applications?' I asked him once when we both had to help do the washing-up in Nishaan after a really big birthday party for a really big one-year-old.

Uzair had focused really hard on drying a bunch of forks. 'I missed the deadline. But –' he smiled; it got stuck somewhere around his stupid cheekbones – 'at least Mum didn't miss her dialysis appointment this week.'

I knew Aunty Ayesha threw up a lot. Whole meals. Whole chunks of roti and pizza, tea and bright orange carrots. I knew Uzair sometimes found her all nauseous, lying limp on the kitchen floor with a plastic bag by her mouth. I mean, when he wasn't going to work at the jeweller's with his dad, then coming back without his dad, then picking up Mikaeel and Shuaib from football, then going to the gym to clear his head.

'Oh,' I said.

We washed up the rest of the cutlery in silence.

After that, Uzair came to Nishaan talking about gym sponsorships and the power of social media. Once, Fiza showed him where to get the extra bottles of Rooh Afza for some business company's giant order of *falooda* and Uzair spent an hour in the back room chatting to her about his new idea of a cupcake-baking business, as well. Thick icing. Frosted icing. Whipped cream. Meringue. Fudge. All on little baked delicacies he was planning on making with his own two hands.

'That would be cool,' Fiza had said, her eyes drifting to visions of all the sugar she was already limited in consuming on account of turning into a sweary little gremlin whenever she'd had too much.

Uzair had sounded dreamy, too. 'Yeah. Maybe I'd even get to make my own wedding cake.'

It was normal for all of us in the Ali family to snap to attention at the mention of marriage. Never mind this really big wedding coming up that summer. Just call it PTSD. We catered so many weddings, hosted so many celebrations, suffered and survived the traumas of so many dramatic families, and so many indulgent recipes, flower arches, balloons, hired Ferraris . . . Even the mention of a three-tiered vanilla fudge cake to celebrate yet another marriage meant to last forever was nauseating.

'Wedding?' Fiza blinked. 'Who, yours? Uzair, who are you marrying?'

Fiza said Uzair's laugh sounded even wheezier than it usually did. 'Huh? Oh no, Fiza. I was only joking.'

He didn't bring it up again though. Neither did any of us. Not what he'd said or the heat that travelled to his face every time our mum – or his – joked about marrying him off to someone.

'Amir,' Uzair kept saying after everything that went down with the police. 'Listen, Amir!'

He followed me into the restaurant that morning after beating me to the shower.

But I didn't want to look at him and his easy boy-band face. His boy-band hair. All the stupid rings on his stupid fingers, and the car air fresheners in his back pocket.

Pretty soon, there'd be a group of girls spread out on the back tables, ordering *halwa puri* and channa and picking at it with their eyes on my cousin. Like Noor Bhatti in my year, and her best mate Tahmina Begum, and all of their stupid friends. They always got all whispery and giggly looking at Uzair. They died over him for no reason.

But I mean, he'd always had this little fan club. Fiza used to beg me to go to the cinema with her, him and his little brothers Mikaeel and Shuaib all the time. Apparently, he paid for the tickets and snacks, and made really funny jokes halfway through the movie if you were paying enough attention. I told her I didn't like it when she talked in movies, so why would I like it when he did? Fiza told me and my big mouth to stop being a hypocrite, said that I did that too. And I said I wasn't a hippo, what was she on about?

'Amir.' Uzair followed after me as we nudged past the people coming in for *desi* breakfast, the crowds blocking off Nishaan's entrance and spilling on to the outside cobbles.

'Listen, Amir. I'm not gonna tell your mum about what happened.' He lowered his voice. 'Y'know, with the graffiti and the police and all that. I'll just . . . help you out, alright? I'll do your deliveries when you're doing your volunteering. You just need to pretend you're still doing the deliveries, and I'll handle the rest. Alright?'

The smell of *karak chai* brewing in the back kitchen was strong and sweet. The heat of the early morning, thickening with the first rush of customers.

'Yeah?' I looked him up and down. 'What's in it for you?'

Uzair sighed. He ran a hand through his hair. Through the window, I saw the girls at that table got even more giggly, fanning their faces with our menus. I rolled my eyes. I wanted to tell those girls that the reason why the menu was laminated was to avoid spills and stains, not collect their dribble and drool.

'I just –' Uzair started again. 'I just don't want *Khala* to be stressed. I think your mum would be if she knew what happened. And, well, that's not fair on her. I mean, maybe we can tell her one day, but not right now. Right?'

He and I glanced over to where my mum was standing behind the counter, tearing off receipts and chatting with the people waiting for a seat in the lobby. There were lots of pens in the pocket of her apron. A few streaks of silver at the very front of her henna-coloured hair. Tiny tired lines at the corners of her eyes.

She'd looked like a statue once upon a time. A stone woman, crying stone tears, on her spot on the sofa. And before that, she'd been all water. I don't know how else to explain the way she looked when she was on the phone, begging my dad through sobs and tears to at least visit sometimes, at least remember he'd always had more than one family that needed him.

'Right, Amir?' Uzair repeated.

I shoved my hands inside the pockets of my basketball shorts. Tore my eyes away from my mum. 'Yeah, I guess.'

The hubbub of knives and forks, warm plates being carried and babies settling into high chairs grew louder like music. I knew better than to just stand in the middle of our restaurant when the morning got like this. But Uzair was still watching me. He didn't look like he was about to move.

'Amir, man,' he said slowly. His voice got all weird and soft as he rested his hand on my shoulder. 'I get it. You miss Zayd. You're about to be the same age he was when . . . when . . .'

I rolled my eyes. I shrugged his hand off my shoulder. 'Table seven need *karak chai*.'

Uzair followed me around the tables and chairs. 'At school, yeah, when I did psychology, I had to read about death, and this chapter in my textbook said grieving is a process that can sometimes take up your whole life . . .'

He was still talking as I walked into the kitchen. Still going on and on as the sounds of spices steaming and onions frying swallowed his chatter up whole.

'Here.' Fiza shoved a rose made out of a napkin in my face as I announced table seven's need for *karak chai*, and a waiter with a tray full of tiny steaming cups went rushing out of the door. 'Mohamed made it for me.'

'What the hell?' I said to Mohamed's busy commanding back. 'Where's my rose?'

'Take the one I gave your sister.' Our head chef was too busy overseeing the big metal pots of meat dishes on the stove, giving a few short commands to everyone flipping *parathas* and frying *puris*, to turn back to me.

'So I get a second-hand one, not one you made just for me,' I said to the line of muscles in his back. 'I see how it is.'

'Wow.' Fiza made a face, turned her head to an angle, screwed up her eyes. 'I was trying to be nice! But fine, be like that.'

I tapped her screwed-up face with the napkin rose. 'Shush, favourite child.'

Her nose wrinkled at the movement, her face splitting into a smile. Even the kitchen gang washing dishes in the back joined in on the joke. Students, ex-taxi drivers and single mums. Men, women and children who just needed a break.

'Oi, leave her.' One of them grinned. 'She's only little.'

I smiled despite myself. 'Yeah? That's what she wants you to think.'

Fiza aimed to kick me. But I was used to that.

She was a big girl. Twelve years old. All angst and being annoying.

Our staff were all used to Fiza's mannerisms, too. For example, the way she always checked over all the dishes before they went out. Just like Mum used to when we first started the restaurant.

My little sister was Nishaan royalty, always tying a too-big apron over her clothes, always fussing with the ends of her sleeves and the straight hairs escaping out of her ponytail. She sometimes stood on her tiptoes on the counter, sometimes sat cross-legged on top of it, fussing with extra napkins, placing freshly cut coriander on steaming bowls of *gosht* or smelling the strong garlic *tarka* in warming bowls of yellow *daal*.

'Yeah, yeah,' I said, dodging another kick Fiza aimed at me. She was sat quite calmly on the counter that day. 'You lot'll still be saying that when she's a wrinkly old fifty-year-old with no teeth and a bad back.'

'Who's still cuter than you,' Fiza sang.

'You wish!' I laughed. 'You wish!'

Fiza rolled her eyes as I took off my delivery cap, squinted at her, bit my bottom lip and told her to say mashallah already, say mashallah.

Then Mohamed started reminding me of the deliveries I had to do that day, told me to check them over already, match the receipts, staple them right.

Pretty soon there were dozens of brown bags packed tight with pressed paninis for lunch, and stacks of cardboard boxes of rice, pan-fried chicken, chips and mash for sides, and various curry dishes to go, along with traditional *desi nashta* and drinks.

Well, those were the deliveries that Uzair would be doing. I just had to pretend like I was. And that was easy enough. My bike was locked out front already.

'Has he gone yet?' Mum rushed into the kitchen, just when Fiza was telling me to put that napkin rose behind my ear for the cycle into town, and I was telling her it'd look better being held in her teeth like a dog with a bone, and she was threatening to bite me for suggesting something so stupid.

I took the opportunity to hand the napkin rose to my mum instead. 'For you, Ma,' I said. 'By me.'

Behind me, Mohamed snorted as he jigged a pan steaming with buttered spices.

'OK, fine,' I relented. 'By Mohamed. But it could've been by me! If I had more time on it.'

'Speaking of,' Fiza interrupted, while our mum's fingers hovered delicately over the pulled-together petals, 'are you gonna help me out with my holiday homework when you get home? I need to write a short story about someone that inspires me, and fast, because when we get the chickens, all of my time will be spent on making sure they're comfortable in their new home.'

'You're not getting any chickens, Fiza,' Mum said.

'Well, not yet,' Fiza said slowly, avoiding Mum's eyes and mine. 'But who knows? Maybe someday ...'

I could tell she was dying to say the word 'soon'.

'So anyway,' Fiza's words got all quick and weird, 'about the short story –'

'Yeah, yeah,' I said. 'We can start it later.'

Somewhere in the past, she was still being carried over Zayd's shoulder in our back garden. She was still screeching and howling while he tickled her side and I readied the surprise attack, a stick for a sword, and he asked an invisible audience if they were not entertained.

Our mum watched mine and Fiza's fist-bumping with wary eyes. She always said me and Fiza were scary when we got on. But the corners of her lips were quirking, ever so slightly.

'Amir,' she said after a bit, 'you're gonna be careful about these deliveries, aren't you?'

'Yeah.' I nodded, packing the brown bags into a backpack I'd be emptying into Uzair's car. 'When am I not careful?'

'Well, when you're doing wheelies on that bloody bike and almost breaking your neck. I don't want any phone calls about people getting no paninis because you ate their lunch orders.'

I rolled my eyes. 'But what if I knock on their door twice and they don't open it?'

'Then you knock three times,' Mum said.

'What if he knocks three times and they still don't open it?' Fiza piped up from the counter.

'Then he knocks four times.'

'What if –'

'You just keep knocking!' Mum said, in such a commanding voice that afterwards we could only hear pans being moved around, muttered orders, instructions to start getting the *jalebi* batter ready for the afternoon, and Fiza being told to re-do the mithai display in the front, as well.

I didn't move when Mum sighed and cupped my face with

her soft hands, though. 'I just want everyone to see you the way I see you,' she said. 'My special boy.'

My whole face went hot. 'They know already,' I said. 'Just look at me, Ma. I'm beautiful.'

My mum laughed. She looked younger when she laughed. 'Remember that poem you wrote for me? In Year Seven? Your teacher said it was the best one in the whole class.'

'You mean the haiku?'

The memory of my mum reading over something I'd scribbled in my exercise book always embarrassed me a bit.

I mean, I'd spent ages trying to get that haiku right. It was supposed to be about something we loved. But I kept scribbling out lines. Writing them out again. Counting syllables on my fingers while my best mate Hassan Jalani repeated one word for his entire haiku – 'football, football, football' – and my other best mate Ben Stockdale kept rereading the instructions, and my other best mate Abshir Mohammed was already on his third one.

My English teacher, Mrs Khan, kept asking me to read mine out, and every lesson, I kept saying it wasn't ready. But she read it quietly when it was done. Just by herself, not to the whole class. Then she called my mum and read it out to her, and my mum asked for a copy straight away:

My Mum

Amir Ali

A tree grows alone
Its leaves protect smaller plants
The tree hugs so good.

Mrs Khan told me to keep writing, as well. Just for myself, if I wanted to.

If there was stuff I wanted to say every time I got told to be quiet in class.

If there were words behind the punches I threw on the playground, the rage that sometimes crept up on me so bad I saw red for a long time before it all dulled to black.

Before I forgot what had happened. Except for the ache in my knuckles, the bruises on the skin of everyone who mentioned my brother to me:

'Is it Zed? Or Zaid? Or Zayd?'

'What kind of name is that? Some alphabet letter non-sense.'

'Sounds like a dealer.'

'Sounds like an idiot.'

I did, though. I wrote sometimes, in a book that went in my underwear drawer. Under the newspaper article. Hidden from everyone's eyes. But my mum always made me feel so awkward every time she mentioned that very first haiku.

'What about it?' I said, my face reddening in the heat of Nishaan's kitchen.

'Oh.' My mum wiped her eyes. 'It just reminds me every day of what a good boy I have. Sorry, I should say man now, shouldn't I? Since you'll be sixteen soon!'

Fiza snorted as my mum wrapped me up in her arms.

'Shut up,' I muttered at her.

My mum laughed. 'Behave, you two.' Then she squeezed me tighter. 'Or you won't get your favourite for your birthday.'

'Red velvet?' I grinned.

My mum didn't confirm my suspicions. She just made a big show of kissing my cheek, and I tried to fight her off, because no one wants to be embarrassed like that in the kitchen of their family business, in front of all these chefs and all the waiting staff coming in and out all the time, and your sister laughing at you. But it felt nice as well. Her hugs really were the best.

Though we were still in July, August couldn't come quickly enough.

Especially because I still had to find Uzair, get in his car, and do my stupid volunteering. The smile on my face dropped a bit on my way out to his Ford Fiesta, passing by a gaggle of guys who nodded at me.

'That was Zayd's brother, wasn't it?' they said as they went through the glass door. Snatches of conversation sounded after the bell on the hinge rang. 'Bro, he looks just like him. Proper gangster. Bet he's dealing like he was, as well.'

Zayd wasn't a drug dealer.

He was actually the most careful person in the world about stuff like that. Always joking and laughing in all the videos he recorded of us lot in bug-eyed sunglasses, rapping along to his favourite tracks, but always so irritated – and not afraid to say so – when me and Fiza got too comfortable with the explicit stuff. Swear words and that.

He was always careful to say *salaam* to all the guys on our street as well. The ones that were in his year at school. But he'd refuse any night-time hang-outs. Zayd used to always mention – with a casual smile, and his hands tucked comfortably in the pockets of his joggers – that there was some stuff those guys did that just didn't make sense to him, some scents and emotions around Friesly he didn't like so much.

In between hitting their vapes, the guys in our neighbourhood used to joke about his big beak-like nose. 'It's because you've got all that nostril space – of course you don't like the smell of this stuff, innit?'

And he'd laugh along, without judgement. A nice guy. Seriously, the nicest. The best brother in the world.

Because, yeah, there were drug dealers that lived on our street by then. Those guys that went from dozing off in the back of a science class with Uzair to having random nicknames – Muzafir became Muzzy, Kashif became Kash – and planning hits on anyone who had tried to take over their territory.

They played music in their cars really loudly when my mum was trying to watch emotional Pakistani dramas like *Hamari Zindagi* on TV. They had all the aunties that lived on our street really worried because they were their sons, and all they did was smoke up, and turn the bass up on their car stereos too much, and rev their engines for fun.

They obviously did other stuff, too. Arson attacks and petrol bombs that got their tyres squealing on the roads. Fights and whispered meetings over Class A's and Class B's that had them swearing really loudly when the kids that played cricket on our street were tucked up in their beds.

That was the stuff that got their mums crying when the sun went down and there were empty seats at the dining-room table. I know that because sometimes there was the smell of blood and sweat on Friesly's street corners. The *athaan* for another kid's funeral, echoing across our crammed-together streets. Bouquets of flowers at car junctions. Arguments on the hot tarmac, and the elderly begging angry young men with bats in hands and razor-sharp tongues to go home already, go home.

We knew about all of that. Everyone who lived in south Friesly did. But Zayd wasn't one of them lot. Those dealers. He never had been. And all I delivered on my bike was food. I thought everyone knew that, too.

I kept thinking about it during volunteering. I couldn't stop.

We were all standing next to where I'd tagged Zayd's name. Me, Kemi Adebayo – the best runner in our school – and that girl Eman, who was good at art, who always got the best grades in sketching even if Abshir tried to do better than her when we did still lifes of flowers and fruit. Sometimes she drew doodles of Sonic the Hedgehog, as well. They were the sickest doodles I've ever seen. We even said so, once. Me, Hassan, Ben and Abshir.

Them lot, all crowded around her: 'Nah, I don't get it. It looks just like him.' And me on her other side, asking her how she was so good at this.

None of us got a response though. Eman jumped, hearing our voices. She spilled the water she was using to mix her paints with. I guess we shouldn't have snuck up on her like that.

Anyway, there were all these random north Friesly kids who'd actually signed up for the Volunteering4Friesly programme with us as well. Maybe so that they had a better chance of getting into uni when the time came. Maybe they wanted to prove they were the good kids the police wanted working with them. I don't know. I just wanted to stand in front of my brother's name and tell everyone to back off, go home already.

'PC Phillips has made it very clear that you are the future of this town, our hope for our new "Volunteering4Friesly" project,' our new supervising officer, PC Chris-something-something, said.

He had a spotty face and a very dead trim. I could tell he was older than he looked though. There was something about his eyes, the way they darted around, weasel-like, that gave it away.

So this guy, PC Chris, started shouting about the buckets of warm water near our feet, the sponges that were supposed to help us clean up that bus shelter, as well as all the nearby ones. His voice got louder every time he started some new mini-speech about respecting Friesly.

He kept glancing towards the police station, as if PC Phillips was watching him. Like she was listening to him go on about how we were the youth, and we're doing the best thing ever for our town Friesly. To be fair, she probably was.

All these other volunteers actually nodded at what he was saying as well. The north Friesly lot.

One of them kept looking me up and down. A weird smirk on his face. I didn't like it.

'Oi,' I said to him. This kid had blond spiked hair which made it look like he was from the '90s. Thick clear-framed glasses, too. 'Is he paying you to agree with him like that?'

Kasmey, you can always spot the rich kids a mile off. There's just something about them. I don't know if it's their looks, their attitude or what, but it feels like they came from another time period. Some place past the past. Whether they mean to or not. Whether they're dressed up all 'vintage' on purpose or not. They just feel wrong for where they are. The time. The place.

'Hmm?' this kid said. Like he didn't want to talk to me, but his eyes were on me all the time. Like I was about to steal something and he was CCTV.

'Y'know,' I carried on. 'PC what's-his-name. PC Chris. Is he paying you to be here? You, that girl in the dungarees, that ginger kid over there?'

They didn't fit in with our graffitied bus shelter, our shops with the half-broken shutters.

They'd go home across the river that separated the north and south, close to the moors and dainty cafés and hike routes that all the tourists from Bramracken and Hent liked to take photos of. They'd complain about how much they hated south Friesly without loving it at the same time.

'Ha.' Posh accent. 'Why would he be paying us to be here?' Posher than mine.

'Well, it's not normal, is it? You lot could be doing anything all summer. Why would you wanna spend your time rolling around in the mud?'

The guy raised an eyebrow. 'Excuse me?'

'Y'know.' I snorted for him. 'Oink oink. With the pigs?'

I saw Kemi start creasing in front of me, the corners of her eyes crinkling when she smiled. She was always jokes though.

Every time we had mixed PE, me and Kemi used to team up for rounders and cheer everyone on and have so much fun getting them out when they batted wrong. Eman looked confused next to her. But that was nothing new.

'Listen, you have to be getting paid to stand here,' I said. 'You can tell me, y'know. Oink once for yes. Oink twice for no.'

I smiled at the guy. It looked like something was twitching inside him. I crossed my arms over my chest. I wasn't surprised when he took a step closer to me.

'I'm not sure who you think you are,' he started, 'but I know your lot are exactly the kind of people PC Christopher is talking about. You need to be taught respect through volunteering schemes like this. You need to be forced into it because God knows no one's brought you up right to properly volunteer like we are.'

'Oh, is it?' I stepped closer to him as well. 'No one's brought me up right, huh?' My hands clenching into fists. 'Are you talking about my mum?'

A pair of ugly dusty black boots stood to the side of us.

'Mr Ali.' PC Chris's voice was right in my ear as the world dipped into shades of red and black before me. 'Is there a problem here?'

I wanted to say why aren't you talking to this guy, too? Why aren't you calling him by his surname? Why aren't you asking him what he meant by 'your lot'? The blood jumped up and down in my veins, my head spinning with all the things I wanted to scream.

Zayd's name glowed brightly behind me. 'No.' I took a step away. 'There's not.'

PC what's-his-name smiled.

'Good.' He patted my shoulder, his fingers like pincers, digging into the flesh. 'Now, you might want to grab a sponge and a bucket before you take your position by the bus shelter.'

He was so close to my face. A burst of pain bloomed beneath his tight grasp. Then he released me and wandered off to the other volunteers. Glasses, Dungarees, Ginger. Those lot who did actually grab the buckets, who were actually mapping out where to begin their cleaning.

I stayed by Zayd's bus shelter though, massaging where the PC had held on to my shoulder. Nearby, Kemi was making a big show of squirting more bubbles inside her bucket. And Eman tried to carry hers over without spilling any water everywhere, sweating from the effort.

I put my hand to where I'd written my brother's name. I traced over the Z and the A and the Y and the D. I thought of the time Uzair's dad – my uncle Nadeem – had given us keychains with our names on them. Tiny plastic ones with cars on them and typewritten meanings of our names underneath: '"Amir,"' Zayd had read aloud. 'Your name means "prince". That's not fair, man. Why do you have a cool name? And you've got a Lamborghini on yours! Bad boy car.'

'Why?' I'd snatched his keychain from his grip. 'What does yours say?'

'Leave it, it's boring. What's the point of having a name that means "growth"? Everyone grows! Ma!' I remember he'd shouted over his shoulder. 'Can I change my name? It's boring!'

He always made me laugh so much. 'What are you changing it to?'

'I don't know,' Zayd had this way of acting old and young at the same time. And when he talked, he used his whole body. Arms going. Feet tapping. 'Something cool.'

'Pappu Laalu the poppadom man,' I said.

Zayd narrowed his eyes at me. 'Proper joker, aren't ya?'

Then we both burst out laughing and Zayd fought me for his space on the sofa. 'Alright, move then! Ah, gerroff! Gerroff!' He forced my fingers from the armrest. 'Let Pappu Laalu watch TV!'

'This isn't playtime!' PC Chris said, his hands on his waist, his police uniform a black speck in a sea of light leaks and sunshine. 'Get those sponges wet! Start cleaning!'

He didn't seem to care that all these people were passing by.

Old ladies like Marta Varga from the antiques shop, old men like Howard Li from the pharmacy. Jafari Williams on a smoking break from his shift at Clean Cutz. Boys and girls we went to school with, entire families, gangs of friends going off to Fowley Park. Everyone talking about the weather and the moisture being sucked from the air, and what was on TV last night, and the theme for the council's town hall meeting that evening.

Until they saw us lot, obviously. Then they just stared and walked extra slowly, grinning like it was something to be proud of, our volunteering. I looked down instead. At a street grate, at the cracks in the kerb, at leaves that had fallen off the trees and were curling in the dusty yellow heat.

'Come on, Volunteering4Friesly!' PC Chris grinned at everyone who went by like he was selling good kids for them all to see up close. 'Push those sleeves up! Get some soap on that glass!'

Across the road, pigeons gathered at Sir William Barker's feet. And beyond that, a new newspaper took pride of place outside Mahmood's Foods.

It was too far away to see properly. And it had been so long since I'd seen an article by Zakiya Bhatti, the journalist with an eye for injustice. But I still strained my eyes, searching for her name amid the waves of heat, the black-and-white lines of the story.

CHAPTER 5
EMAN

Lunchtime with Volunteering4Friesly was different from lunchtime at school.

Noor and Tahmina weren't there, for one thing.

And there was no cafeteria food, no long lines of steamed vegetables and sandwiches, plates of jelly and cake, and dribbly pots of pasta to fill in with arrabiata sauce and cheese.

And I didn't sit a few seats away from where those girls ate at our shared table, while I played *Ball* on my propped-up phone, sneaking glances towards them and their smiling mouths, their inside jokes. Sometimes I'd laugh when they laughed, too.

'What's funny?' Tahmina had asked me once, over the cacophony of ordinary cafeteria sounds.

I remember staring at her, hesitant, a leftover smile still on my face. 'Huh? Oh – just – the same thing you guys are laughing at.'

Noor crossed her arms and leaned forward on them. 'And what are we laughing at?'

My *Ball* game continued on in front of me, the clumsy sounds of missiles and cartoonish blasts echoing as I stammered for an answer. I was glad when their attention was stolen by the clatter of another student dropping their plate of fish and chips, cutlery and all.

It was after midday in the middle of town when our stomachs began to grumble. The tourist traffic had already slowed, the streets sleepy with parked cars, as PC Chris led us to the picnic tables on the hot tarmac outside Mahmood's Foods for lunch.

His uniform was bright and black and blue in the heat. It was easy to follow.

But the sight of him made some of the men outside Clean Cutz stub their cigarettes quickly and lean less easily against the yellow brick walls and concrete. Others stared, eyeing PC Chris up and down, wondering if his appearance would part the crowds on the cobbles like Musa's had with the sea in the Qur'an story.

The bus shelters we'd been put to clean were shining now. My arms hurt with the effort of making them look like that. They glowed bright as fire in the afternoon sun.

Well, all of the bus shelters did except for the one we'd graffitied with Zayd Ali's name.

That one still had the blue spray paint on it, but now it shone cleaner than it had done when we'd graffitied it. I didn't know how I felt about that.

'Hmm,' Farida aunty had said on the walk to Wash 'n' Wear that morning, her eyes narrowing at the newly graffitied name that caught her eye, her mind blissfully ignorant of my law-breaking. 'Now who would write a criminal's name on the glass like that?'

I'd stared at her, confused. 'Criminal?'

'You know, I did hear he was involved with drug abuse,' Balqis aunty said, while Nani insisted the gossip be swapped for mosque chat instead. She still had an awful lot of donations for the homeless to sort out.

Still, Zayd Ali's name was familiar to me. I recognized it in the same way I recognized a line in a long Greek poem we'd studied in English: *Dear branch in bloom, dear child I'd brought to birth* . . . Vaguely. With no real awareness of what that line was about. But enough curiosity to want to know the details.

PC Chris also stared at the graffiti while Kemi, Amir, and the teenagers from north Friesly sat down to eat their supermarket meal deals. 'I guess that must've been strong spray paint.'

Amir unwrapped a Nishaan panini from its Nishaan paper covering. He had a little box of ketchup. He fussed with the flimsy peelable top. 'Yep.'

PC Chris started wondering out loud about other ways to cover up the graffiti. The teenagers from north Friesly had some helpful suggestions. Like using stronger cleaning products or covering it with posters for the Barker Summer Festival. Or even with quotations from Sir William Barker's many speeches on child labour laws.

'I will use my influence for good,' he'd stated once, in the Victorian era. *A festival for good* apparently sounded like a very good tagline.

'Ow!' the blond spiky-haired north Friesly boy said after making this point. 'PC Chris, Amir just kicked me!'

PC Chris looked questioningly at Amir and his still-half-opened ketchup.

Amir looked back at PC Chris. Then he sighed. 'Look, it was an accident, alright? I've got long legs. He doesn't have to start crying about it.'

'But you could be more careful with your long legs, couldn't you?' PC Chris said through gritted teeth.

Amir shrugged, his face half in the shade of his delivery cap.

A vein pulsed in PC Chris's temple.

'It's hard when you're tall,' Kemi blurted from the other side of Amir. 'Trust me. People always think you're tripping them up when you're not.'

She and Amir exchanged a look. Something passed between them. Some thought I desperately searched my own mind for. But I couldn't find it. It wasn't shared with me.

'Yeah,' Amir said. 'It wasn't on purpose.'

The wood of the picnic table expanded beneath us, warm and riddled with tiny moving insects.

I watched PC Chris stare at Kemi and Amir like they were a puzzle he was having a hard time figuring out. A jigsaw that needed a careful eye. I saw his hand turn into a fist and wondered – dimly – if he was the sort of person who forced pieces to fit when they didn't.

Then again, the entirety of our first day volunteering had felt like playing *Ball* on expert level for me. Especially this bit. The sudden silence, the meal wrappings in front of us, my awkwardly moving hands.

The way everyone was looking at Kemi and Amir was new, too. I couldn't apply gaming logic to it. No coding tricks. No cheats.

'Y-yeah.' I nodded enthusiastically. 'Yeah, it's hard when you're tall.'

Suddenly all eyes were on me. I guess because I'd forgotten I wasn't tall. And I realized again how different this was to school lunches. Similar as well, though. How was it that Kemi and Amir could communicate without a single word?

Desperately, amid the hiss of Coke cans and water bottles being opened, I hoped for them to like me for more than simply whether I could comment on a bit of graffiti about a criminal like Zayd Ali.

'Ugh,' said the girl in the dungarees. She had freckles and curly brown hair, and she clamped her fingers around her nose. 'Sorry, I don't mean to be rude. It's just that something smells awful around here. I just –' She turned to me. 'Sorry, but how can you eat that?'

'Huh?' I said, looking down at my half-eaten *aloo gobi* sandwich.

Nani and I did all the food shopping for our house as Mum's shifts at the hospital were so long. But recently, Nani had been so busy with the launderette, and with organizing for the mosque's homelessness project with the aunties, and with all her regular duties that she hadn't had time to buy tuna sandwich filler or peanut butter or anything like that.

She and I quite liked *aloo gobi* sandwiches though. They were a good snack. You took the potato and cauliflower curry, and you spread it on two bits of bread, and you pushed it all down, and it was delicious. Definitely a bit fragrant. The smell of spices travelled further than any cling film wrapped around the bread. But it wasn't bad.

I thought everybody thought that. So I didn't know what to say now, and the only figure of authority had just headed inside the supermarket to grab an extra bottle of water.

PC Chris's silhouette moved behind the automatic doors, his tall figure easy to spot beyond the bright star-shaped special-offer signs and the newspaper stand displaying some article about the architecture of the train station.

'Oh –' I started. 'Well . . . Um . . .'

Amir's hand reached over and tore a bit from my sandwich. 'It tastes banging, alright?'

He spoke with his mouth full, then turned to the girl in the dungarees. 'What are you eating anyway?'

Kemi stopped spearing her pasta salad. She stood up to inspect the girl's sandwich. 'Looks like just cheese in there, Amir.'

The two of them shared a disapproving look, noses wrinkled, their heads shaking, before they went back to eating their own lunches.

I couldn't help staring at Kemi and Amir. They were just sat there looking under the rings of their Coke cans for whether they'd won any prizes, but they'd stunned the teenagers from north Friesly into silence.

Something was rising, steadily, like the bubbles in their drinks, inside of me.

I stared at the corner of the sandwich Amir had ripped off.

For me? Had he done that for me? Did that mean we were friends? Amir caught me staring at him as he sipped from his can. He winked at me. Lightning quick. So confident. Lips quirking at the corners. My stomach leapfrogged over itself.

I dropped my gaze. I didn't look at him for the rest of lunch. But his smile was so bright. I felt warmer than usual in the thick July heat.

I headed home after volunteering that day all soapy and sticky with sweat. But I thought it hadn't been so bad considering it was punishment for being what the police thought was a troublemaker.

There were kids in Friesly who hung around a lot more than I did on street corners, by abandoned churches, beside the newsagents with all the ringing mobile phones on the front desk.

There were kids in Friesly who knew a lot more than I did about fast cars and jewellery and whatever it was that made people like Danny *Dangar* beg for money on street corners.

Maybe they liked video games too though.

Maybe they also had favourite sandwiches and jokes they liked playing on their friends.

Maybe they were just like me, or Kemi, or Amir. Only different.

I think that was why people wanted more for them. Especially Nani, and the aunties, and everyone else that went to the weekly council meetings that were held in the town hall on Mondays.

Usually, me and Mum would wait for Nani to tell us about

the arguments, the uncomfortable plastic chairs, the detailed itinerary the mayor and the council never got through, the Q&A sessions that went on for too long.

We always listened to her descriptions about the metallic taste in our water supply. The empty buildings on our side of town. The construction work that never led to anything. The state of the falling-apart cemetery by the river. The long lines at the Job Centre, and how the youth centre had shut down, with no plans to open another one, and how the running club for Friesly South had run out of money to send people on national competitions.

Then there were our dangerous roads. The state of the river on our side, all full of crisp packets and shopping trolleys. Our falling-apart streets. Our homeless. Our poor.

'Honestly,' Nani had said the last time Mum was home to help her take her loafers off in the hallway afterwards, 'if these meetings are supposed to tackle Friesly's poverty, our high mortality rate, and all of these other long *angrazey* words, why does it feel like nothing gets done in them?'

'Let me guess,' Mum said. 'The mayor just started talking about the August fair again. What's it called again? Barker Summer Festival? You know how she thinks it makes people happy. Gives us more tourists. Gives the posh business owners up in north Friesly something to look forward to. And a visit from the local MP!'

The mayor always welcomed a visit from the local MP.

'Pah!' Nani laughed in her daughter's face. 'You know what would make me happy? If that crazy-*pagal* lady took the Barker Summer Festival and shoved it up her –'

Mum smiled and hit Nani's arm just as I joined them in the hallway and asked them why they were talking about high morality rates.

'Mortality rate,' Nani corrected me from the almost-bottom step on the stairs. 'Not morality rate. What are you learning in school these days? Hmm? You know it's –'

'– something everyone in Friesly knows about already so we don't need to go through the details all over again,' Mum said, giving Nani a look she thought I didn't see.

She ushered me into the living room, begging me to turn the TV to Channel 868 so we could watch another emotion-filled episode of *Hamari Zindagi*.

I never minded though. Being ushered away from the grown-ups. Things were always so good in those moments with Mum and Nani.

With Nani still grumbling about the mayor's meetings.

And me in the middle.

And Mum passing along the box of *jalebis* we always bought from Nishaan, stifling her yawns to complain about the sugary syrup dripping into her tea. It was the highlight of our evenings together.

That was usually when I noticed that the bruises under Mum's eyes weren't as dark as they had been when we'd lived with my dad. She was just tired from working. And I knew from all of her blinking, and from the skew-whiff curve of her work hijab, that the possibility of her falling asleep in the first ten minutes of the show was for definite. But she was happy.

Me and Nani always sang along to the already-shrill theme song, our hands waving sweet *jalebis*, Nani's gravelly voice always a bit louder than mine.

Hamari zindagi, ho . . . Hamari zindagi . . .

Our life. The life we share together. The life we cannot help but share together. And Mum always laughed and moaned and covered her ears.

After work, there was a line of people outside our house. I stood outside the front door, all ready for another episode of *Hamari Zindagi*, another evening with my mum and nani. But for a second, my heart rate spiked. I thought I was in trouble again. That the police had come for me again. That I'd done something wrong.

Then I recognized the gaggle of kids in *topis* and little-girl hijabs standing at our front door, swinging their book bags so they hit the wooden door, yelling for their *apa* to let them in for the mosque lesson with Nani they thought they were supposed to be having that evening.

'*Assalamu alaykum*,' I said. But only because Nani insisted I did, instead of the usual 'hi' or 'hello' to that *besharam* – bad-mannered – lot.

Still, Juveria Bhatti, Iqra Khan, Awais Farooq, his older brother Baasim, and all their cousins and siblings said their *salaam* back. They stood up straighter than they had been, when they'd been nudging each other and chattering, and pretended like they hadn't been banging on anything at all.

'*Baji*,' Juveria said eventually, '*Baji*, I told them there's no mosque-house on Mondays! But they didn't listen to me!'

'Oh … Ah!' I said, shifting awkwardly from leg to leg. 'That's right, because of the council meetings …'

Baasim glared at Awais. 'I told you, didn't I? When we were putting the cricket stuff away? I told you I thought we were forgetting something!'

'Well, how was I supposed to remember?' Awais shoved his fingers in Baasim's face. 'I'm six years old!'

And then, when they'd all turned back to stare at me again, and I couldn't find an answer for the questions in their eyes, I said, 'Um, I guess … Well, I guess you'll all have to go … home?'

The mosque-house gang seemed OK with this though. They knew me well. They were locals, after all. The sons and daughters of our neighbours, pilgrims on a very familiar journey, some very intimate streets. They always used to complain about how tired they were and say how much they couldn't be bothered with mosque-house when their parents dropped them off at ours. Usually, I'd usher them inside awkwardly, silently.

And in the sitting room, Nani would peer at them through her big glasses, waiting for them to take out their books.

Then they'd be sitting down in seconds. They'd be rocking on their legs while reading over their Arabic, waiting for one of them to start asking the questions they knew Nani loved to answer as much as they liked to ask them:

'Apa, is it true there's gelatin in the sweets at Mahmood's Foods? Is there? Oh, apa, don't … Don't say that! Wait, even in the cola bottles? But those are my favourite!'

'Apa, can you say "pig" out loud instead of spelling it? Or does that mean you're going to hell? Um, I mean – *Jahannum*? Swear it means you're going to hell?'

'Swear it means Pakistani-International-Gangster!'

'Shut up, Awais. My best friend Fiza says you don't know anything –'

'You shut up, Juveria! I know more than you and Fiza!'

It was funny, overhearing their conversations as I sat on the stairs outside the living room. And seeing – through the hinge in the door – how this old lady, who just lazily sat up on a tasselled cushion and smacked her lips when she talked, had Juveria, Iqra, Baasim, Awais, and all their cousins and siblings spellbound. Their heads nodding. All of them hanging on every one of Nani's words. Even if they hadn't had that experience that evening I came home from work. The kids left, chattering along the way, silently disappointed with the absence of their *apa*. I heated up leftovers in our very empty house and waited for Nani to come back from the council meeting myself. Mum from work, too. Sitting on the sofa without them felt strange.

Minutes passed with the channel loaded up and ready to play. And then hours. Until they'd missed that evening's episode of *Hamari Zindagi*. I checked my phone for texts. It had none.

Then my head started drooping. And I think I must've fallen asleep, because I started having this really weird dream. It wasn't like any of my usual ones.

Nani used to tell Juveria, Iqra and the rest of that lot that some of our dreams came from God as warnings or blessings, and some came from the Devil – from the Shaitan – to scare us, and some just came from us and our bored minds.

I knew most of mine just came from me. When I closed my eyes, all the memories of what I'd already done in the day played in my head like a 'What You Missed Last Time' segment.

Usually, I got the toast I'd eaten for breakfast.

The *Ball* loading page.

Nani and Mum's faces.

So I think it would've been normal if I'd seen Kemi and Amir's faces that evening. Or the glow of blue police car lights. Even machine number twelve leaking soap bubbles everywhere in my memory.

But none of that came up. I recognized what I saw though. The beginning of a true story Nani used to tell, unfolding behind my eyelids. It was really weird to see it developing there like a movie. But I think I saw it because Juveria and Iqra and everyone liked to hear it so much. It went like this:

There was a patch of green wilderness just outside Nani's village in Mirpur, Pakistan, full of tall plants and uneven soil. You had to be careful and watch your feet if you were about to cross it. Keep an eye out for clumps of dried dirt and too-tall grass, avoid ditches, snakes, scorpions and biting ants. You could never even see where your feet were going, what with all of the overgrown shrubs, but you got good at it with practice.

Most of the villagers crossed that green on foot on their way to dirt roads that led to nearby towns, or on old motorbikes that stumbled all over the place, loaded down with the baggage for some long journey. It didn't really matter how you crossed it. Just that you knew that you had to, to get to and back from places. And that you did cross it.

Apparently, the air smelled fresh in that wilderness in a way that it just didn't in Friesly.

The Pakistani sun gave off a really strong kind of heat.

It made you feel like you were surrounded by baking dirt, sweat and strong wild jasmine plants. Sweet, heavy breezes passed through the trees and disturbed the crows sitting on the branches. Big hugs of warmth surrounded your body, and made the crows start stretching their ink-black wings.

But there was something off about that patch of green as well. A bad feeling. A sadness that made people feel sick. After all, there were rumours that the patch of green was in fact an unmarked graveyard.

This half-knowledge froze some people halfway across it, until they were stuck in the warm-damp shadows, unable to see a way out of the tall grass because they were filled with so much emotion, so much fear. That was usually the point in the story when one of the kids would butt in. Juveria did, the last time I remember Nani telling it.

'*Apa*, are you sure it wasn't a jinn living there, messing around with everyone's heads?' she'd said, with the front of her little-girl hijab falling into her eyes. 'They do exist, y'know. There's one in my house. It moved the fridge away from the wall in the middle of the night, and –'

'Juveria, man. Why would it do that?'

'I don't know, Awais! Why are you asking me? Maybe it was hungry!'

Nani had cleared her throat. 'Let me ask you a question. What do you think is scariest? A big fat spider on the wall when you're on the toilet? A *jinn* moving a fridge from a wall in the middle of the night? Or a field buried full of the dead? A field full of people that were just like you, living and breathing and laughing and joking, until God decided it was time for them to leave this world?'

Everyone had gone really quiet after that. We'd watched Nani fuss with her glasses for a bit, her eyes big behind the lenses.

'Look,' she'd said, smiling, 'we're not supposed to be scared of death. This life is temporary. The Angel of Death will come for all of us one day and bring us back to God. But I won't pretend that it isn't a bit . . . difficult to think about. Especially when you've never had to think about it before.'

No one argued about the stories of young farmer boys leading their cows through the wilderness after that. About how it was said they'd felt chills down their spines as they remembered dead relatives lying under the soil, being punished or blessed for what they'd done in this life, a cool, knowing wind pinching icily at the thin fabric of their *shalwar kameez*.

Suddenly, there were no debates to be had, I think because we all knew that she and the aunties knew every detail of death. They'd lived through it. They told these stories while loaded down with the memory of their own loved ones returning to God, may they be forgiven and granted *Jannah*, *inshallah*.

Farida aunty's twin brother had suffered a heart attack after a rigorous school-wide cricket match. Balqis aunty's old friend had stumbled off the crumbled edge of a verandah by accident. A wild dog-turned-pet named Pollu's tongue got dry as he dehydrated to death in the school courtyard. My nana turned cold in his bed before he even got to board the plane to England and meet me.

Nani said most people who came back from washing their clothes by the dam or selling guavas on the side of the road didn't like that wilderness for how it made them feel. They said it brought back the names and lives of those the village had lost. Faces of family members, friends and people they missed and loved so much they'd never even realized how much they missed and loved them when they were alive.

But they had to make their way through the green. They had to be hit by the realization that they would go one day, too. Be buried in dirt, and return as a soul to the sky and the creator of it. Just as it was written to happen. People did get upset at the thought, though. Not Juveria, Iqra, Baasim or Awais, who I heard playing on our street, screaming, 'This life is temporary' over every little thing.

But Nani did mention the people who got stuck in the wilderness. The ones who stood crying in the green, lost to reason until their friends and families heard them and came with oil lamps, their quickly moving chappals slapping against their cracked heels, the village mosque playing the *athaan* for Maghrib, and quietly led them out.

She never sounded like she blamed anyone who got stuck, though.

'Things are written to happen by the grace of God,' she'd tell her students. 'And there are blessings in every bit of suffering we receive. In every bit of horrible, drawn-out suffering. But you've got to try to be a blessing, too. To other people, if you can. No matter how bad it gets.'

In my dream, I was standing on the edge of the green.

The sun was beating down on my head. I could feel the heat rising from the baking dirt. I could smell my own sweat. Sweetgrass. Barley. Strong wild jasmines, fire ants, goat droppings, dry stone. And it was weird, because I knew, even as I was dreaming, that I'd never dreamt anything that felt as real as this before.

Nothing I'd imagined before had prepared me for how the dream wilderness looked exactly like the real one Nani had described. Down to the crows in the trees, and that sadness coming up from the grass like invisible steam. The goosebumps puckering on my arms while a sweltering warmth smacked my face.

Then I took a step into the green. Dream-me took a step into the green. And this horrible feeling took over. A tear rolled down my face. Then more tears, as I realized I was stuck. Right there, sun-gold in the grass, overwhelmed by an unforgettable fact of life. Right there, with my head chanting death's name, my heart chanting death's name, and no one coming with their oil lamps, the heel-slap of their chappals, or any background beautiful village *athaan* to lead me out.

The feeling woke me up, it was so horrible. And I realized, as I blinked away the daylight coming in through the living-room curtains, my head spinning with sleep, that there was a prayer on the tip of my tongue. A plea to God, looping over itself, as I cried, and sat up, and realized, with a start, that the house was very quiet.

Mum wasn't home. Nani wasn't home. But my phone suddenly had a lot of text messages, a lot of missed calls.

CHAPTER 6
KEMI

Ada's accent went back to normal as soon as it was just me and her. All the vowels and consonants she'd sawed off inside the police station hitting harder and heavier when it was the two of us pounding the steep Friesly streets.

'Why'd you sound like that in there?' I'd asked her that day.

'Like what?' my sister replied with her eyes on the ground. That's how I knew she was embarrassed. I mean, whenever Ada messed up and under-peppered our dinner, or took too long to stop texting on her phone when Mum asked her to, she clammed up like a shell. Kept her eyes down. Refused to greet our faces with her own.

I joked around with her anyway.

I wanted to know if her university voice was also her telephone voice. If it was a softening of something rough, an erasure of sounds considered spiky by others. Even though she couldn't ever be spiky or rough to me.

I mean, my sister flinched every time I joked that I'd fight her. She'd always jumped with fright whenever I hid around a corner on the landing, hand clamped over my mouth to hide my deep breathing, ready to spook her before Mum came home.

'Never mind all of that,' Ada said eventually, her braids swinging with every step she took towards Say It With Flowers. 'I thought you wanted to raise the money for that residential. Why don't you get a job so that you can go next year?' Then, after a beat of my silence: 'Go on. Tell us why you're in trouble with the police, as well.'

I bit my lip.

I thought of all the shops I'd planned on knocking on the doors of before I'd seen Amir by that bus shelter.

Marta Varga's antiques shop, full of dusty old furniture. Howard Li's pharmacy, and his kids running around the well-stocked aisles. That shop that repaired broken mobile phones and sold new ones. The one that sold plastic toys which made really loud noises, electric fans and cheap electric blankets.

'Face it, Ada,' I said calmly. 'People around here don't want employees they actually have to pay.'

She and I often moaned about the many weekends I'd spent sweeping up hair at Clean Cutz just to be paid in chocolate coins, in jazz recommendations, and by Chris and Fady buying me strawberry laces on their lunch breaks.

I remember even back then – on my less-than-minimum-wage pay – just staring at the gold tooth in Uncle Jafari's mouth.

It had shone and flashed so brightly when he talked. I'd wondered – since this was how I thought back then – how he'd managed to be born so rich, so valuable. At home, I'd passed a finger around my own gums, desperate for the hard ridge of something other than bone. Then I'd asked Mum how people got gold teeth. She'd laughed me into going to bed early on purpose – I got so annoyed with her.

It got to me sometimes though. Especially that day we got in trouble with the police. How I wasn't a dazzling shade of yellow in a row of white. How I wasn't something better than just regular old bone.

I'd even stamped my Reeboks on the cobbles. 'Ada, it's really not fair. You know, some people are born lucky, right?'

'I know.' She'd poked her finger into the dimple in my cheek. 'But listen, those people are unlucky in lots of other ways. They just won't show them to you. They won't give you their full story.'

I grimaced. 'You aren't gonna start talking about university again, are you?'

Our relatives in Nigeria wanted all the stories. What college, what degree, what book list, what lecture, what library . . .

Ada was polite in her responses, friendly, sweet, her usual self. But sometimes I heard something different. Our grandad mispronounced some old politician's name, and she was so quick to correct him. The family genius, stunning me into silence instead of my usual applause.

Then one college's tradition got muddled up with another's and she stated – with the tight smile I only saw on her face when Mum wanted her to try contacts instead of her usual thick glasses – what the truth was regarding all the pomp and poshness of her university.

I pretended like I didn't hear it though. The emergence of another tongue on the tip of her old one.

'The point is,' Ada said, the two of us panting in the muggy air, 'what's lucky to you might be unlucky to someone else. I mean, do you know how many people know what Friesly's actually like at uni down south, Kemi? Like, none. This one girl even said she's seen pictures of beautiful north Friesly but she heard the south is a "dangerous" place to live because of all the shanking and crackheads.'

I made a face. 'Sorry, but isn't it dangerous to be that stupid?'

Ada had laughed at that. And I'd laughed too, seeing her throw her head back like that. Throat to the world, light as a feather.

I think that was because that was the same way she'd looked when our dad would pull coins out of our ears.

He'd always show us his big gummy smile whenever he was supposed to be angry with us. Like when I'd streaked baby-butt-naked in the garden or when Ada had drawn on the walls of the rental in crayon. The rage never came with him. Not once. Even his grip on mine as I struggled with my maths homework, guiding me to do better, to stop making a mistake into a mess, was firm but not rough. Never rough.

The tourists all fresh from visiting the green fields of north Friesly wandered past us in their hiking gear, ready to buy ice cream from the van parked down the street.

Mums chased after children whose summer dresses billowed behind them like butterfly wings.

Dads waited by the ice-cream van, their big climbing shoes tapping a rhythm, impatient for everyone to decide on their orders.

Ada and I glanced at one another, our eyes catching in a streak of sunshine. I knew in our minds we'd both just seen our father sitting casually on the concrete kerb outside our flat.

Once, after his shifts working machinery at the bread factory in Lowbridge, he'd greeted us with two Mr Whippys in his hands and we'd had to be very careful not to stain our clothes with the milky cream, the flaky chocolate we'd only ever dreamt of tasting before that moment.

'You're spoiling them,' Mum had groaned upon seeing us, she herself fresh from hanging the laundry out of the windows, smoothing down her very strong arms.

Dad had only laughed. 'It's food. Let's not be picky about food, hmm? The bills will not stack up simply because my girls are eating ice cream.'

His lion rumble had always had her rolling her eyes.

But that day, he'd surprised Mum with a plastic-wrapped Screwball to match his own. He'd gone to Mahmood's Foods and bought her a hefty lump of vanilla ice cream swirled with raspberry sauce and – at the very bottom – a tiny round bit of bubblegum that was incredible for only really having two good chews in it.

Our parents ate them with wooden spatulas, Dad laughing at the cream all over mine and Ada's mouths, Mum begging us to let her close enough to wipe it for us. Dad smiling his secret contagious smile at Mum. Mum rolling her eyes again. Shoving him away.

But that was how we knew she loved him.

And that's what I remember of my dad, Opeyemi Adebayo. His big heart. How he came to all of my Sports Days. And how he shone – so bright – before the darkness of death took him whole, and let Emmanuel Achebe, from the Jacob Pentecostal Church, wander into our lives.

'Come,' Ada had said after a bit, watching the ice-cream van sell its Mr Whippys all doused with sprinkles and syrup. 'I think that there's still loads of Screwballs in the freezer at Mahmood's Foods.'

I'd grinned, chasing after her.

'That is a beautiful bouquet.' Emmanuel Achebe's strong accent hit me more than the colour of the orange gerberas my mum was pruning on the back desk of Say It With Flowers.

It was the evening after I'd finished my first day volunteering for the police with Amir and Eman. Washing bus shelters. Getting my fingers all wrinkled with soapy water.

But Mum's strong dark hands were making light work of a bunch of gerbera stems, smoothing the happy petals with ease while a combination of dusk and street dust shone in the shade outside.

'These flowers must know that a beautiful woman is taking care of them,' Emmanuel said, and I immediately wanted to throw up.

But, of course, my mum blushed. 'Don't say such silly things, Emmanuel!'

The gap between her two front teeth showed when she smiled. The young woman who'd stood her ground and rolled her eyes at my dad's charm offensive swallowed up by a new awkward old lady. This one was shy. This one's hands shook when they arranged stems. This one giggled to herself at men who didn't know how to be charming at all.

I don't know if she remembered confessing her love with an eye roll. The batting of an eyelash against a cheek. A playful shove into a lap that was always there to receive her.

Ada nudged me as she went by the table. 'Fix your face.'

'Yeah, but when is Emmanuel gonna fix his?' I muttered.

I don't know how to explain exactly why he felt so fake to me. An artificial light bulb next to my dad's real fire, real flame. A dull glow next to a burst of life.

It always made matters worse that Emmanuel thought he was such a ladies' man. With his flimsy little glasses. The thick tweed jacket he always wore, even when it was really hot out. Bargain aftershave. And the church leaflets he was always handing out to everyone.

I think if my dad hadn't been a wedding portrait in our hallway by that point, he would've taken one look at Emmanuel simpering after Mum in Say It With Flowers and burst out laughing. I think if my dad was still here, he would've thrown his head back and laughed so loud it would've felt like thunder was shaking the ground. My dad would've had to bend down to see him better, too.

Emmanuel was short. His hair was flecked with white. My dad was twenty-nine forever. He would've smirked, with his large flour-smelling hands on his waist, saying: *Really? This guy? This guy is my competition?*

Once, Jasmin asked me what I dreamt about the most. She'd already told us about her flying dreams and Michael had mentioned feeling like all of his teeth were falling out of his mouth. Me, I said flying, too.

I didn't want to tell Jasmin or Michael that I saw my dad stepping out of the picture frame in the hallway at night. His long legs clambering over the ornate gilt frame and heading down to my room in the dull glow of the setting world outside. I didn't tell my best friends that I dreamt I saw him sitting on mine and Ada's bed, waiting for us to come home from school, or the flower shop, or the corner shop at the edge of our piece of Friesly.

His head in his hands. His eyes meeting mine first, and filling with disappointment that I'd kept him in the picture.

It's all different, he'd say. *It's all different now that you've let the world go on without me.*

Because that's what I've done all this time. Let it keep spinning while he lies covered in dirt and Emmanuel takes his chair at the dining table.

I stared at that man's hairline in the flower shop. *Oily.*

The sweat patches under his armpits. *Disgusting.*

His crusty leather sandals, his long leathery toes. I had no words for them.

I looked at Ada, who was waiting for Mum's shift to be over with me. She always screwed up her face, knew my unspoken words. Usually at exactly the same moment they came to me, as well. But Ada's face was hidden by her braids as she scrolled on her phone.

'How's Nathan?' I said, just to be annoying.

Ada turned her screen so that I could see the news headlines she was so preoccupied with. 'You know, I don't just text Nathan Eze all the time.'

You used to, I wanted to say. But the prickle of her tone was enough for me to simply raise my hands and say nothing more. My sister, with so many different voices, and venom in some.

I mean, Nathan was my sister's boyfriend for the longest time. Is. Present tense. For a while, she never let us forget it. She wore his black fleece every day for a month. I guess it smelled like home. Literally, because Nathan lived in the flat beneath ours. Number 13 to our Number 24. And all our flats smell like plaster and wood varnish.

I watched Ada push her glasses up her nose and wondered – at the sight of the pulled thread in the sleeve of her T-shirt – where Nathan's black fleece was now. At the back of our flatpack wardrobe? In her university room? Well, that didn't stop her sleeping with the fluffy fabric pressed up to her cheek not so long ago.

My phone hummed with a notification from mine and Jasmin and Michael's group chat. Their day had been filled with sports science lectures. Discussions of muscles and ligaments and stretching exercises. Presentations on computers, group work, and a running track with paint so fresh I felt I could smell it by looking at it.

A biting feeling clawed at my stomach.

A twinge I did my best to ignore.

I sneakily took a photo of Emmanuel leaning on the side of my mum's work desk in Say It With Flowers. His mouth all gummy and open, mid-compliment. His glasses skew-whiff, and that weird thin moustache of his lifting as he talked. Jasmin and Michael didn't know that much about him. Or, really, much at all. But they recognized a funny photo of a funny guy. They would've known I'd want them to laugh.

I liked that they spammed me with exactly that. So I didn't have to respond to the photos of their new red running bibs, or of the croissants they were snacking on, or to the shots of the Eiffel Tower obscured by their new branded water bottles.

It was still light when I got home at the end of the next few days of volunteering.

My whole body aching with exhaustion. The block of flats rising up out of the pale light of the sweltering summer evening like giants.

The neighbours were too busy chain-smoking and beating their carpets out over the railing to really stop and say hello, ask me about Ada, congratulate me on her homecoming.

I heard snatches of conversation though. Snippets of Czech, Albanian, Kurdish, Swahili, Somali, Pashto ... It was all jumbled together with little bits of English.

Full stops didn't exist in the flow of the languages of the flats, the small worlds rushing into one another. Instead, we had those English words, 'isn't it?' and 'alright?' Those were the pauses. Those were the bits we nodded at and knew about. Like how a blind person knows that the bumps in a bit of paper are where the meaning exists. I knew 'isn't it?' and 'alright?'

A hand up as I walked the path up to the steps – not waving, just up – meant I was recognized. Number 24. The youngest girl of the three that live in Number 24.

Smiling eyes that had left the hills and valleys of their homelands to find new ones to climb meant I was welcome. Weathered hands twirling spoons in night-shift-stained mugs of coffee meant I was accounted for. Present, like how that one weird teacher at school always wanted us to answer the register with. Present. At home.

But the kids' playground . . . the kids' playground where me and Ada and Nathan and the twins that lived opposite him grew up . . . That was like a hug. That was what drew you in, made you so sure you were where you were meant to be.

Number 13. His name was Nathan Eze and he liked books almost as much as Ada did.

Number 48. The twins were Precious and Aron Mba and they hated books as much as their parents hated English mashed potatoes and other people's concepts of well-made food.

We all liked playing on the swings though. Us five.

We all liked stretching our legs and spinning on the roundabout and comparing timetables at the very same school. Doing impressions of our neighbours who would age with good humour like everything does.

When we were little in the flats, it didn't matter that I was the youngest at eight, and Precious and Aron were two years older, and Nathan and Ada were the oldest by three years, Ada beating Nathan by exactly one month. We just sat and swung our legs together after dinner. We all got tired of our parents shouting and of the slam of doors – or for me and Ada, of our mum's nervous silence. So we swung and swung and swung.

'Hey!' I waved, seeing their three familiar silhouettes by the climbing frame.

Precious waved back, kicking stones aimlessly. Aron did, too. But goofily. With too much enthusiasm. I immediately knew he was being sarcastic. We liked to annoy each other like that. Nathan squinted hard behind his glasses. Or at least I thought he did. The glasses were just big on his face. They were all anyone saw when they looked at him.

Still, seeing those three like that made all the memories of PC Chris, and all the posh kids from north Friesly, and the ache in my wrist from washing bus shelter glass go away.

Suddenly I wasn't so angry at Amir for getting us into all of this with that stupid graffiti.

I wasn't so curious about that girl Eman not sticking up for herself when people tried to make fun of her food either.

'Ada!' I rushed into the shared space of our bedroom, my socks skidding lightly on the floor. She sat painting her nails. 'Ada, everyone's out in the playground. Let's go after dinner.'

Mid-polish application, my sister froze at the sound of my voice. Then her fingers flowed back into motion. 'Maybe next time, Kemi. I have a lot of things to do.'

She reminded me that Mum knew about the police volunteering, as well.

She said I had to be on my best behaviour, and not get involved with any bad influences because obviously Mum wasn't happy about it, and would prefer not to speak to me for fear of hurling her flip-flop at my head that evening.

'*Kemi!*' Mum's voice rang in my head, echoing from the one time I'd got detention for forgetting my PE socks and I'd heard her whole face shake in rage. '*Kemi, don't get in trouble. It scares me to get phone calls about you.*'

I pulled on Ada's sleeve, grinning. 'Well, I'm not the one she needs to be worried about. Ada, you love bad influences. Remember that time you and Nathan were kissing in the community allotment and you thought no one could see you, but me and Aron did, and –'

'Kemi.' Ada looked at me hard. So that I knew she meant it. 'Don't.'

The venom in her voice. Another tongue.

I faltered, tripping over my words. Then I walked off. Out of the flat, letting the door slam shut behind me. Not heading to anywhere in particular. Just out on the balcony. I stood in the humid evening air, the chirp of insects, the buzz of midges and flies. Then I shook my head. I breathed deep. I walked back into the flat.

'Kemi,' Ada said at the dinner table, interrupting Emmanuel's stale church sermon about the benefits of good manners easily. 'Do you want some more Fanta?'

I didn't say anything. Then I glanced at her. Saw the raised arc of her brow. I shrugged. She poured it into my glass for me without the usual chat about hurting my teeth with all the sugar I inhaled all the time.

I couldn't shake it though. The way a part of Ada felt far away, still at university. Ghostly, gone away, and refusing to come home. Properly, I mean. Back to the flat, and the kids' playground, and us in Friesly.

A year ago, it was so easy to spot her shadow moving to the window in the middle of the night, phone kept like a secret near her ear.

'Where are you going?' I said once in the dim light, because she and Nathan had been whispering too loudly on the phone she'd told my mum she didn't have.

'None of your business!' Ada hissed.

I'd raised an eyebrow. 'Isn't it?'

And I remember I'd inhaled so she knew I'd scream. Then she was shoving my windbreaker on me and helping me out of the front door and down the stairs to where Nathan stood, chewing his nails in fright, nervous as a nervous system. It was fun to hang out with them though. The twins too, once they caught wind of our shadows dancing by the creaking chains of the swings from the dull corners of their rooms.

'Hey,' I used to say a lot in those days, feeling the cool air chill the insides of my lungs as I swung on the swing, with Aron waiting for his turn while Precious took hers, and Nathan and Ada pretending like they weren't purposely huddled together on the bench.

'Do you think everyone in the flats is asleep right now?'

Aron always snorted at me. 'You mean like you should be?'

Precious rolled her eyes at her brother. Ada tried to kick him.

'Shut up,' I said, 'or I won't show you my superpowers. They're sick, you know.'

'Go on then.' Nathan smiled. 'Show us your powers.'

I liked how he always took me seriously. I liked how it felt to be looked after by someone who wasn't in my family. Ada was always the first to follow my finger to where the light in one of the windows glowed yellow like the morning. Nathan was always next.

'That one's going to go out nnnnnow,' I used to say, stretching the word until I was sure the light would dim.

And Ada would laugh and do the same thing with another lit-up window, and so would Nathan, and then Precious, and Aron. We'd all point up at the windows and will the world into darkness. I mean, as dark as it can be when there are still bright and shining stars. Aeroplane trails. Faint and wispy clouds.

'Nnnnow!' we used to shout together. We used to forget how old we were supposed to be together.

'No, now!'

'Wait, wait, wait. Nnnnnow!'

Until someone's upstairs window slammed shut, a wordless protest against our noise, and the distant wail of sirens somewhere further into town hushed us into a giggly contented silence. Bodies aching. Cheeks hurting from smiling.

'Now,' my mum said, in between heaping Emmanuel's plate full of *jollof* rice, 'Kemi knows the value of good manners. I think she knows them even better than your congregation does since she has decided to join a volunteering programme for the summer.'

I glanced at Ada, hoping she'd be just as dully impressed by our mum's positive spin on my accidental criminal activities. Bingo. My sister's mouth lifted a little, wry, genuine.

'Really?' Emmanuel said, while licking a stray piece of rice off his thumb. A shock wave of disgust went through my entire body at the lip-smacking loudness of the moment. 'I hope it's better than that Volunteering4Friesly scheme the police are doing for the wayward youth in this town. Lord knows they need it more than the north Friesly lot who're using it to boost their university application forms.'

I think Mum, me and Ada had a heart attack at the same time.

'D'you know,' Ada said clearly, saving my mum while she choked on her water, 'I think Kemi's volunteering might be related to that. But only because she is such a good role model for other people on that scheme. The north Friesly opportunists and the south Friesly strugglers. She's the real deal.'

'Hmm.' Emmanuel served himself some fried plantain. Looked at me through his dusty glasses. Sprinkled his meal with pepper. 'Yes, I would agree with that.'

I handed him a napkin so that he wouldn't lick his fingers again. He took it. He dabbed his sweaty forehead with it. A groan threatened to come out of my mouth.

I glanced at Ada again. I wanted her to see the Dad-was-never-like-this look in my eyes. I wanted her to be my older sister again. But she was looking away, her brow creased in concentration, too busy trying to stop Mum's dress sleeve from dipping into a lamb side dish.

PART TWO: FAMILIAR FACES

featuring:

chickens – a fall – a coma – litter-picking – paper cuts –
a wall of arms – a hurricane – a disappearing sister – the
perfect delivery boy – police leaflets – the second haiku –
a pair of sunglasses – a Gucci pouch – a tidal wave – a pet
called Quiet – leaves pulled off trees – the aunties'
argument – the sun/a stargirl – a sweatshirt instead of a
fleece – the best view in Friesly – the Bible – a £5 note – a
very old friendship – and a party in the drinks aisle

CHAPTER 7
AMIR

Fiza's chickens arrived on a drowsy Tuesday morning. A collection of speckled round-eyed hens and a rooster with a red crown on his head. A few tufty baby chicks that cheeped and pecked and crowed and cawed from the inside of a giant cardboard box. Courtesy of one of Uncle Nadeem's friends, of course.

'Why?' Mum groaned, eyes bruised with lack of sleep.

Her brother smiled a kilowatt smile. It felt too bright for the time of day. 'Well, she's been going on about it for ages, hasn't she?'

And that was all there was for an explanation.

Then Uncle Nadeem hopped back over the fence, returning to his own house so easily, one arm resting on the slates of the stone wall that separated our two concrete gardens, all of him inflated with a sense of only-uncle pride. In return, he asked for eggs – fresh ones, with curling brown or black feathers stuck to the shells.

'I'll egg you in a minute,' Mum muttered to him. Light danced in her eyes at the sound of my laughter.

It was me who had to go and wake Fiza up though. Me

who had to help her and Uncle Nadeem raise a barbed-wire cage over the hard slabbed ground of our back garden, ripping up the little patch of grass and mud we had, to let the fork-shaped stencil of chicken feet roam free.

The Nishaan phone had been ringing for a while, and Mum needed to answer it, so she said it was up to me to make sure Fiza didn't throttle the chickens in her enthusiasm when she saw them. But when she came down, my sister just stared, skidding to a stop halfway across the kitchen floor. Big sobs began dripping down her nose and cheeks and all over her pyjama sleeves.

'*Yara*,' I said, proper confused. 'I thought you wanted these chickens.'

The rooster stared determinedly at Fiza's hand. Pecked the birdseed I'd slowly poured on her palm.

'I do want them,' she sobbed, her chin all wobbly when she picked it up and held it in her arms. A heartbeat in her fist. So quick, so small. 'I d-do . . .'

I wanted to laugh at her ugly crying face. But then she started talking about what it would be like if no one was looking after the chickens, and how we were the ones that got to do that, and what a big deal that was. I ended up just going to get her a tissue for all her snot. I made her blow while she fought me off, puffy-eyed, irritated, ignoring the rooster pecking at her fingertips. Then I watched the chicks and hens in the box with Fiza as well.

That warm mass of feathers.

Black, brown and orange.

I realized how fragile their bones were. Birds are so light. Like human beings. They can't fly away in hard situations. They need protecting.

My mum's face was thunderstruck when she finally put the phone down.

'What?' I said.

'The accident last night.' She sat down on the kitchen chair beside mine. 'The one outside our restaurant.'

Her eyes got big with unspilled tears.

'Amir ...' The white of her hair caught in the light. Like paint stains. Unignorable. 'Amir, it's worse than I thought it would be.'

This is what had happened the night before.

Old Maariyah Malik, who taught Qur'an to the neighbourhood kids, had come to Nishaan to buy a bag of freshly made *jalebi*. She and my mum even had a conversation at the till about how it was a tradition in her house, having the sticky orange swirls on the table when the theme tune for *Hamari Zindagi* was on. Old Maariyah Malik particularly enjoyed watching her granddaughter feel how sticky her fingers got with all of that syrup on them.

The till's chimes. The sound of pennies and pounds for change. Dusk outside. The day winding to a stop. Neighbours and strangers heading home from work and summer activities, all tired, some defeated. The July heat, clammy like sweat on skin.

Old Maariyah Malik paid for the box of *jalebi* and hobbled her goodbye, her walking stick a helpful third leg on her way out. Mum went to check the back after she was gone, their chat about the old Pakistani drama fading from her mind like cigarette smoke on the wind. She really needed to talk to Mohamed about inventory. And the thick walls that separated the kitchen from the front of our restaurant made it so that she didn't hear the way old Maariyah Malik smacked her lips as she put the last of her money inside her cracked leather wallet, her old eyes squinting at the notes and pennies in her wrinkled hands, her walking stick misjudging the safety of the weathered cobbles outside. They'd felt the force of so many pairs of shoes, boots, trainers, sandals treading on them over the decades ... They were run-down. Slippery. We knew that already.

Mum felt the air inside her body change when a half hour lapsed into a full one and the walls of the kitchen began to reflect the blue and white lights of an emergency vehicle. The moaning wail of an ambulance siren, echoing in her ears.

She and Mohamed glanced at one another.

They'd run towards the congregation of neighbours and strangers gathered outside, all wide-eyed and whispering, watching as old Maariyah Malik's still lips and wrinkled hands were loaded on to a stretcher. One foot had lost its leather loafer. Her stick a phantom limb now. Her lips not smacking. Her blood staining our doorstep red.

'It's sad,' Abshir said on our *FIFA* call later. 'Our neighbours used to go to hers for mosque all the time.'

'I bet it was better than having my sister teach me.' Hassan's voice came out crackly because of his microphone. 'You know

Neelam shouts at me every time I don't pronounce *ain* and *ghain* properly.'

Hassan's sister Neelam was known for being a loudmouth. Both in her home and on the pitch when we all played football together. She was around the same age as Uzair, long-limbed, long-haired, and nowhere near as boring. Almost married, for one thing. And the sickest striker we ever had. She once kicked the ball so hard it almost fractured Uzair's nose while he was in goal.

'I'll shout at you too if you don't score right now, Hassan,' Ben yelled. 'Missed it! Again! Oh my days!'

'Well, the old lady's in a coma now, not dead,' I said, trying to throw Abshir an assist and missing myself. 'Maybe she'll make it out alive.'

I heard the smile in Ben's voice. 'And maybe this'll be Liverpool's second victory today.'

Groans on the line. Swears and insults. 'Oi, keep chatting when you've got better stats than us.'

'Than who?'

Abshir burst into song despite Ben and Hassan's jeers. I joined in despite the bad taste in my mouth. 'Man U! Man U!'

They moved us on to litter-picking in the park once the bus shelters were clean enough. Me, Kemi, Eman and the north Friesly kids. They gave us those giant hand-looking grabber thingies and bibs and black bin bags to put the litter in.

'Hey.' Kemi grinned when she saw me coming. Behind her, Eman was still struggling with her bib. 'Watch this.'

She tucked her arms into the sleeves of her T-shirt. She used her grabber thing and mine to do a little dance. Waved her arms around all crazily, pouting and waggling her eyebrows all the way. I burst out laughing.

'Wait, wait,' I said. 'Give us one.'

We tried to do a handshake with our grabbers. It didn't really work that well. But we both found it funny anyway. I mean, until the north Friesly kids turned up, and PC Chris pointed out where we were, and they completely ignored us. I even nodded at that kid with blond spiky hair and glasses. Just to be polite. But he bumped his skinny shoulder against mine on his way to pick up an empty crisp packet on the long grass.

I threw my grabber thingy after him. 'What d'you think you're doing?'

The guy didn't turn around. 'Relax. It was an accident.'

I could've sworn I saw a smile on his face though. Or at least the look on someone's face when they're about to smile but they're trying to pretend they're not. Kemi looked at me. She shrugged. Behind us, Eman was still trying to get used to the grabber thingy. It wasn't that hard to use, but it looked like it was giving her some trouble.

'Eman,' I said. I think at that moment she needed my help as much as I needed hers. 'You saw that too, didn't you? He did that on purpose.'

'Hmm?' Her eyes were so big they made her look surprised all the time. 'Oh, um. I don't know.' She wiped her nose on the back of her hand. Her fingers were shaking a bit. I guess because of having to hold the grabber thingy. 'I wasn't – I wasn't really watching.'

'Here.' Kemi bounced over with her usual puppy-dog energy. She helped Eman stretch her hand, open the claw grip. 'It's like this, see . . .'

But I was still watching that blond kid. I was watching him and his friends, and how they were picking up chocolate wrappers and fallen leaves, taking photos, and posing to put all this on their social media accounts. Like, *look at us! We help out! We're good people, volunteering in the bad part of Friesly!* So what if they dropped the chocolate wrapper right back where it was when the photo was done? And they didn't even notice because they were too busy checking to see if the angle was just right? To make sure you could see enough of the rusting sign for Fowley Park in the back, the lake that was one-half duck city and one-half someone's giant abandoned shopping trolley, and the red-brick terraced houses, the wire pylons, the shoes tossed over the telephone line, and in the distance – so faint, so grey – the weight of Sir William Barker's stone hat?

If they saw the bus shelter, my bus shelter, Zayd's, all coated with a giant poster for the Barker Summer Festival, they didn't say anything about it.

But there was still a little blue spray paint on the side of my palm, no matter how many times I tried to scrub it off. Sticking there.

Like him, on the top shelf of the bunk we used to share, wafting a breeze with his legs and his bedsheets, telling me to get him some water from downstairs.

Like me, half-asleep, kicking the slats, telling him to get it himself.

'So,' PC Chris said, his hands in the pockets of his uniform trousers. 'Is Mr Amir Ali going to get rid of any rubbish today? Or is he too busy staring into space?'

I had this weird need to use my grabber thingy on him. Just pinch his side with it. Piss him off. But I picked it up and stabbed some stringy tissue paper instead. I put the bits that were clinging to the grass, spoiling the path, all the way inside the black bag.

'You're a pro,' PC Chris said. He dusted off my vintage Ronaldo shirt. 'But that's what we're good at, isn't it? The Red Devils always take the rubbish out.'

It was weird. I didn't know he supported my team. 'Yeah,' I said. 'They do.'

The even weirder thing was he was smiling at me. Thin lips curving up at the edges. I mean, they were until he walked back to where PC Katie Phillips was standing by the big trees that always rained green on people walking the path. I watched their mouths go as they talked. I saw PC Phillips' lips go big and small, biting and chewing, as she looked me up and down. Mimicked the way I'd thrown my grabber down. Angled her shoulders like an angry kid. I heard it, just watching her lips. The same stuff I heard about me when I was in detention at school for making the class laugh at a spelling mistake on the board. The bad shit that got thrown around on Parents' Evening, behind my back, and in corridors when me and my mates were being 'too loud' when we were talking. Whether we were talking football or comparing scores on our English assessments or listening to Abshir imitate his grandma and how loud she shouted when she wanted water at dinnertime because she was going deaf and misjudged the volume of her voice all the time.

'Hey, what happened outside Nishaan last night?' Kemi interrupted the noise in my head, her grabber now being used to scratch an itch on her back.

'Oh yeah.' The north Friesly girl in the dungarees made all the vowels in her sentences really long. 'We heard about this too. Drugs, right? A deal gone wrong, and someone got stabbed –'

'No,' I said. Maybe a bit too loudly. But it pissed me off, how everyone was always talking about us lot like that. Just because we walked a certain way, looked a certain way, lived in a certain postcode. 'No, it was nothing to do with that.'

That was Zayd's brother, wasn't it? Bro, he looks just like him. Proper gangster. Bet he's dealing like he was as well.

But Zakiya Bhatti knew otherwise. And there was an eyewitness. An actual living breathing person who'd seen the truth and knew it even better than I did. I'd double-checked her press profile again. My messages showed up as delivered. Double-ticked and already gone. But not opened. Not read. I'd sent another message about Zayd, and the article, and who had seen LOCAL BOY, 16, die like that anyway?

Now Kemi was scratching her head with the grabber. 'The accident outside Nishaan, right? I heard the cobbles outside are stained red now. Are they, Amir? Y'know. With blood?'

'Yeah,' I said. 'We couldn't open Nishaan today because of that. It's probably gonna stay closed for a week. Maybe two. This old lady that taught Qur'an to the neighbourhood kids slipped and almost died, and –'

Eman shoved past me quicker than I'd ever have thought she could. She wasn't very good at PE. I mean, she was always the slowest at running, and the worst at the beep test and at catching things. But her shove was more painful than the blond kid's. Barged right past. Left her black bin bag behind, all coated with juice cartons and rotting fruit.

'Hey, where are you going?' PC Chris yelled at her retreating back. She didn't respond. He turned to the rest of us. 'What just happened?'

'See?' PC Phillips jabbed a finger in PC Chris's skinny chest. 'I told you! That boy is a negative influence on the rest of them – you have to be harder on him!'

I felt my heart beating quicker in my throat. My grip on the grabber thingy tightened, threatening to splinter the plastic in two. I threw it down on to the ground. 'What do you lot know about negative influences?'

PC Chris spluttered in front of me. 'Pick that up, Amir!'

I ignored him. I wanted to jump on the grabber, break it, break anything.

But Kemi picked it up off the overgrown grass, and she tried to make me laugh by dancing with it, and something in her eye told me to be careful, relax, chill out.

I didn't want to. I knew a boy who was the chillest, a nice guy, proper smart, sick at *FIFA*, and the worst singer in the world. Had it made a difference for him? To be all of those things? Had it made anyone think differently about him at all?

It was a good thing that PC Phillips went to check where Eman was. She would've killed me for ignoring PC what's-his-name like that.

But she was too busy with Eman, who was a tiny speck by the barbed wire of the tennis courts. I watched as Eman kneeled down, and hugged her knees, and rocked back and forth like a kid who'd just had a bad dream. To be honest, I didn't want to be the reason for that.

PC what's-his-name's voice drifted in and out of my ears, an annoying buzz that I wanted to swat away, a constant drone forcing its way, insect-like, into my brain.

I gritted my teeth. Then I heard Kemi sigh behind me.

'Oh no,' she said.

I forced myself to turn back to her.

There was so much sadness in her voice. It sounded like a disappointment worse than being picked last for team sports. I tried to ignore how everyone else was looking at me – PC what's-his-name, the north Friesly lot, the people walking their dogs on the winding park path – while I forced the pieces together in my mind. I mean, there'd been an old lady with a walking stick and a gummy smile, two smacking lips, when we'd first been in the police station, hadn't there?

The realization hit me later than it had hit Kemi.

'It must've been her grandma,' I said finally. 'The slipped-and-almost-died lady.' My hands rested wearily behind my head. 'Shit, man.'

'Oi.' PC Chris wasn't smiling at me any more. 'Watch it.'

CHAPTER 8
EMAN

'I just don't get it, Mum.'

The bright hospital lights had started to give me a headache. The endless rows of too-clean corridors, nauseating in their pristine glow.

'You said she fell outside Nishaan. But Nani always came straight home after the council meetings in the town hall. What was she doing there?'

Mum looked tired that morning. The usual signs of her exhaustion: her work hijab messier than she would've liked it to have been, the safety pin that held it in place poking out against the sharp of her jaw.

She took my clasped hands into her own. 'Well, Eman ...' Her eyes turned into two shining pools. 'We were out of *jalebis*, weren't we? You two can't watch *Hamari Zindagi* without those.'

The glow of the ceiling lights got brighter. My thoughts, too tired to keep swimming, started floundering, sinking and swallowed up, and then, still. Still as a tripped-up girl on a playground floor.

'Th-that's what she went to buy?'

I pictured the sweet sticky spirals hitting the ground at the same time that Nani did. The smooth of those well-weathered cobbles outside Nishaan stealing her walking stick out from under her. Then her skull hitting the ground. The skin protecting it suddenly as fragile as fallen leaves, burnt yellow and curling by noon.

The cobbles had said nothing while Nani lay there, her breath knocked out of her. The fallen leaves had alerted no one to the old woman lying stiff out on the street. A single leather loafer, no longer jammed under our living-room sofa by accident and needing to be prised out by me and Mum, but just loose on the sole of her foot. Not moving. Not moving at all.

'That's why ... that's why she's in a coma now,' I said dumbly. 'That's why she has a blood clot in the brain. Because I wanted *jalebi*.'

The smell of the grass in my dream swept over me. Stuck. Stuck right there, sun-gold and overwhelmed. Right there, with my head chanting death's name. My heart chanting death's name.

My mum squeezed my hand. 'Eman, listen.' She fought to keep our eyes connected. Brown on brown. 'None of this is –' Her pager beeped loudly in her lap. 'Oh.'

She hesitated. Glanced at me – once, twice – as she checked over the information. Silence stretched out before us, easy as a relaxed back. Then, more of it.

'It-it's OK,' I said, when Mum wouldn't say anything more. But her hand was still in mine. I shook it, hoping with some stupid optimism that she wouldn't let go. 'You have to do your job, don't you? Go. Really, Ma. Go.'

Ours was a grip on a quickly changing reality.

Mum's eyes were bleary. Slow to find mine again.

I squeezed her palm. 'Go.'

But it still hurt somehow. How easily she stood up. How quickly she left me alone.

It was the fact of my own weakness that had me sobbing beside the barbed-wire fence in Fowley Park. It was because of the cobbles turning red outside Nishaan. It was because of the *jalebi*, all sticky in our hands. And how when I was little, my knees covered in fresh bruises, Nani used to click her tongue against her teeth, grab some tissues and wipe my fingers individually, one eye trained on the TV, the other on my mess.

'What are we going to do with you?'

Always a tease on the tip of her tongue. A smile on her lips.

A promise that *I'm coming, I'm coming* when the busyness of the TV noises and my own giggling ineptitude were interrupted by neighbours rapping on the door, by children in mosque *topis* and little-girl hijabs begging to come in for a lesson.

I was sobbing because we were at the beginning of a season which involved those same neighbours rapping on our door for a different reason. And I was wiping my eyes with the back of my hand despite PC Phillips crouching down beside me all confused.

She didn't know about the little hands lifting the letter box, the children's voices calling through the thick black brushes, asking if mosque-house was on or not, it looked like rain was coming, they'd have to rush home and not get damp and sodden if it really wasn't on.

But I didn't have the words to tell PC Phillips that. Nor could I tell Baasim and Juveria and all the other little kids that she wasn't here, and she might not be here tomorrow, or the day after that.

For so long, Nani had been as dependable as the one streetlight on our corner that always switched on early. It illuminated the way for kids looking for lost things in the dark, searching for hair ties and their youth, missing shoes and forgotten memories, deep in the velvet shadows. It served as a sign – following long shopping trips to Mahmood's Foods after school, my fingers straining hard to grasp heavy plastic carrier bags – that we were home.

I'd sobbed, throwing the wallet the police had returned to us hard against the kitchen wall in those first few hours of the news.

It had fallen like night. The leather crackling like old skin. Then I'd pressed my palms into my eyes, ignoring the sting. I'd stood up and picked that wallet up from where it had slid behind the cooker, near the bin, ready to – almost immediately – collect dust.

Little fingers still rapped impatiently at the door.

'Helloooo? *Baji*, are you in there? *Apa?*'

Thunder rumbled up ahead. A summer storm, electricity. Or was it the sound of a bin being taken to the kerb? I couldn't tell the difference.

'Listen.' PC Phillips held out a pack of tissues to me. 'I don't know what the big deal is, or what Amir Ali has said to you – the little bugger – but you need to ignore it. You've got a job to do. Several, in fact. Volunteering4Friesly is not something that should be taken lightly. In fact, I'm expecting a big black bag of litter with your name on it by the end of today. I'm expecting more than one. OK, Eman?'

Tears dripped down to the edge of my chin. The grass in Fowley Park was taller than it should've been. The green around us, all rough to the touch. Half in darkness, half swamped with sun. Like my dream. A wave of sickness washed over me.

'Just look at this place!' PC Phillips yelled over the sound of my sniffling. 'A strong girl like you could clean up those crisp wrappers over there in a heartbeat!'

The distance between us was too wide to be comfortable. Our shoulders not brushing. Her tissues requiring my effort to reach for them more than they required anything from her. But I did reach for them. I wiped at my eyes.

PC Phillips seemed pleased about this. 'I'll give you sixty seconds, OK? Then you come back and get rid of those crisp packets.'

I took a shaky breath. I nodded. It seemed like the right thing to do. And I watched her walk back to where PC Chris stood waiting, his arms crossed over his chest, while PC Phillips' lips mouthed a countdown.

'Thirty seconds!' she yelled, her thumbs-up all faint in the distance, her eyes fixed on mine.

There was an ache in my skull. My brain rattled around. I ignored it. The wet *slosh* echoed as I walked back to where Kemi and Amir were jabbing at the grass and depositing the rubbish into their bin bags. The wet *slosh*, *slosh*, *slosh*.

*

The tasks for volunteering changed as the weeks went by. We went from having wrinkled fingers from washing bus shelters and pasting Barker Summer Festival posters on walls in the middle of the town, to developing calloused hands from litter-picking in the park, to getting paper cuts from doing admin work in the police building, to having tired feet from delivering leaflets for the police themselves.

We were expected to put in our very best effort all of the time.

Despite the stale heat, the sweat gathering in a sickly strand at the nape of my neck.

We were expected to learn from the graffiti stains on our skin at the very beginning of this ordeal and never do anything as troublesome, as disrespectful, ever again.

Well, that's what the state of my hands and feet said to me. I don't know what the message was to Kemi, who always laughed when someone did something stupid at school. I don't know if the soap, the glue, the litter, the paper, the leaflets shone very brightly for Amir, who already knew the vivid language of school detention by heart. Was fluent in it.

I'm not really sure what tasks the kids from north Friesly were given to do after Fowley Park was divided into sections for our litter-picking, either. I think I should have paid more attention when PC Chris was talking to us about it, our bright volunteering bibs all collected in his hands, our litter-pickers lined up by all the bin bags we'd filled that morning.

Honestly, all I could focus on was how there were so many bags that had my name stuck to their sides. All these double-knotted black ones, lumpy with soggy cardboard and empty drinks cartons, with my name written in permanent ink on their little sticky tabs. In a very familiar style of handwriting. But I couldn't place where I'd seen it before.

'Huh?' I said, when PC Chris congratulated me on my speedy work.

He and PC Phillips exchanged a smiling glance. 'See? We knew you had it in you. You've really put your fellow volunteers to shame, Eman. Well done!'

Then PC Chris excused us and said we'd be starting our organization of the reprographics room in the police building tomorrow, and to get there really bright and really early so that we'd have plenty of time to organize the files and folders that needed it. He looked especially at Amir when he said this. But I don't know if Amir had been late to volunteering yet.

I remember Kemi patted my arm before she zipped up her windbreaker. 'See you tomorrow, Speedy.'

'But I didn't –'

I frowned at the black bin bags. I counted them all. I had two more than Kemi and Amir did.

'I didn't pick all of that up . . .'

'Yeah?' Amir shrugged his backpack on. He fussed with an inside-out strap. 'Who d'you think did then?'

The handwriting on the tab really did look familiar. Sharp and spiky.

'I . . . Hmm . . . Well . . .'

Kemi laughed. She beamed with all her teeth as she waved goodbye. I glanced between her retreating shadow, and Amir in front of me, and the heap of black bin bags. Frowned down at them, my shoulders heaving with the force of a contemplative sigh.

Amir's smile showed a really sharp incisor. Like a vampire's tooth. 'You're funny, you,' he said.

Then he walked across the grass to where his bike was locked up against a grocery shop's railing. I didn't expect him to look back at me, but he did. Twice.

And I tried to imagine Nani was still here, not stuck in a state of deep unconsciousness, lost to a terrible fall, an accident-induced coma. I tried to imagine her face, seeing Amir's thick eyebrows, and the razor slit in his right one, and how he looked golden in the afternoon sunlight, wrestling his bike free, and standing beside its glow, smiling at me. Twice.

'*Mashallah!*' my memory of her whispered to me, her phantom limbs nudging my side. '*Smile back at him, won't you, Eman? You know your grandfather smiled at me like this every time he was in front of me, walking in the alley back from school, just us two.*'

I turned around quickly. I remembered Farida aunty. The seriousness of her one eyebrow, which moved vividly as she spoke about Zayd Ali. A drug dealer. Amir's brother. A thug. Then I walked home along the back streets, past green wheelie bins and bricks used for cricket stumps. My heart skipped like stones on water. Warmth rushed to my cheeks.

'Stop it,' I told myself. 'Just stop.'

A pile of Tupperware boxes greeted me at our front door. A Jenga-pile of Farida aunty's sabzi and *daal*, Balqis aunty's *pakorey* and lamb *biryani*.

I made the roti to go with everything myself. It was drier than Nani would've liked it to have been. But no one clicked their tongue against their teeth and dragged up their walking stick and had me make the atta, roll out the dough, heat up the *tava* again. The realization made me cry all over again. Tears that sizzled dry on the hot metal.

I turned up at the police station to tidy up the stacks and stacks of recyclable paper in the reprographics room with everyone else only slightly late. I guess because I felt tired. Like a Tuesday morning, which sometimes feels like a Monday morning but worse.

'Eman!' Kemi hissed, then patted the space next to hers.

Somewhere in the past, I watched Noor and her friends laugh together at our lunch table. The pull of girls' arms when they're together, a wall that feels impenetrable. My own arms, on the outside of that lunch table, so limp. Scooping up pasta. Watching *Ball* repeats. One pair of arms can't be a wall at all.

Kemi hooked her elbow round mine. 'Don't worry,' she hissed. 'You didn't miss anything important.'

I looked at the criss-cross of our arms.

Then, after hours of PC Chris speaking at us, we were called to lunch. And out by the oak trees dropping leaves on our shoulders, the dappled sunlight stencilling temporary tattoos on our skin, Amir stretched his arms up and out and reached one of them all the way around the back of me. My stomach lifted like bubbles in fizz. They spread everywhere. Like in the tenth level of *Ball*, when it starts getting hard, when you have to start putting the work in. That game felt so far away from me now.

'Sit up, Amir,' PC Chris said sharply, his voice echoing over the wooden table. 'I'm explaining something important, and you're acting like you're at a bloody picnic.'

Kemi glanced at me, her teeth biting at her bottom lip. She pulled her feet back from where she'd been resting them out all relaxed in front of her. But PC Chris didn't say anything to her about that.

He started explaining which files went into recycling, and which ones into spare paper, and which ones into the shredder. Then the freckles on his nose danced. He wrinkled his entire face in disgust.

'For God's sake, we've given you notebooks to write in.' PC Chris took the pen that Amir was using to write on his palm and threw it in the bin. 'You don't need to do that.'

My hand was smudged with the notes I'd written on it, too. I clawed at the ink with the tips of my fingers, hating the reedy thinness of PC Chris's words. Cold as violence. They cut extra hard. But PC Chris didn't say anything to me about my hands.

And when we stood up to head back to the police station, shaking off the pins and needles in our feet, it was Amir that PC Chris yelled at for forgetting to put the wrappings of his panini in the bin, even though we'd all experienced the same drowsy after-lunch feeling that made us all forget these things. If I'm remembering correctly, it was usually Amir who remembered to swipe up his mess and who made a big show of tossing it into the bin in the first place. I don't know if PC Chris saw that though. I don't know if he ever did.

'Maybe he's having a bad day,' Kemi said, when the three of us were on the carpeted floor of the reprographics room, organizing the hard-copy equivalent of Friesly Metropolitan Police's spam email inbox into piles to recycle, reuse or shred.

The window was cracked open a little. No breeze outside. No clouds in the sky.

Amir didn't move from where he was lying horizontally, a piece of printer paper shielding a heavy burst of sunlight from spreading its warmth on to his face.

'Or maybe he just has it in for me.'

Kemi kicked the sole of his shoe. 'At least look like you're helping us out. Me and Eman have shredded loads of these already. Innit, Eman? She's got bare paper cuts already!'

I looked down at the plasters Kemi had helped me place around my fingers. And then at the sharp tongue of the shredder, waiting for the paper pile we'd been instructed to move.

'Yeah,' I said slowly, flexing my finger joints.

Amir groaned before he stood up. He walked over to me while fussing with the Nishaan delivery cap on his head. 'Alright, Eman. Why don't you go and help Kemi with the paperwork and I'll deal with the moving and shredding?'

He smelled like mint shower gel. Is that what all drug-dealer family members smelled like? A whole garden of the plant Nani used to stew and add to the *kava* that cooled my headaches? Fresh like pavement rain? Amir leaned down to hear me answer. I forgot I was supposed to talk.

'OK,' I said suddenly.

Amir laughed his vampire laugh. He leaned around me to turn the shredder on, and I saw that the eyes that always looked so angry, that always got caught in the shade of his delivery cap, were light brown.

Like tree bark. A place to rest your palm on, call your sanctuary, during games.

Kemi beamed at me again.

'What?' I said, sitting cross-legged next to her beside the big window, the traffic jam on Long Road harmonizing with the sound of the shredder.

'Nothing,' she hummed, as I began to leaf through the pile of recycling. But she still kept looking at me. She poked the part of my cheek between my jaw and my teeth. Smiled until I did too.

'What's his problem anyway?' Amir yelled, throwing his arms around all irritated. 'This PC Dickhead, what's-his-name, Chris guy?'

He fed the waste into the razor tongue with reckless abandon, even with a little bit of joy for how it came out on the other side, spaghetti thin and white as ice. 'Just because his trim's dead. What does that have to do with me?'

'Go on then.' Kemi neatened the corners of her waste pile with her hands. 'Give him your barber's number if you're bad.'

Amir snorted. 'My barber's my uncle's best mate. Uncle Feroze.'

I could hear the smile pulling at Kemi's lips. 'Go on then. Give him your uncle Feroze's number if you're bad.'

The two of them burst out laughing at the idea of PC Chris ringing up for a regular Friesly boy haircut. Short back and sides. A touch-up. One blade on the top and another under. Even a fade at Clean Cutz, or 360 waves, or locs. He'd wear all of that with none of that strange sweet magic, that trick with no name which made some Friesly boys – with their awkward intentional limps, their joggers and too-big hoodies, their cheeky loudmouth grins – so beloved to us that knew them.

Kemi and Amir looked at me, inviting me into their joy. Was this it? A wall of arms?

'Yeah,' I said, desperate to hold them up with me. 'Imagine him. Imagine . . . PC Chris . . . with a good haircut!'

There were more bubbles inside of me. Fizz and fizz and fizz, as Kemi and Amir and I fell over laughing. But they grew smaller when PC Chris appeared in the doorway of the reprographics room, grim-faced, his car keys dancing around the top of one finger while his free arm carried a heavy box of leaflets.

'What's so funny?' he said, in the wake of our silence. 'Go on. I like a laugh. Tell us a joke.'

None of us did.

An old woman walks into a wild field of green echoing with crows.

Or is it a young lady?

A young lady walks into a field of green echoing with crows.

CHAPTER 9
KEMI

The flat was heavy with chatter and rose-scented perfume. Large bottles of red wine, reflecting shards of pink all over our living room. Like stained glass. A church for St Valentine's or something. But Aunty Sunbo and Aunty Ifeoma's cackling was less respectful than any behaviour at a regular church service.

'Kemi,' Mum said, her hands quick to steady mine at the door. 'Go wash up.'

The jerk of her head backwards – to the full sofa, the sounds of bodies in the kitchen – emphasizing the importance of guests. Of good manners to greet guests. Good manners to greet guests well – no sweat on your upper lip, no smell of too-full recycling bins. Whether Emmanuel was still busy leading the rest of the flock at the Jacob Pentecostal Church or not.

I looked past Mum's small body to the copy-and-pasted reflections of her family who showed their gaps in their teeth when they laughed, who stopped Ada from perusing the folded-over corners of their Bibles to congratulate her on her success.

'OK,' I said.

Even though a part of me wanted to warn Ada about the flute of wine in her hand, and a part of me wanted to get washed down the shower drain and fall asleep somewhere, and a part of me wanted to help Mum clean the reddish spill growing bigger on the glass table.

I even hesitated, watching the tired sway of her hips, the hand on her back which signified pain in her joints again.

'Kemi,' Mum hissed, jerking her head backwards again. There wasn't any fire in her eyes. Nothing that made her seem like anything but a woman ageing under the duties of her culture. I went to the hallway anyway.

'Remember what you used to call her when she got like this?' I said to Dad's smiling face.

Hurricane, the man in the wedding portrait laughed, catching his wife around the waist, desperate to taste even one of the many *puff-puffs* cooling on the counter, the delicacies of a primary school party I'd pleaded and begged for. She'd smacked him away of course. A wry smile at the corners of her lips. *'They're for Kemi's class. For children. You are not a child, are you?'* Maybe it was a good thing Dad wasn't. Those *puff-puffs* were deep-fried and wrapped in foil and didn't place any position on primary school palates more accustomed to samosas and pakoras, fairy cakes and iced gems. Jasmin had already eaten enough fried stuff, apparently. Michael was the pickiest eater in the world. So the Tupperware container holding the fried dough bites had been only slightly less full on the bus ride back from school – and what was missing was only because of a kid called Hassan Jalani's endless appetite, and my own sad snacking. I remember Ada shaking her head at the sight. *'You shouldn't have forced Mum to make so many.'* How I'd pursed my bottom lip, stared out of the bus window, knowing she was right. I'd let the wind-whipped trees see me cry and no one else. I'd gasped a little at first, too. Feeling the shake of the Tupperware container in my hands, the lid being unsettled and my dad's factory hands taking *puff-puff* after *puff-puff*. He'd handed them out to me and to him. Then he'd winked at me: *'We'll tell your mother everyone loved them.'* I'd taken a bite, smiling, watching him point to me and then to him: *'Everyone. We're everyone.'*

'Now, Jesus died for us all because we are sinners.' Aunty Sunbo was a little unsteady on her feet, the glass of wine sloshing in her grip, the other hand hooked casually around Ada's shoulders. 'A God-fearing woman like me, I know what my sins are. But you, my girl. Smart, tall, beautiful. What are yours?'

I watched my sister search all the faces that worked at the flower shop for my mum, her eyes hunting past the laughter in the living room, Aunty Ifeoma bragging about her eldest niece to everyone sat beside her, Aunty Sunbo pressing Ada for a response.

'Well,' she said eventually, when the tired flutter of Mum's eyelashes, and the way she shrugged into resting on the sofa, suggested any response was a good one, 'I can't always do more than one thing at a time.'

Aunty Sunbo walked and talked under a hazy grape-scented cloud. 'Busyness is not a deadly sin, Ada.'

'Oh.' Ada's voice got all soft. 'Isn't it?'

A series of stumbling and slurring: 'No, preoccupation with the good keeps you from distraction with the bad! It is a blessing from the Lord!'

There were chants in agreement, a cacophony of voices asking about what Ada had to eat at uni down south, the cost of a taxi over there, her gown size. And then, what it was all for, her job in the future, a career so that she could cement her place elsewhere, so that she could always live right with the good and not wrong with the bad.

'Somewhere else?' I asked Mum, wiping the table beside me. 'Is that what they mean by her living right? Somewhere that's good enough for her? Not here?'

'I don't know, Kemi.'

There was no hurricane beside me. There was only a breeze struggling with a rag and a spray bottle.

I sighed. 'Give us that, Mum.'

The breeze relented so easily. Like it had never been different. Like there had never been a strength inside it at all.

Nathan, Precious and Aron jumped a mile from where the kitchen counter stood tall with various bottles of juice. Some a darker shade of dandelion yellow, others brown as soil and just as rich. The cans of fizz at their lips clearly heavy with mixing.

I laughed despite myself. 'I'm not even gonna ask.'

But they laughed, too. Told me stories of Uncle Jafari's influence, Aron and Precious's boredom, and how Nathan could never – no matter how hard he tried – hold his liquor right.

'Where've you been all summer anyway, Special K?' Precious said, ignoring Nathan's protesting, her fingers quick to help me run the cleaning rag under the tap.

Police sirens flashed blue and white in my mind. Graffiti stains on my fingers. Bin bags in the park and the whirr of the shredder in the station's reprographics room. 'Around,' I said.

The gang cooed over nothing, just so I'd know they thought I'd sounded cool. I pretended to throw that cleaning rag, joked to keep the smiles on their faces.

'Listen, listen, listen.' Aron pushed past his twin, hopping up on the counter beside me as I rinsed glasses. The rest of us side-eyeing him like usual.

'Kemi, you're an athlete, innit?' Running Right residential in France or not. The goofy grin on his face or not. 'So you know how important it is to eat properly. Would you tell these lot I have to have the big bits of the rotisserie chicken from Mahmood's Foods because I go gym and they don't?'

Precious narrowed her eyes, her arms crossed over her chest. 'You don't go gym! You just flex in the mirror at the gym, it doesn't count!'

'No, look!' Aron tensed his arm, trying to define the muscle.

'Where?' Nathan fussed with his glasses, Precious following his lead and squinting behind him.

'Here!'

I squinted too. 'Where?'

We were just waiting for Aron to roll his eyes, shove us away, call us idiots. His tantrums were only ever thirty seconds long. Usually followed by an invitation for desserts at the tea and doughnut place on Long Road, as well.

'Ada,' I said, watching her carry a stack of plates to the sink after me. Her eyes stuck on balancing a knife right and not on Nathan's stuck on her. 'You're coming too, huh?'

'Hmm?'

'Long Road. For desserts.'

'Ah.' My sister's smile stopped at her cheekbones. 'You know, I don't know if I'd remember the way there. It's been so long since I've been. I feel like I don't know Friesly as well as I know other places now.'

I wanted to tell her it was a simple journey. A simple path. One I'd once trusted more with her feet than with mine. But she left the kitchen so quickly.

I wondered if it was all gone to her now. Or going, quick and fast. The geography I'd thought impossible for her to forget. A neighbourhood attraction like Nathan's name so bright she'd carved it into her desk once. The surrounding land of her and mine and Mum's broken heart.

I mean, back when we first heard about Dad's cardiac arrest at the factory, Mum used to lie in their bed for days on end, just a completely silent, unmoving lump under the duvet.

And OK, I'll admit it. It used to scare me a lot, seeing her like that. But it was Ada who used to dress me for school and make me toast spread with margarine. It was Ada who I showed my book bag and the week's library choices to. We'd get home from school, and the flat would still be in the dark. Blinds down. Windows shut. Mum still lying in bed. But Ada would raise the blinds, and set the table, and tell me to go and pour a jug of water.

The woman who lived upstairs played more records to sweep her flat and lay out her washing to than Uncle Jafari did inside Clean Cutz. In the afternoons, a husky voice escaped the needle on her record player, a deep melody travelling down the floorboards, crooning, almost crying, disturbing the dust with the promise of a better day.

'Ada,' I used to say, while we ate more toast, only now with beans, at a table too big for the two of us. 'Ada, what's happening to Mum? It's not happening to her too, is it? The same thing that happened to Dad?'

I used to hear my mum wheeze and cough and struggle to breathe in her bed. I used to hear her cry for hours, weep for hours, and give herself a panic attack from doing that.

'Nothing's happening, Kemi,' Ada always said. She'd scrape the beans from her plate on to mine. 'Eat your food.'

She'd spend ages going through breathing techniques with Mum as well. That cheeks-full, in-out breathing technique I got taught for running at school. The one that helped me win so many medals. Inhale. In. Exhale. Out. She'd sit with Mum for hours, unravelling the cocoon of her blankets, rubbing shampoo into her hair, humming along to the melody coming from upstairs.

Ada would talk to Mum, too. Small stuff. Like the smell of fried plantain, the vegetable plots in the community garden, the colour yellow, and Screwball ice cream, and how much Mum had liked the flowers at Dad's funeral. Weren't they nice? The roses she'd spent so long pressing her fingers over? Well, the new flower shop in town grew roses just like that. Soft to the touch and sweeter than Mum's own sharp scent of sweat and coconut oil.

It worked, what Ada did. The softness of her voice, the clear way she explained things. My sister handled my mum's really bad months so well I thought only she should do it. And all while I sat in the hallway with my dad's portrait, listening to their conversations, talking to him like Ada talked to Mum. He was my own personal moon, hanging on that wall, so close yet so far.

'Things will get better,' I'd tell him. 'Mum will be back to normal soon. Don't you worry.'

I really believed that. I really believed in her rolling her eyes again, shouting at anyone who crossed her, smacking their fingers when they needed it. Hurricane woman. Hurricane woman who could live again to blow hard and fast on any house belonging to any man any day.

But the Jacob Pentecostal Church belonged to God. And Emmanuel Achebe.

'Hey,' I mouthed to Ada hours after everyone had gone home, glancing between the unscrewed salt and pepper shakers at dinner and Emmanuel reaching for them.

If I squinted past her, I saw three shadows hanging around the children's playground, arms heavy with fried and sugared doughnuts, beckoning us – like some fairy-tale figures – to come out to play.

'What?' Ada said. She dog-eared the thick university book in her lap.

I waited for her reaction.

But there was no laughter from her at all the salt falling on Emmanuel's chicken and peas and rice. No smile at the excess of white granules he groaned at while Mum coddled and cared and went to grab him some extra napkins and a fresh plate.

Ada simply stared. Then she continued to read.

Didn't she find it funny? Emmanuel's shock at the mass of salt landing on his plate? His big eyes? His flimsy glasses falling off his face? I stole a glance at Ada in between spooning up rice – while the shadows outside chatted and joked and laughed without her.

There were a lot of leaflets in the box PC Chris had under his arm. Displaying, at Friesly Metropolitan Police's request, a wide array of bright colours and easy-on-the-eye graphics. They dealt with important issues like JOINING THE POLICE and EYES OPEN: ESTABLISHING YOUR OWN NEIGHBOURHOOD PATROL.

Me, Amir and Eman read through the ones at the bottom of the box as well. HELMETS ON, HEALTH RIGHT: CYCLING SAFELY, surrounded by clip-art pictures of cycles, helmets and a specific scenic cycling route in north Friesly. HOME SAFE: PREVENTING HOME BURGLARIES, on a black background, with the information about locked doors and home alarm set-ups displayed in the glow of two-dimensional street-lamps and torch lights. DON'T OPEN THE DOOR: 7 STEPS AGAINST DODGY DOORSTEP CALLERS used a red and white combination to make it look even more urgent, even more vital to be shoved through someone's letter box by the three of us.

'You should count yourselves lucky,' PC Chris explained while surrounded by the paper smell of the reprographics room. 'Delivering these leaflets won't be nearly as bad as picking up litter or staying inside this room.'

'OK,' I said. 'But will it be boring?'

PC Chris instructed us to come straight to the car park behind the police station the following day.

'Don't you know, Kemi?' he said to me when we were stood at the police reception, getting our jackets and bags to leave. 'Only boring people get bored.'

PC Phillips' voice climbed out from behind his skinny frame. 'And those who are too stupid to realize they're being taught a lesson about the rules and respecting them. This isn't for fun.'

PC Chris nodded. 'Exactly.'

But it was PC Phillips' eyes that flashed blue and piercing in the hustle and bustle of the police station. I felt her gaze follow me, Eman and Amir way after we made our separate ways home.

Or, I mean, the things I think she was trying to say with her eyes followed us home. Words about who we were to her that stuck in her irises. I'd seen her look at other people the way she looked at us.

At carjackers coming into the station in handcuffs. At kids running to get the ball that had been kicked behind a parked police car by accident. At Danny *Dangar*, stuck at a zebra crossing, waiting to cross the street, not knowing when a car was giving way to him, nudged by school kids on bikes, cut to pieces by their words. And there was always a pause in her steady stride outside Clean Cutz, a little too much curiosity about the Black man sweeping up hair inside, a little too much enthusiasm in her waving hello to my uncle Jafari.

CHAPTER 10

AMIR

I never thought I'd actually be saying this, but I missed doing deliveries for Nishaan. I proper did.

I mean, I used to complain about it all the time. I used to get annoyed because people took the mick with their orders, asking for extra mayonnaise, wait, no mayonnaise, barbecue chicken in their panini, more ketchup on this, hold the salad, another can of 7-Up with this, didn't we get the Buy One Get One Free deal with that?

I got annoyed, too, when a neighbour on a particularly difficult delivery stopped me and asked me what I had in my backpack. His phone in his hand, his eyes looking me up and down like CCTV.

'It's a simple question,' he'd said, this one man, with his arms crossed over his chest, acting like he owned the street I'd cycled up and down so many times. 'What are you delivering here?'

'Food,' I'd said. 'Haven't I told you that already?'

The cap on my head was black, embroidered with the Nishaan logo. My bike, stencilled with the very same. But the man became a building, trapping me in his shadow every time I tried to move.

'Alright, fine. You don't believe me? Fine.'

I'd shrugged off my backpack. Opened up neatly packaged brown bags. Waved the insides around in the muggy air: a chicken panini doused in mayonnaise, a bag of masala chips. I took bites. I chewed hard. Hummed in delight and licked my fingers until the man scoffed and took his leave.

I thought I'd dealt with that pretty well, too. But then the customers for those orders started rattling the blinds in the windows and banging against their windowpanes. I couldn't understand the way some people looked at you with magnifying-glass eyes. Turned you into an easily destroyed ant. So I ate more orders. Well, I was hungry delivering every few minutes up and down the hills of Friesly! And waking up early to do it, too!

'Amir.' Mum used to call me every time I was on the busy intersection which looped back around to town. 'Can't we go one day without a complaint about a missing order? Whose did you eat today? Just tell me. No, no more excuses. Just tell me so I can refund them now . . .'

It always hurt a bit, hearing the frown in her voice, and how she didn't find me funny at all.

On the phone, I always promised that I wouldn't do it again. I wouldn't eat Howard Li's salt-n-pepper chips because he was late opening the door. I wouldn't take a sip from Qasim Mahmood's can of Rubicon mango if I could help it.

But then I'd be stuck cycling around bends and avoiding tree branches, having to wait too long at a junction, seeing someone frown while reading the receipt for their order, and neighbours staring me up and down, and I'd feel it again. This weird feeling inside me that jumped out when I couldn't help it. It came from deep inside. Not from my heart exactly. But maybe around it.

The Hard Feeling
Amir Ali

Bike spokes on the ground.
The sound of a loyal son.
STOP. 'Why are you here?'

Shutting that feeling down was like trying to shut your wardrobe after you've shoved all your stuff inside it cleaning up one day. I just couldn't do it. Not as well as Mum, and Miss Khan at school, and Fiza wanted me to.

Mum was smiling on the day that Nishaan reopened to the public though. The banner in the window written and Sellotaped with Mohamed's expertise. The cobbles outside our shop scrubbed free of any redness, any old woman's leather loafer.

That morning, Mum didn't shout at Fiza for taking too long to feed the chickens in the morning, but with calm and ease let her tell us that Maximus – the rooster – demonstrated his leadership skills every time he ate his breakfast much quicker than the other hens. That morning, Mum didn't push me to make a start on helping Fiza with her short story instead of playing *FIFA*. There was no mention of GCSE Results

Day coming up around the corner. No mention of my approaching birthday celebration requiring my very best behaviour. No stressful discussion of the preparations for the big wedding – Neelam Jalani's – at Nishaan either.

She yawned over a frying pan. 'D'you want eggy bread?'

I stopped tying my shoelaces at the kitchen table. Felt my sister come thundering in, all covered in chicken feed and feathers. We matched each other in our shock.

'But Mum . . .' Fiza said slowly. 'You always say that's such a long breakfast to make!'

'And everyone always says that Amir would never be able to make a delivery without eating at least one thing in the bag! But look at him now! D'you know, Fiza, in the week before we shut up shop, Nishaan got so many calls praising our delivery boy! They said you're so quick and so polite!' Mum leaned forward and pinched my cheeks. 'So handsome, too!' She set the cooker going and fried the butter with ease. 'I knew you had it in you.'

I saw the light in her eyes. I heard the warmth in her voice. I wasn't brave enough to tell her Uzair had been doing my deliveries. So I just smiled and sat down and rubbed my cheeks in silence.

'Um,' Kemi said, ankle-deep in the thick gravel of the car park a few hours later. Her hand at her brow to shield her eyes from the gleam of PC Chris's ugly white six-seater. 'Haven't you got a normal car for us to deliver those leaflets in?'

PC Chris urged me, Kemi and Eman towards the sliding doors and seat belts. 'Normal?'

'Yeah,' I said. My arms were starting to cramp from holding the cardboard leaflet box. 'Normal. Not one that looks like it belongs to your great-grandma.' I groaned as I set the box down into the boot. Sniffed the interior. 'Ugh, it even smells like your great-grandma!'

'Adam.' PC Chris's voice came up from behind me. 'You really need to watch yourself.'

I made a face. 'It's Amir, not Adam.'

PC Chris looked at me. 'That's what I said, isn't it?'

He matched my footsteps back around the car to the sliding doors, closing up the distance between us so that our shadows had no choice but to overlap on the grey ground.

'Look, I'm just saying,' I said, tired of his bullshit already. 'Alright, so you can't afford a Bugatti Veyron. But anything's better than this.'

PC Chris's gaze was steady on my movements. 'And you think you could afford a Bugatti Veyron, Amir? A lot of the boys around your side of Friesly have fast cars, don't they?'

I thought of all the boys the women in my neighbourhood worried about. Muzzy, King Khan, Kash. I thought of the money in their pockets and their mothers' prayers for them. And how my brother had always offered them *salaam* despite disagreeing with their choices, said there'd been a time when they'd been the ones to loan him their pens in form.

'I guess,' I said.

'Where do they get all that money from?'

'I don't know.'

'You do.'

I laughed, just because I was beginning to feel like I couldn't breathe. The air was a little too warm outside, his voice a bit too serious.

'*Kasmey*, man. I don't.'

The burst of the steering-wheel horn came from inside PC Chris's ugly white six-seater. 'Hey.' Kemi's two buns popped out from the passenger window. 'Are we delivering these leaflets or not?'

I stepped away from PC Chris first. I let my Nikes leave scuff marks all over the gravel and the interior of that six-seater as I took my seat in the back with Eman. My head was pounding. I felt my hands shake, all clammy with sweat. I turned them into fists. Was this it? The fear that had made Zayd run away?

'Are we all set?' PC Chris said to Kemi, and then to Eman in the back, and me next to her. His voice, like some radio frequency, now tuned back into Regular Strict. 'Seat belts!'

My fingers fumbled over themselves trying to find the metal clip. The six-seater jerked unsteadily as PC Chris wrestled with the gear stick and forced the vehicle forward. I found the clip, cool against my fingers, as the six-seater tumbled over a set of speed bumps. Then I lost it again.

'Sorry,' PC Chris grumbled in response to our groans.

He started talking again about how important it was what we were doing. He said that delivering these leaflets really would show everyone how the Volunteering4Friesly scheme was all about giving back to your community, being a part of your community, and showing the people within it that you cared. Never mind the fact that Dungarees, Glasses and

Ginger didn't have to do the same jobs that we did. Never mind the fact that they wouldn't have considered our cobbled streets and ramshackle stone walls home at all.

The metal clip of my seat belt jumped out of my hands again. I grabbed it, but it didn't stretch around me properly. I had to pull it so it could fit into the red lock. Then PC Chris braked harshly as we came up to a main road, all blocked up with the usual summer traffic, and I almost lost it again. But two hands, gentle as a whisper, helped me place the metal clip into the red lock.

I glanced over at Eman. 'Thanks.'

Her smile was tiny on her face. Then she turned to look out of the window. She didn't see the burning red tips of my ears.

'No, but seriously –' Kemi's voice drifted back on the stale air from the front of the vehicle – 'this is your car, right? Why did you pick . . . *this*?'

PC Chris adjusted the smiley-face scent diffuser hanging off the mirror. 'I like it.' He grabbed his too-big sunglasses from the glove dispenser. Turned on the A/C. 'I think it's cool.'

Kemi caught my eye in the side mirror. I could tell she was trying really hard not to laugh.

Kemi was the first one out of the van, too, when we had to stop and deliver to our first street.

'There's one special house that really needs a reminder about preventing home burglaries,' PC Chris said as we crunched up to an uphill kerb. 'And the one next door to that house, well, that one really needs a reminder about police-mandated cycle safety. Come to think of it, the whole street needs reminders of Friesly Metropolitan Police looking out for them. Might as well deliver leaflets to everyone.'

PC Chris's tone made him sound like a stranger to the street, a tourist. Someone who could think of our slanty, hilly bit of town as more of a project than a final product. He looked like he didn't fit in, too, sitting up all sweaty in the driver's seat, elbow out of the window, a layer of sun lotion shining white over his acne-dotted skin.

Seeing him, the hard feeling came up from inside of me. I wanted so badly to go home, abandon Kemi and Eman, do anything but this. Then I pictured my mum's face. I saw her seeing me, a police volunteer, a kid so good at messing up. I pushed the hard feeling down.

'How fast do you think we could get this street done?' Kemi said, with this big-dimpled smile on her face. Her entire body poised like a spring, all ready to go. That was usually what she looked like in PE lessons on the school field, too. 'D'you guys think there's a record for delivering leaflets? Shall I time us?'

Me and Eman just stared at her. That street was packed full of overgrown hedges, green flies and midges just waiting to bite us. It stretched out, rows and rows of terraced houses. The kerbs, dusty and dry. Tough as a sore throat.

'However long it takes,' I said, as I brought out the leaflets from the back. 'It still won't be quick enough.'

Kemi grinned. She took double copies of everything. 'Is that a challenge?'

She ran to as many houses as she could, posting the shiny paper through the doors like the front gardens we crossed weren't obstacle courses of cheap plastic toys and half-sunken trampolines. I don't think she even cared about whether anyone was watching her from the inside. Net curtains twitching a bit. Sunshine reflecting off loft windows. Shadows and the sound of moving feet behind all the peeling front doors.

She was just back in Sports Day mode. The girl I'd seen win countless races, carry countless medals, wander aimlessly around the school field with the end-of-race ribbon still colliding with her waist, searching for a family member to gloat to. I don't think she ever stopped being in Sports Day mode.

It looked like PC Chris never stopped being in Bad Driver mode either. Later that day, he forgot to pull the handbrake up when we were parked even higher uphill on that street – so busy with summer-break traffic – and the car started rolling back. The rest of us were outside, watching it move. I yelled at him to pull it up already as he panicked at the wheel.

He pulled it up. Then he just stared at me from inside the car. 'You haven't got a licence, Amir. Why do you know how to do that?'

I stared back. 'And you haven't got a brain. Otherwise you would've known to pull the handbrake up.'

I carried on delivering the stupid leaflets so that I wouldn't have to hear him ask Kemi and Eman about my attitude, my anger, the 'thuggish' razor slit in my eyebrow, the possibility of my underage driving. Had they seen me driving around? Had they reported it? Had anyone?

'What an idiot.' I stood outside an untidy front garden, cap off so I could wipe the sweat dripping down my face, the tarmac below my Nikes almost bleeding from the heat. 'Who doesn't know to pull the handbrake up after you finish parking?'

I felt eyes watching me though. Sizing up the angle of my shoulders, the back of my head. Almost-familiar whispers in breezeless gardens as Kemi and Eman followed after me.

'Just ignore him,' Kemi said at my side. 'He's not that bad if you just don't take him seriously. Right, Eman?'

Eman looked at Kemi. 'Um, yeah.'

I started walking away from them. 'You lot don't get it.'

Kemi and Eman shared a look. I didn't know what it meant. To be honest, I didn't care. The heat was at its worst at midday, coating all of Friesly in a disgusting sort of thickness, while PC Chris's sunglasses glinted harshly from inside the car. And we still had so many leaflets to deliver.

But those eyes I'd felt on me, tracking me in between hedges and overgrown weeds, suddenly appeared out of nowhere. Those front-garden whispers not whispers any more.

'Amir?' I knew Hassan Jalani's voice straight away. On a *FIFA* call and in real life. 'Amir, *yara*. What you doing on my street?'

He looked confused, all round around the stomach and panting from the run up to the kerb. Sweat separating the strands of his hair and plastering them down on his forehead. My best mate since nursery.

Of course I'd know him anywhere in the world. Me, Hassan and Abshir used to play tig at the mosque when my brother and their dads were doing extra sunnah prayers. Us three went everywhere together. Ben Stockdale too, who's Abshir's next-door neighbour, and funny because he's fostered and he knows more swear words than even me and Hassan. In bare languages.

Sure enough, Abshir came running after Hassan, a half-deflated football in his hands, his limbs so tall and thin, his wiry hair moving, as he told Hassan to hurry up already, they were already thrashing Ben and his foster sister Kay 3–1.

From somewhere behind the mess of low stone walls, overgrown hedges and peeling front doors, I heard Ben yell at them to stop lying, the echo growing clearer as his head emerged over a red-brick garden wall, blond-haired and swearing and – eventually – walking towards us.

'Eh?' I stared at all of them in turn, confused.

It only took a few seconds of looking around – noticing the same sawed-off trees in the back gardens, the same lines of washing going from wall to wall, the same creaky electric pylon out front, the same massive barking guard dog down the road – to realize I was on Hassan's street after all.

'Oi, man,' I said, prolonging the 'a' like a yawn. 'I thought you lot were too busy with your families to hang out before Results Day. Isn't your sister getting married soon, Hassan?'

Hassan started fiddling with the string on his fake Gucci pouch. 'Yeah, Neelam the big giant's getting locked down. So what?'

Abshir held the half-deflated football protectively in his arms. 'We all had today free, innit. We thought you were busy helping out at Nishaan, being a good son and that.'

Hassan let his fake Gucci pouch rest by his waist. He puffed up his chest, wandering closer and closer to where Kemi and Eman were standing.

'Yeah, it's not our fault you lied to us.'

He missed the awkward look the two of them shared.

'What are you even doing these days?' Ben's eyes zoomed in on the leaflets. 'Selling pound phone cards to call Pakistan? Our neighbour does that. Give us some then. I'll call your grandad. Give us it!'

Abshir ignored Ben and Hassan trying to wrestle those leaflets out of my grip. 'Leave it.' He grinned. 'Obviously, he's only doing it to impress these girls. *Astaghfirullah*, bro. That's bare haram.'

I really didn't want to look back at Kemi and Eman. My stomach felt weird, thinking of Eman's hands, so careful with the seat belt.

'Chill out, alright? I'm not trying to impress them.'

Ben's freckles got darker in the sun. He bounced his eyebrows up and down. 'Are you sure about that?'

I didn't know what to say.

'Why do you lot care anyways?' Kemi called over, crossing her arms over her chest. 'Are you jealous? Are you jealous you don't hang out with girls? Eman, I think they're jealous.'

'Yeah.' Eman looked at Kemi. I didn't know if she was already looking back at me. It was hard to tell because of the sun. She crossed her arms, too. 'You're jealous.'

Hassan, Abshir and Ben lapsed into an uncomfortable second-long silence. Then Abshir let out the donkey-braying sound I recognized as his fake laugh, the one he did when his dad told him off for putting his feet on the table at home. Hassan and Ben joined in pretty quickly. The three of them wiping tears from their eyes, holding their stomachs, practically begging Kemi and Eman to be serious, stop making them laugh. My best friends, the worst liars ever.

I tried to think of an excuse for my not hanging out with them.

I tried to think of something that wouldn't have their mums shut the door on me at future birthdays, their dads 'humph' and sigh and mention my cousin who seemed better, more honest, a worthier friend, at the mention of my name.

I mean, I knew my mates didn't think of me like that anyway. No matter what their parents thought. Or how many detentions I had at school. Or what people said about Zayd. But I wanted them to believe it fully. Properly. Not when they were defending me from other people, but beyond that. Even in the quiet moments, when they were just thinking of me. Just me, Amir Ali, who they'd known since nursery, who always got the ball when it went flying over a wall, who always had gum and a good laugh for them.

PC Chris pressed hard on the middle of the steering wheel. 'If I don't see movement in the next ten seconds, you've all failed the Volunteering4Friesly programme! Chop-chop!'

Kemi and Eman jumped to deliver the leaflets, their heart rates picking up in a second. I'm not gonna lie, so did mine.

'Who was that?' Abshir said before I could turn around and just get on with the leaflets. He was already tall, but he made himself even taller to see who was sat in the driver's seat. Then his eyes got big.

'Amir, man.' He lowered his voice. 'Are you in trouble with the police?'

Hassan shook his head. 'Nah, he's not. He's not, they're just targeting him, innit?'

I smiled. He really was my best mate.

Ben bumped my fist with his. 'Safe, g. Look after yourself.'

'You lot,' I said, 'text me when you're playing *FIFA*.'

The trees on Hassan's street brought up a lot of dappled sunlight. Little bits of gold and yellow, shimmering like bits of glitter in the art box in nursery. It felt like it was coming down on me, twinkling, warming my eyelids, as I set to delivering the leaflets again. I reached the doors on the opposite side of Kemi and Eman's route with ease.

'You sure you're not in trouble with the police?' Hassan yelled from the tarmac, the last of my mates to head back to their football game.

I put up a thumbs-up, just joking around. 'You know I only give them trouble!'

He laughed. PC Chris was a faint shadow sat in the parked car. But I recognized the thin line of his mouth. The downturned corners. I bit my lip. I shoved a bunch of leaflets through the letter box before me. And again. And again. Again, again, again.

'Amir,' Eman said when our route started to become the same, right at the very bottom of the cul-de-sac. I glanced at her, in next door's front garden. I don't know how long she'd been watching me, but my instinct was to see if she needed more leaflets. I went to give her mine.

'Wait,' she said.

And I paused, halfway through putting my stack of dodgy doorstep caller and neighbourhood watch leaflets into her hands. 'What?'

Her words came out all awkward. 'I heard what you were saying to your friends just now. About ... About giving the police trouble. And, well, y-you aren't trying to turn out like your brother, are you?'

I froze. 'What?'

A drug dealer. A criminal.

While we stood shaded by front-porch roofs, by too-tall trees and the birds cawing in them, I wondered what she knew about him. I wondered what anyone knew about him while they were all running their mouths.

Kemi barely seemed out of breath after hopping over someone's creaky side gate. 'I've got more leaflets if you guys want them.' She glanced between the two of us, her eyes settling uncomfortably on Eman and then on me. 'You know, these ones? The cycling ones? I don't think you guys have those ones. Let me check –'

'Wait, what do you mean by that?' I held my hand up for a second. Suddenly everything seemed so loud. PC Chris hammering down on the steering wheel. Lights and sirens in the distance. 'About my brother? And not turning out like him?'

Eman's gaze was big and round. She was all eyelashes. And rubber bracelets, different-coloured ones, on her wrist. She pulled at them awkwardly. It irritated me somehow, how new she felt to this conversation, how she didn't already know Zayd by heart.

'Farida aunty says he died because he was a drug dealer. He was in trouble with the police. And now ... you're ... Well, I don't really want that to happen to you, too.'

I heard her say that. But everything in the world sucked itself free of sound straight afterwards.

So I didn't hear PC Chris get out of the car, door slamming, telling us to get a move on. I didn't feel Kemi dragging my shirt sleeve, saying none of us knew the full story, none of us knew what had happened to Zayd, so I couldn't be mad if Eman didn't know. Well, even Kemi didn't really know if he'd been a dealer or not.

The people on that street came out in their sun-bathing vests and thin linen *shalwar kameez* to ask us about the leaflets, complaining about their blocked letter boxes. Aeroplanes hummed up in the sky, left trails of white smoke behind them like angels' wings. Cars revved in and out of drives. Blocked the road. Caused arguments. Somewhere in town, a thief set off a shop alarm. Qasim Mahmood came out yelling about the CCTV. Tourists clicked their photographs around Sir William Barker's statue.

The whole world went on, messy and loud and shouting at me. Yelling at me. Even Eman's big eyes. Even her eyelashes.

She blinked and it was a tidal wave of noise, and lies, and rubbish.

She blinked and I looked away.

I didn't mean to slam our front door later that evening. But I did.

'What's going on?' Fiza said from where she sat in the living room, feeding Maximus tap water with a child's medicinal syringe. I ran up the stairs to my bedroom, our old bedroom, and to the underwear drawer in the corner.

'Amir!' She followed after me, stood in the doorway as my fingers felt for the familiar ink, the familiar smell, for Zakiya Bhatti's name, and then Zayd's. Zayd's. 'Amir?'

CHAPTER 11
EMAN

I don't really like it when things are quiet. The backstreets, lit up by a single streetlamp, no animals howling or insects chirping because it's too warm to move even a single muscle.

It's funny, in its own way. Because the quiet seems to follow me around. It always has. But I've never wanted it to. I don't want it to.

Yet it shoves itself into the walls of my life. Like mould. Like moss. It gets past the locks of other people's loudness in my life: Nani's laughter while telling me to stop skidding with my socks on the kitchen floor and the slow murmur of my mum's car driving over the small gravel stones of our driveway.

The aunties speaking without apology in the launderette, bickering over care packages for the homeless and who'll deal with Azrah aunty's dramatic demands next. The light from the TV in our living room and my video games nestled under my pillow. The neighbourhood kids practising their Qur'an in the other room, rocking on their heels, letting the Arabic alphabet give them some momentum.

The quiet pushes itself around all of that. It makes itself at home in its absence. Like a thief in the night. Like an intruder.

So that even when my ears start hurting from too much loudness, my head suddenly heavy with it – in our old house, from the chaos of my mum's shrieks and my dad's punching swears – I still don't miss the quiet I'm so used to. It hurts. Amir's silence – his hands shoved inside his basketball shorts, his eyes cast down to the ground on the drive back to the station – bruised like a shove to the ribs.

And I was sorry. I really was. But I didn't know what I was sorry for.

It was an early finish after we'd delivered leaflets to a few streets. The centre of town was still busy with afternoon shoppers, Danny *Dangar*'s familiar loping figure there among them as usual. The summer heat drying the leaves on neighbourhood trees and dropping leaves on to the roofs of parked cars. Shop windows made pretty with striped summer awnings, glinting mercilessly in the sun.

'I expect tomorrow to be better,' said PC Chris, battling against the sound of a mechanical fan in the stuffy warmth of the police station. He had a map filled with leaflet delivery locations safely downloaded on his phone.

'I expect I'll only have good things to report to PC Phillips tomorrow.'

He did the whole thing of looking at Amir when he said that.

He even made him stay behind so that they could talk about Amir's friends distracting him. Something to do with 'focus' and 'being a negative influence'. Kemi and I left him sitting on the stained sofa alone, the defeated curve of his neck suggesting a lack of appreciation for PC Chris's words.

I remembered where I'd heard it before though – that stuff about his brother. It was in the launderette.

Nani had always hated how the police tried to lead her and her walking stick home if they came across her on one of her evening walks in Fowley Park, always smiling at the trainers glowing white under her *shalwar kameez*, always scaring her with their politeness.

Once, those good manners made her trip so bad in the cool twilight that her thick googly glasses almost fell off her face.

'*Soorney,*' she'd sworn at them afterwards from the safety of the tiny wooden bench in Wash 'n' Wear afterwards. 'What do they think I am? A weakling who can't find her own way home? I'm old, not stupid.'

'Now, Maariyah, don't be so disrespectful,' Farida aunty had interrupted. 'The police are only trying to look out for us. You've noticed them cracking down on the drugs around Friesly, haven't you? Taking some of these boys off the street can't be anything but a good thing. Leave them be.'

I remember Nani rubbing her chin. 'What about Zayd Ali . . . ? Hmm . . . ? He lived near Mahmood's Foods, didn't he? The tall one? Who always did the shopping for his mum?'

'You're sure that he dealt drugs too, Farida?' Balqis aunty had said.

'That's what the police said, didn't they? Don't ask silly questions!' Farida aunty had snapped at her while folding a pair of children's socks.

So we didn't ask any more questions. Not me, or Nani, or

the other aunties. And then the tinkling of the bell on the hinge brought a sudden burst of fresh conversation, meaning no one had any further time for the previous one.

I suddenly wished I'd asked though. More questions. Just like in English class, with that long Greek poem, and not understanding all of the lines: *'Reckless one, my Hector – your own fiery courage will destroy you!'*

Kemi fell into step with me on the walk home, our footsteps tracing the beaten path of the pavement together.

Families ahead of us chattered casually while fussing with sun hats and passing around forgotten sunscreen. And the quiet. That quiet was my pet. A stray cat, nestling up against both of our legs.

I glanced at Kemi. We crossed the road. I glanced at her again as the sun lit up her dark hair, her two fluffy buns.

'About Amir –' I said. 'I didn't mean to –'

'It's OK.'

She was concentrating on something. Her eyes, wandering past the dropped leaves on the ground, the humming bees fallen from some height. Her Reeboks, with the double-knotted laces, jumping from slab to slab. Avoiding the cracks in the pavement.

'Hey, do you have any brothers or sisters?' she said, still focusing on her game.

I shook my head. 'No.'

Kemi glanced up at me. Stopped jumping. 'Oh.'

She started again. 'I do. I have an older sister. Ada. She's cool. But she was cooler when she didn't go to a fancy university.'

Kemi pulled a leaf off a low-hanging branch. I wished I was tall enough to do that too. The quiet nestled up between us again. Too close. Too much.

'I wish I did,' I said. 'Sometimes I wish I had a brother or sister.'

Kemi glanced at me. 'Yeah?'

She avoided the cracks so easily. The rhythm was right there in front of me, so I copied it, jumping over a crack on the opposite side of her. 'Yeah.'

'What would you guys do together?'

I thought of Kemi's older sister. I imagined a girl taller than me, there when me and Mum and Nani sat in the living room together, chiming in with confidence on what we'd just watched on TV. Then I thought of Amir's older brother. I imagined a boy taller than me, there when I remembered it was my job to mop the hallway, standing over a soggy floor, daring me to come closer with my shoes still on.

'Talk.'

'Talk?' Kemi repeated.

'Yeah.'

It hadn't occurred to me before that I could do that – talk without being spoken to first. And now it was all coming out. No hesitation.

'We could talk about things, like school, and waiting for Mum to come home, and my green-field dream. And how I don't understand the aunties sometimes. And missing Nani. And we could cook together.'

Kemi smiled. 'And not burn anything.'

'And not burn anything.'

The two of us jumped from slab to slab together. We walked wavy together.

'And if I got stuck on something . . .' I stopped, a little out of breath, looking for the words. 'They could help me.' I turned to her. 'Does your sister help you? When you get stuck on something?'

Kemi chewed the inside of her lip. Above us, a flight of birds called to one another. An entire community in conversation.

'Sometimes.'

Then she shoved me without even saying anything, with nothing but her dimpled smile. She sped off – quick quick quick – across the street. Her touch still warm, still lingering on my arm. I didn't think about it. I laughed. I ran after her.

'I told you I was going to make the *saag aloo*, Farida. You were supposed to fry the *parathas*.'

'But, Balqis, I remembered Eman likes my saag aloo. I thought she'd like mine better.'

Balqis aunty's larger frame eclipsed Farida aunty's on our front doorstep. 'Didn't I tell you to plan this properly? Now Eman has my *saag aloo*, my pilau *chaval*, my *raita*, your samosas and pakoras, your *daal* and your *saag aloo*! Who even needs two boxes of *saag aloo*?'

The aunties squabbled in their usual Mirpuri language, a whirl of cream *shalwar kameez*, leather loafers and beige cardigans, blind to me unlatching the garden gate.

'I organized this as best as I could, Balqis! Don't you shout at me! You are far from perfect, Balqis! Your nephew doesn't even know how to drive yet!'

'He's doing his best! And you can't talk, Farida, your niece might as well be a nephew considering she doesn't shave her beard!'

The aunties' squabbling grew louder, fiercer, sharper even as I tried to interrupt, as I tried to give my *salaams*, force them to see me.

But without Nani's calming influence the volume rose quickly, and the insults grew harsher – about relatives with no education, about sons marrying women who gave them no children, about stolen wealth, stolen wives, stolen homes, stolen language. It was like the middle of the room we'd stood in for so long had fallen away. And now we were just floating. Anchored by nothing. Holding on to no one.

'We have lots of food still in our fridge, Balqis aunty, Farida aunty,' I said in the face of this war, the constant jangle of their gold bangles. 'Thank you so much. Really, it's OK about the *saag aloo* –'

Balqis aunty jabbed a finger. 'We all know the real reason why you're so nosy, Farida! You were always such a busybody when we were young, and you still are now!'

'Oh, enlighten us, Balqis,' Farida aunty sneered, 'since you had so many good grades at school. No, I'm misremembering. You had none! That's what happens when you're married off to the first person that comes knocking!'

'Well!' Balqis aunty said. And then – I felt it, too – that sharp intake of breath that comes before something that should never have been spoken, never uttered aloud. 'At least someone married me!'

It came back to me again. The quiet. It got bigger, no longer a pet cat, but now a sprawling monster of a thing. I knew everyone felt it. Everyone saw it. The same joke Farida aunty had suffered her whole life, cutting her to pieces all over again. The quiet that followed made worse because Farida aunty no longer had the desire to interrupt it.

I reached out my hand to rest it on her shoulder. 'Farida aunty –'

'Make sure you put all of these Tupperware boxes in the fridge, Eman,' Farida aunty said. 'Your mother works hard. I'm sure she'll be happy to see it all there for the both of you.'

She dipped her head low. She walked across the garden path, unlatched the gate and didn't look back at Balqis aunty's stubborn frown or at me struggling to hold all the Tupperware boxes I'd just been given.

My mum's nursing shifts always finished late. Even on weekends. That was something I'd been used to ever since we moved to Friesly though.

When I was little, the sound of the car meeting the gravel in the driveway was magic to my ears. It got me out of bed on the nights Nani tucked me in and disappeared to make a cup of tea and drink it alone downstairs. I imagined my mum's arrival. I fought off sleep, my eyes puffy and strained, always ready to see how she really looked when she dropped her keys on the hallway table and unpinned her hijab.

My mum always looked so tired. But happy. She looked happy, and safe, with no dad-shaped bruises on her face, no busted lips or blackening eyes. And she always turned around, caught my eye, then winked at Nani:

'She still isn't in bed yet?'

I loved that sentence. I loved how it was my cue to laugh when she said it.

Then I got older, and I slept past the sound of the car meeting the gravel in the driveway, and I only saw her on weekends. My mum and I slept in. Then we'd go shopping.

'Let's get you some new ones,' Mum once said while guiding me and Nani to the jeans aisle. 'Yours have so many rips and holes in them now.'

I remember I'd begged Nani to come with us with my eyes. I'd begged her to fill in the gaps – the things I desperately wanted to say but got stuck on, couldn't utter aloud, to my mum and her no-nonsense tone in that clothes shop.

'Fozia,' Nani had said calmly, 'I think Eman's jeans have rips and holes in them on purpose. It's the fashion now.'

Mum had glanced back at me, her eyebrows raised. She'd looked like she'd wanted to say something to me.

But then Nani had led us out of the shop, one hand directing us on where to go, the other resting happily on her stick. I would've followed her anywhere. I really would have.

Back in the kitchen, I stacked the new Tupperware boxes full of food on top of the old ones. I wanted to text Mum about the aunties and all they were doing for us. And when I heard cars come crunching into our gravel driveway, I thought one of them was my mum's. Until I opened the door and realized it wasn't. None of them were.

'Eman!' An aunty I hadn't seen since I was a baby – and who hadn't bothered to keep in touch – hugged me to her.

'Eman, you look just like your mama! Where is she? We heard about Maariyah. Aren't you going to invite us in? Is she at work? Can we come in and wait?'

'Eman.' An uncle whose name I could've sworn I'd heard Nani curse before – because he'd called my mum stupid for leaving my dad – rested his hand on the crown of my head. '*Assalamu alaykum*, Eman. We're sorry to hear about your nani. She was always such a loud – um – passionate woman.'

'Eman,' more aunties and uncles and distant cousins and friends chorused. They shrugged their shoes off and left them in the hallway, and hugged me to them again, and again, and again. 'We heard about Maariyah. We're so sorry about Maariyah.'

I didn't know what to say. I didn't know what to do. Our house was suddenly warm with our relatives, all of them having made trips from faraway towns to greet me with teary eyes, with sloppy kisses on my cheeks, and with well wishes for my nani's health. Her upcoming operation, her leg, her brain. She was going to survive, wasn't she? Or did we know better? Had we been told any news? Was there to be a funeral to attend in a few weeks' time?

'Please,' I said, with fear rising in my throat, and the knowledge that there were definitely not enough Tupperware boxes of food for the dozens of people flooding into our hallway, and a text being hastily sent to my mum. 'Come in.'

CHAPTER 12
KEMI

My dad told me something really important when I was little. It always comes back to me when I'm running.

My feet pound the pavement. The early-morning sun always makes the back of my neck feel as warm as the colour yellow. It's like I bring it to Friesly. It's like I move and morning opens up, fresh like the centre of a daisy or birdsong at dawn. It spreads slowly, over concrete yards, over unmown grass. Electric gates. Stone walls. The wooden benches outside Mahmood's Foods and the stone smile on Sir William Barker's face.

Running brings it all back.

What he said before he had his heart attack.

How I felt the day Mum took the bus on her own for the first time just to come into school, just to wait awkwardly in the reception and tell us that his colleagues had found him all still and not moving on the cold factory floor.

I had art that morning. I remember because me, Michael and Jasmin had been putting PVA glue all over our hands and peeling it off. But as soon as Mum told us what had happened, my fingers felt heavy. Irritated. They felt colder than they should have. Ada sat next to me on the bus back to our house afterwards, sniffling as she peeled the white flakes from my fingers, and Mum smoothed down the back of her school jumper. She made sure her collar was clean and white. Like that mattered somehow. I don't know. Maybe to Mum it did.

Heel, toe. Heel, toe. Breathe in. Breathe out. My dad's words are unforgettable. I carry them with me like I carry the morning, like I bring the sun. I remember them like I remember he taught me to double-knot my laces in the mornings.

'Not too tight –' his voice always that warm rumble in his throat – 'but not too loose you fall over.'

I remember how it felt that one Sports Day when I'd spotted him in the crowd of parents. My dad, who could never make any school events because of work. My dad, who insisted he'd try. And now he had. I'd adjusted my competing bib and decided I'd win the hundred-metre sprint especially for him. I also remember how much it had made my heart ache when I was so close to winning – the fastest kid in reception, the fastest kid in all of Friesly – and someone pulled at my back and sent me hurtling on to the ground.

Standing back up, grass stains all over my knees, had felt . . . wrong. That was all I felt. The wrongness of it. I saw everyone else who'd been shoved down like I had. Five-year-olds with fresh bruises, with pulled-on ponytails, with bibs too loose around their necks. Some of us crying. Some of us confused and looking around.

'*Baby*,' my dad had said afterwards, hugging me to him. '*You did so good. Don't cry. You did so good.*'

I remember sniffling into his jacket. It smelled like Old Spice and soap. '*But I didn't win,*' I said.

'*Listen to me.*' My dad's smile was the brightest smile in the world. '*You only lose in life if you give up on yourself. Huh? Like that kid. The one who cheated. You only lose if you stop being who you truly are.*' He held my hand just right. Not too tight. Not too loose. '*And who you are is incredible.*'

'*Even if I lost?*'

He scooped me up into his arms. '*Oh, I don't know if you really lost.*' His laugh rumbled in his throat. '*I don't know about that.*' He kissed my cheek. '*My little girl, my shining star.*'

There's a quiz show that Ada and my mum watch together on Saturdays. It's not anything special really. It's just one of those usual quiz shows, with a host that asks general knowledge questions, and guests that guess answers, and a cash prize which has confetti and streamers come falling down from the ceiling if anyone's lucky enough to win it.

One particularly muggy morning, I saw the two of them sat on the sofa in the living room together. They sipped tea. They dipped biscuits into the lukewarm beige, only barely aware of the soggy halves falling in.

Ada answered the history questions before they'd even been fully read out. She got them right. The lady playing for the money on the screen didn't.

My mum squinted at the TV, drawing the trunks of her legs forward to analyse the lady's defeated face. 'Was that for five hundred pounds?'

The cash came out of a chute in the ceiling, fell in a circular whirl, disappeared into the middle of the quiz-show set. Gone. A wrong answer and it was all gone.

What if you never had the right answer though? What if your whole life was a series of questions you'd never been prepared to have the right answer to?

'Ada, why don't you just sign up and win us some money?' I said, all sweaty from a morning run, and watching her get three in a row right, and my mum started smirking over her mug, which was her way of bragging about Ada's big brain, and Ada smirked too.

She never looked away from the TV. 'Why don't you? Kemi, you know all the same answers I do.'

I bit my lip. Then I looked at her, sweeping up biscuit crumbs into the palm of her hand and putting them on to the centre of a plate that had held sliced-up apples and pears yesterday.

I thought of how Ada pressed down so hard with her pen in all of her exams that the backs of all the papers went bumpy with her handwriting. My pens were always leaky no matter how much I practised with them. I thought of how she could read a book and finish it in a day. I only read books for school and always needed her to help me understand them. I thought of the walls of our bedroom, all covered with revision posters during her exams, and how Mum beamed when our family in Nigeria mentioned Ada's name, and how Nathan bought Ada a bookmark with her name on it, and how she showed it to me once, with a secret smile, while we got ready for bed. The medals and cups I'd won for running hung limply on the corner of a wardrobe door, the shine of the cheap plastic never brighter than the shine of Ada's golden glow.

The host of this quiz show had really slicked-back hair. He smiled all the time, even when people said they needed the cash for their daughter's life-changing operation, or so that they didn't have to remortgage their house, or to save for a new car after theirs was in an accident.

He asked a question about sports. I thought hard. The name for running at full speed over a short distance.

'Sprints!' I yelled at the very same time as Ada.

Mum let out a big belly laugh as the contestant answered incorrectly. 'Was that for a thousand pounds?'

'See?' Ada smiled at me, warm as the weather. 'You know these, too.'

'Yeah.' I smiled back, surprised to find I did.

The money poured down the chute again and vanished. Ada cleared the table and set the tap going in the kitchen, humming to herself over her own simple pleasures, her own personal victories. I watched the rise and fall of a university sweatshirt Mum had forced Ada to buy. How well it fit her. But how much was it exactly? How many borrowed notes? Copper-smelling coins? And did she love it as much as she had loved Nathan's black fleece?

'Hey, Trouble,' Mum said to the dramatic curve of my neck. 'Church is in half an hour. Don't forget you volunteer for life with Jesus Christ. This is no choice, Oluwakemi. It's a blessing.'

Her voice followed my grumbling all the way down the hallway, past Dad's smiling face, his eternal and everlasting joy. 'And wear something nice to the Lord's house!'

I don't think God cares very much about whether His people wear running shorts, or denim shorts, or the dungaree dress I always pick out of mine and Ada's wardrobe for church before she can.

The corduroy material comfortable. The dress part smart enough for my mum to be satisfied with, casual enough for me to think of as still somewhat cool.

But the Jacob Pentecostal Church had always had a reputation for being well attended by more than half of the Naija community. Its services were considered to be the perfect mix of devotion to the Lord – all 'Praise Jesus' and 'Hallelujah', stamping feet and wavering voices – while still being accessible to all. Rhythmic. Joyous.

Even – if you were really into it, if you actually liked God – fun.

That was why Emmanuel was so proud of it. That was why Mum and Aunty Sunbo and Aunty Ifeoma considered it their personal duty to have the pews filled, the high ceilings reverberating with our singing voices, our clapping hands.

When we were little, before 9 a.m. the block only ever smelled like hair wax, like coconut oil. The hiss of irons being switched on, kettles bubbling, voices yelling for Precious and Aron to get up and wash already, an expected rhythm. Then we'd all walk down together. Whole families. Parents and grandparents and children and uncles and aunties. A snaking line of well-washed, Vaseline-moisturized faces in our best clothes, with our greatest intentions.

When Dad was here, we went to a different church. One that didn't have as much rhythm and shouting and joy in its pews. One that had more because he was still alive.

I'd let myself be carried by him. High on his shoulders.

The best view of Friesly's backstreets in the world.

Mum always fussed that I'd fall, and he'd smile and insist that I wouldn't, and she'd end up smiling back despite herself.

From that height, I usually saw the aunties helping Precious's mum hunt for a spare hair tie along the low brick houses in the backstreets. Nathan and Ada jumping away from each other in fear of accidentally bumping hands. Aron earning more than a few questioning glances from the elders at the too-short tie around his yawning neck. And him sticking his tongue out at me when I teased him. Eventually, when we'd picked up Uncle Jafari too, there'd be a whole-group tussle to get him to wear it properly.

'Let the boy have some style,' Dad used to say when it got a little too heated, when Aunty Sunbo looked close to cursing out Aron completely and his parents were shaking their heads at him.

Dad once stopped by a peeling front gate, next to an alley that smelled like drainpipes and days-old cooked spices, to help Aron.

'Here.' His hands stopped holding on to my legs, his voice leaving the song we'd been singing together. 'This is how Jafari and I wore them in the good old days.'

Soon enough, Aron's tie hung long on his little-boy chest. But it looked smart somehow. Cool. Like there was magic in Dad's hands, like something sweet twitched in his every move.

Aron's dad and Uncle Jafari snapped their fingers approvingly, and spent the rest of the walk up to that quieter church showing us kids how to do it properly – how to hit your thumb against your third finger just right.

Just so we'd get given up-and-down looks, frowns and glares when we tried to do it in that quiet church later on. I did it quicker than Aron, than Precious, than Nathan, even than Ada. I looked at my dad. And then at my fingers. He looked at me. And then at my fingers. The organist paused, squinting over his half-moon glasses.

My dad hugged me to him, grinning despite the disapproving looks. The pastor cleared his throat. He began his sermon.

'The Lord is my shepherd,' I recited from the leather-bound Bible in my hand, the Jacob Pentecostal Church already alive with nods of approval at my words, already thundering with stamping feet. 'I have all that I need. He lets me rest in green meadows; he leads me beside peaceful streams.

'He renews my strength,' I read, while Emmanuel mimed at me to open my mouth more, to quit mumbling my words. 'He guides me along right paths, bringing honour to his name.'

I know that I should've been grateful that Mum had put me forward to recite when Emmanuel had needed a reader and was willing to pay for one, and Ada had reminded Mum that I needed the money.

But the sight of him in his church robes – his newly wiped

glasses ... his presence among the stained-glass windows, the lectern, and the pews so full of people – all of this frustrated me. I tried to focus on the faint song of pennies and pounds being dropped into the donation box as it was passed around the congregation. I tried to think only of how it would feel to be paid for this.

And not just with good deeds, which my ever-Christian mum was careful to remind me about.

With cash.

Notes.

Pounds.

Something I could fill my pockets with.

Something that could go towards the Running Right residential in France next year. Maybe even in the winter months if there was still space on the training sessions in Yorkshire.

If I just kept reciting. If I could appease the old ladies with their reading glasses, the old men squinting hard at their Bibles, Mum, and Aunty Sunbo, and Aunty Ifeoma, and Aron, and Precious and Nathan, and ... and ... Where was she? Where was Ada? I squinted across the pews. Emmanuel urged me on, all thumbs-up and joyous at the very back of the church, his thin pencil moustache lifting on his face.

I sighed. Then I cleared my throat. I planted my Reeboks on the carpeted floor. *Think of the money, Kemi. Let Jesus give you lots and lots of money.*

'HE renews my STRENGTH!' I said, with my fist up, and all the rhythm that I'd seen Emmanuel himself use. Fresh energy. Freshest in the world.

'He GUIDES me along RIGHT paths!' I paused,

nodding to myself, encouraged by bursts of agreement from the pews, louder humming, claps and whoops. 'Bringing HONOUR to his NAME!'

It was almost fun, watching Mum and the aunties holler up at me, seeing Aron burst out laughing, and Precious and Nathan gape. The gum inside Precious's mouth glinted pink and chewed-up. It showed like Uncle Jafari's gold tooth did at the very back of the hall, his good humour exploding in applause, in 'Praise Jesus' and 'Hallelujah', which I knew he only half-meant, because Uncle Jafari wasn't the biggest believer in God. Not Nigerian. Not wholly Christian. Not even our real uncle. That man attended our church to keep a promise to a best friend he'd never see again. Not in this life. Maybe not even the next, because Uncle Jafari didn't completely believe in heaven and hell either.

What was the real reason then? Something that defies logic? Something like love?

I clambered down the front steps, closer to the pews, pausing along those enraptured young faces. 'EVEN when I walk through the DARKEST VOLLEY!'

'Valley!' a voice corrected.

I pointed into the crowd. 'Yes!'

A burst of laughter followed. It spread like the warmth of a hug. And I saw her. My sister, smiling at me in the front row. Half-covering her mouth with her hands, her face flushed with either pride or humiliation. It was difficult to tell.

I marched closer to her. Ignored the vocal recoil of the microphone.

'EVEN when I walk through the DARKEST VALLEY, I will NOT be afraid, for HE is with me!'

Hands met hands. Skin touched skin. Applause fell, beautiful and bountiful, and heaped itself on my shoulders. My chest heaved up and down with the force of my own performance. And I watched as Ada stood up, just like everyone else did, all of our family. But it was different, too, because she wasn't sat with them.

I wanted to ask her why.

We were bound by eye contact, two pairs of dark brown eyes. I wanted to ask her why she wasn't sitting with her boyfriend, her old friends, her past.

'Praise Jesus!' My uncle Jafari grinned, emerging from the sea of faithful church attendees with his usual too-calm swagger. 'Hallelujah, Amen! Who would've known our Kemi would be such a great Bible reader?!'

He was such a jumpy old man. Skinny, with that shiny gold tooth in his mouth, and a patterned shirt for every occasion. Whether it was buying me scratch cards to share with him at lunch or coming to church or trimming men's hair with his colleagues at Clean Cutz.

There were even old snapshots of him and my dad when they'd first become friends in Friesly, and Jafari had first discovered patterned shirts and chains to match his teeth, and my dad, in football shorts and a simple T-shirt, had grinned at his sense of style.

They knew how to get along though.

They knew how to deal cards, and drink rum, and mock each other's choice of shoe all the time.

They knew how to help Ada with her homework when Mum was out, and her introduction to her times tables called for their attention, too. And they knew to give me the simple task of collecting Ada's pencil sharpenings so I could feel included, as well. I usually wore them – with pride – around my neck.

'Don't,' I said, grinning despite my shyness at accepting Uncle Jafari's compliments.

'No, you were great,' Uncle Jafari insisted. 'You really volleyed us into a new understanding of God's work.'

Then he threw his head back like a hyena, dying over his own joke.

I rolled my eyes. 'You just couldn't help yourself, could you?'

Uncle Jafari insisted he was only joking as he ruffled my hair, his hand warm and open on the crown of my head. 'Aw, don't be sad, Kemi girl. Here, I've bought you a present.'

He dropped a new scratch card into my open hand and howled when it showed up used and lost against my palm. I just shook my head, the ghost of a smile on my lips as I watched him go, me insisting on a dinner invitation which he casually waved off.

Then I scanned the people making their way out, the gaggle of coats and shoes, searching for Emmanuel. I'd seen the many notes and pennies the donation box had been stuffed full with as it had made its way around the plastic chairs that filled the church. It looked like it was at least £300. I could handle Uncle Jafari's teasing if that was what I was getting in return. And

Emmanuel's beaming grin, too, his rapturous applause along with everyone else's.

So I was already smiling when I heard the shuffle of his leather shoes from behind me.

'See this, Kemi?' Emmanuel sifted through the notes and pennies and pounds. He handed me a single five-pound note. 'This is what your godly hard work has given you!'

I tried not to let the smile die as he went on and on about blessings, and good intentions, and how this was enough money for me to go down to the supermarket and buy a big bottle of Fanta for my family to enjoy with their dinner. I really did. But it was no use.

One moment I was the best Bible reader in Friesly, celebrated for minutes which felt like an eternity – and should have – and the next I was standing in an aisle in Mahmood's Foods, shopping despite Qasim Mahmood's eagle-eyed gaze from the checkout. And the weight of Precious, Aron and Nathan's request to get them some pick 'n' mix. And the dull hurt of being smiled at only by Ada as she fell into step – outside the churchyard – with Mum.

'Stupid Emmanuel,' I muttered to no one in particular.

I dropped the paper bag of strawberry laces, cola bottles, white mice and tangy rainbow stripes into my basket. It was heavy enough anyway with the big Fanta bottle in it.

I felt for the creased note in my pocket. 'What am I supposed to do with only five pounds?'

Well, I knew I could save it. I could see how many scratch cards Uncle Jafari could buy for me. Maybe we'd win on one and that would be enough for me to get a personal trainer for the Olympics. If I didn't bomb my GCSEs, of course. Because then I wouldn't be able to study sports science at A level. I grimaced, all caught up in worry about my future, and about my sister, and about the weight of the basket in my hands.

The note looked like it could rip in my hands, it was so worn and well-folded. Some strange pen marks defaced the paper. Uncles and their notes. Their money always looked like that. Not new and shiny, like the money in the quiz shows, catching in the light and disappearing down a cylindrical funnel, far away from grabby hands, a stranger's, or mine.

'Oof!' The sound filled the supermarket aisle as I collided into someone.

'Sorry!' came the hurried response.

I was all ready to argue with whoever it was, I was in that sort of mood. But then I realized Eman Malik was standing in front of me. A bit shakier looking than usual, but still just Eman from volunteering. She was carrying two cartons of juice in her arms. No basket. An orange carton and an apple carton, and a carrier bag in her back pocket.

'Hey, it's alright,' I joked. 'Party in the drinks aisle in Mahmood's Foods, huh? Wait, what's up? Why are you crying? What's wrong?'

She tried to use the end of one of her shirt sleeves to wipe her eyes, but it was hard when her arms were full. 'Nothing. I'm O-OK. I'm f-fine.'

'You don't look fine,' I said. 'You're not still upset about Amir, are you? Look, he'll get over it. No one really knows what happened to Zayd, and people say stuff like that to him all the time –'

'No, it's . . . it's –' Eman was puffy-eyed and biting the inside of her cheek. Then she took a deep breath and all these words came tumbling out of her mouth.

'Kemi? What drink would you get for all the people visiting your house because your grandma had an accident outside Nishaan and now she's in the hospital in a coma with bleeding in her brain and no one knows if she's going to survive or not?'

I looked at Eman. I looked at her tear-stained face, the cartons of orange juice and apple juice she was hugging so tightly, the bits of change resting dully in the palm of her hand. Then I took the five-pound note out from my pocket. And the carton of orange juice, so her arms were freer.

'Both.'

'Both?' Eman hiccupped as I steered us towards the checkout.

'Both.'

PART THREE : FRIENDS

featuring:

a wall of banned customers – proof – Zakiya Bhatti's press
profile – guests – a get-together – shadow-boxing – a puddle
of mango juice – shisha pipes – boys – unwelcome cousins –
another *aloo gobi* sandwich – snow-white *shalwar kameez* –
Neelam Jalani's wedding – the third haiku – the wrong
Elvis – a poorly Maximus – the second accident – justice for
Zayd – PC Chris's story – the death of clown number
three – a roll-up cigarette – a chopped-off tulip head –
the rain – and Nani

CHAPTER 13
AMIR

'Amir?' Fiza crossed over the threshold of mine and Zayd's room, ignoring the KEEP OUT sign like it wasn't there. 'What are you looking for?'

I didn't say anything. I just pulled out the entire wooden drawer, letting clean boxers, blankets and bedsheets fall on to the vacuumed floor. Then the newspaper article I'd so carefully cut out dropped down, flimsy, feather-like.

Fiza's socks padded across to me softly. Hesitantly.

Like, somehow, Zayd's bedhead would lift from the upstairs bunk and he'd ask us, with bleary eyes and a dry throat, exactly what we were doing. The sheets remained still. He slept on. But his school photograph showed up black and white in my hands. Strong jaw, big smile, short tie, white collar. All teeth and thick eyebrows.

'Huh?' Fiza read the headline over my shoulder. '"Fatal traffic accident leaves local boy, 16, dead".' Her brown eyes were paler than mine. In the sunlight, they looked golden. Warm like honey. 'Is this . . . Is this about . . .'

'Zayd,' I finished for her. 'Yeah.'

Zakiya Bhatti's block of black-and-white ink seemed softer when my sister read it. It became easier. A pool of words she dived into slowly but carefully. She stumbled a little though. Fought over the lump in her throat. Looked at me.

'D'you want me to?' I said.

Fiza nodded. She dropped down next to me. I took a deep breath:

An anonymous eyewitness reports: 'Zayd was often seen leaving the supermarket with the weekly shop for his mother. Few in our tight-knit community heard a bad word about him. This is a devastating loss for the Ali family and for Friesly itself. An innocent young man was accused of a crime which he did not commit. Zayd was not given the respect of being known for more than his unfortunate death. He was and is much more than this tragedy.

I let Fiza lean her head on my shoulder. I felt the wet warmth of her tears on my shirt sleeve and couldn't be bothered cussing her out for that.

I had no answer when she asked me who had said all of that about Zayd, either.

My sister's homework tasks were always giant projects that needed an expert's eye on them.

'Amir,' my mum said when Fiza needed to complete the construction of a motte-and-bailey castle over half-term. 'Remember when you made a castle? Yours was pretty good, wasn't it?'

She repeated my name and the stilted compliments I'd received for the effects of Coca-Cola and vinegar on hard-boiled eggs, for multiplication challenges, and for a historically accurate Roman shield.

And then there was the short story about someone who inspired Fiza ... Well, that was the easiest challenge in the world. Even though it required a snack trip to Mahmood's Foods first.

That place was always so well polished, so busy, and glowing with the fluorescent ceiling lights that showed up everyone's faces in detail on the CCTV footage.

I mean, old Qasim Mahmood took that place seriously. He'd built it from the ground up. Uncs had used all the money he got from winning boxing competitions in his youth to stock up the shelves, clean up the aisles, find a place that could sell everything from twenty types of spice mixes, to rotisserie chicken on the side, slush drinks, ice cream, *halal* meat, frozen samosas, frozen pakoras, frozen *parathas*, frozen burger meat, to metal and clay bowls, pots, pans, spatulas, graters, cups, mugs, jugs, knives, forks and spoons ... Basically, everything. Everything you could possibly want. Anything anyone could possibly need. Including more chocolate and fizzy drinks than were really necessary for writing a short story.

'Be careful, alright?' I said to Fiza as she double-checked the sell-by date on a packet of spicy crisps. I glanced up at the CCTV cameras in the corners. They zoomed in and out easily. 'I told you we should've gotten a basket. No one can hold all this stuff ... Fiza! Watch it!'

'Oops,' Fiza said.

We both watched the crisp packet drop to the polished floor, hitting the girl in front's Reeboks. Of course the packet was open. Bits of fried potato sprinkled with chilli spice, ready to crunch and split under a stranger's feet.

'Oi, you know that Qasim Mahmood has a whole wall of banned customers, don't you?' I hissed, tugging Fiza closer to me while scanning the aisles for the old man. 'Leave it. Or he'll take your photo and put it up there for everyone to see.'

Two fluffy buns turned around in front of me. Picked up the crisp packet.

Kemi held the scrunched-up silver wrapping towards my sister. 'Amir, you're not just scaring her for no reason, are you?'

Fiza accepted it shyly, looking up at Kemi from under her eyelashes.

'Eh?' I said. It was weird seeing Kemi in Mahmood's Foods all of a sudden. And even weirder to see she wasn't alone. Eman stood beside her, hugging a carton of apple juice to her chest. I saw her at the same time she saw me.

'Oh.' I looked past their shoulders to see if the queue for the self-checkout was even moving at all in the evening rush. 'It's you two.'

Fiza tugged on my sleeve. Whispered loudly. 'You know these girls? Who are they?'

I made her let go. Whispered loudly, 'Nobody.'

Kemi's eyebrow raised a little as the queue shortened. We shifted forward. 'What are you lot buying anyway?' she asked. And then, with a shake of her shopping basket: 'I'm on snack duty. Eman, too.'

I watched as Eman glanced at Kemi. Wide-eyed. Tapped

her fingers nervously on the side of the apple juice. Lifted the corners of her eyes to smile at me. I thought of what she'd said about Zayd. What her aunty had told her about him. I didn't smile back.

'We're on snack duty, too,' Fiza said proudly.

Kemi glanced over at the thick bag of pick 'n' mix in Fiza's arms. 'Milkshake bottles.' She grinned. 'Nice.'

I could practically feel Fiza glowing beside me. Her arms and legs getting bigger and brighter. Her gaze shifting between me and Kemi, as if to show off a new toy, a new friend. Once, Fiza told me that flowers grow towards a source of light. Right there, in Mahmood's Foods, it was like Kemi was that light. To Fiza, she was warmer than anything else.

The self-checkout on the right side was free.

'Come on.' I sighed, with my hands in my pockets, feeling the flimsy thinness of Zayd's article in there while Fiza still stared up at the girls. I rolled my eyes, suddenly desperate to go home. So I let the article drop back down into my pocket and forced myself to just scan our stuff. Put it in a carrier bag and go.

'Wait.' A small hand rested on my shoulder.

I sighed, turning around.

Eman looked down at something in her hands, her brows narrowed, confused. Then she was scanning my face. 'I think you dropped this.'

'Huh?' Kemi came up from behind her. 'What is it? A newspaper article?'

I shoved my hands in my pockets again, confused, turning them inside out. Then I stared at the black-and-white writing being clutched in a grip that wasn't my own. The hard feeling came up from deep inside me. It bounced up and down. Like a flame. Like a small one, getting bigger. A candle turning into a bonfire. My hands became fists. Then they loosened.

Suddenly I was pocketing the change coming out of the machine. Suddenly I was setting Fiza's sweets down and turning around to face Kemi and Eman.

'Proof,' I said.

'Proof?' Eman still sounded confused.

'Yeah.' I looked between the girls. 'Proof that my brother didn't do anything wrong. Y'know, since this town, and you lot, and everyone who lives here doesn't get it. Zayd wasn't a drug dealer. He wasn't a thug. He was just a kid, sixteen. Sixteen like I'll be soon, and a shit singer, always napping, always joking around, and good at school. Not good for nothing like they make out.'

The newspaper article stared up at them. I wasn't begging them to read it. I was just asking them to. With everything I had in me. With all of me.

'Never good for nothing.'

They did though. Kemi and Eman. They read it.

We sat outside, on the wood-warm benches where we'd had lunch together all those weeks ago.

Fiza sat with us, too. I watched her count up the special-offer signs on the automatic doors, the glowing neon lights casting the black-and-white shots of banned customers in an unearthly glow. And I waited, with my leg shaking, with the bonfire burning inside me, for Kemi and Eman to get it, to see it – what had happened to Zayd – like me and Fiza did.

'Wait.' Kemi was the first to look up. 'So who's the eyewitness who said all of this stuff?'

Fiza and I shared a glance.

'We don't know,' she said.

'And Zakiya Bhatti?' Eman said, her fingers holding the article to the wood, pinning it out of some light breeze's reach.

The newspaper stand outside the supermarket looked like it always did, the dark criss-cross mesh locking in a sheet about some MP set to make his annual visit to the rides and roller coasters of the Barker Summer Festival. Beside it, the piles of too-ripe apples and bananas, green chillies, garlic and onions sat limply in saggy cardboard boxes which Qasim Mahmood was double-checking for mould.

'I found her press profile online. I've sent her about fifty messages.' I took my cap off. Ran a hand through my hair. 'It doesn't work. She doesn't reply.'

Kemi and Eman shared a look. Both of their shoulders fell hard, like disappointment. Like mine had for years, looking for someone who knew something, who knew everything, and who was hiding from me.

The messages sent from my guest press profile were long at first: grey-box variations of 'Hi, did you write about Zayd Jahan Ali's death?' to 'I saw the article. I'm his brother' to shorter and more direct lines, just because I wasn't sure of what was professional and what wasn't, if I was boring her, if journalists didn't reply to big personal essays in their inbox, or to any messages at all.

'Wow,' Eman said, seeing them show up on my cracked phone screen. 'That's a lot of messaging.'

Kemi squinted at them from behind her shoulder. 'Why are half of them in capital letters? "HI", "HELLOOOO", "CAN YOU REPLY PLEASE??????" Why are you screaming at the lady?'

I took my phone back, scrolled through the more desperate messages. 'Well, how hard is it for her to message me back?'

'Not hard if you spellcheck what you send before you send it,' Kemi said, patting down her edges. 'Amir, you know "article" ends with "cle" and not "cal", don't you?'

'It does?' Eman and I said at the same time.

She and I moved in to check my spelling at the same time, bumping heads, and groaning at the light pain. I scrambled to excuse myself at the same time that she did again, putting space between us, coughing awkwardly, while Eman tried to explain her dyslexia to an unimpressed Kemi and I pretended I didn't care about spelling at all.

'Hey, you guys could help us look for Zakiya,' Fiza said brightly, interrupting the chaos with ease. 'And if you hear something, anyone mentioning they know her, or who that anonymous eyewitness is, you can just let us know. Which one of you is his girlfriend?' She looked at Eman. 'You, right? Just call up the restaurant. Nishaan on the high street. Or better yet, come over, you can meet our mum. Our house is fifty-six Greenwood Lane –'

I covered her mouth with my hand. Ignored the eye-crinkling smile on Kemi's face, the awkward way Eman reddened, and grimaced, and looked away from me. I wanted to tell them to ignore her, to just pretend like Fiza didn't exist, but then old Qasim Mahmood's voice came out from behind us like the grumpiest blessing.

He dropped an old leather wallet on to the stained wood of the picnic table. 'You lot. Don't litter on my premises. Unless you want a spot on my wall.'

Our four heads shook in denial as we watched him go. His wall of banned customers was well known for ruining any good reputation, even if yours was based on a weak foundation in the first place. Barely strong. Barely holding on.

'Sorry, Uncle!' Fiza yelled to the back of his white shalwar kameez, billowing like clouds. Qasim Mahmood waved her off, despite the threat of his still agile arms, still strong shoulders.

Eman gasped, suddenly standing up and patting down the pockets of her jeans. She grabbed the hard leather wallet, feeling along the cracks, the well-worn seams. 'It's Nani's. I-I take it everywhere with me. I must've dropped it inside.'

'Oi, it's fine,' I said, watching her fingers check inside the wallet all over again. 'You didn't lose it. It's right in front of you.'

'Right.' Her breath came out shaky. 'You're right.' She picked up the carrier bag she and Kemi had packed together. Two cartons of juice, bulky beneath the flimsy white plastic. 'I need to go anyway. We have guests over, and my mum's entertaining them on her own.'

She picked up her grandma's wallet, too. It was thick, the sides heavy with bus passes and discount vouchers, a shiny photograph of a chubby-looking baby, tons of credit cards. A scrap of paper hurtled to the ground. We all reached to pick it up.

'What is it?' Kemi said when Eman's fingers clasped on to it first.

I watched Eman frown at the tarmac.

'An old receipt?' Fiza eyed the piece of paper all weighed down with pencil scratches. It looked like there were names written all over it. 'Why are you so bothered about an old receipt?' she asked her. 'What's so good about it?'

'Leave it, Fiza,' I said, reminding her to put her jacket on properly. 'It's got nothing to do with you.'

'No.' Eman's voice softened as she stared down at the creased receipt, at the mess of tiny printed words. 'No, this . . .' She faltered, before clearing her throat. 'This is to do with Nani.'

CHAPTER 14
EMAN

The phone in our house for as long as I can remember has been a really old model with a curling – and extremely long – wire.

It lives in the hallway, in a corner next to the coat rack, and the radiator that we line our shoes under. It's set up for all kinds of calls.

Anonymous and irrelevant ones, which Nani always told me to avoid, mouthing and pantomiming with her arms to let the receiver drop on the occasions that I was barely thinking and lifted it, muttering my hesitant 'Hello?' Familial connections that I barely understood, like long-distance relatives crackling their Mirpuri language over the line, or immediate – but not exactly immediate – cousins asking for Nani, asking for Mum.

Sometimes there were genuine wrong numbers, callers searching for the pizza place on the high street which was one number off of ours, or a willowy-sounding elderly person muttering their gratitude for Christmas cards my family weren't religiously obliged to send, or a younger voice declaring their affection for grandparents who definitely didn't have names that were mispronounced as much as Nani's was.

I was used to it though.

The rush of my grandma's shorter leg, her average one and her walking stick as she pulled herself along from the kitchen to pick up the receiver. Her just-washed hands, smelling faintly like chopped garlic, always wiping themselves on the neutral cotton of her *dupatta*, and her accented English, hemming and hawwing to be heard.

It was usually just gossip from the aunties. Facts about Azrah aunty and her estranged too-rich sister in north Friesly, or everyone's favourite tomboy, Neelam Jalani, and her love marriage to a very rich boy she'd met at university.

Most of the time, however, it was Friesly Grand Mosque that called our number. It was that combination of green glass and pillars, gold-painted minarets and the tiny wood-heavy room which they had for praying women that knew our phone number by heart.

'Maariyah,' I'd sometimes hear a thick Englistani accent escape from the receiver, sighing in a mix of heavy South Asian consonants, a lilting Yorkshire rhythm. 'These fundraising events are difficult to organize. We're doing the best that we can.'

And Nani's usual enthusiasm, her fighting spirit: 'Well, keep doing that! And in the meanwhile . . .' At this point, she'd pat her cardigan pockets, search for the shape of her leather wallet, her large old Nokia, then continue, 'I'll do the best that I can, too!'

It was, after all, Maariyah Malik who'd decided for years on end that Friesly Grand Mosque could place their efforts into raising funds for orphans across the world, into building wells in impoverished countries, into financing the careers of women who weren't strangers to domestic violence, and into caring for people like Danny *Dangar*.

'*Acha meri gal sunno!*' Her voice came back to me as I read over the receipt on which she'd scrawled the details of her donations drive for the homeless. '*Are we telling people to donate their unwanted things to make the mosque look better? No! We're doing it because we know the homeless need blankets and food and the things we take for granted!*'

I thought of the calls she'd made in Wash 'n' Wear all those weeks ago. The way she'd sat on the wooden bench in the middle of all the washing machines and dryers, ticking off the individuals who'd said they'd drop off the extra toothpaste they'd bought by accident, their worn hats, scarves and jumpers.

Tinned cans they'd bought on special offer which they'd never been able to finish.

Soup, lentils, tuna, risotto.

Discounted soap, discounted shampoo which came out of a dispenser.

Facial wipes, scented and unscented. Water bottles. Roll-on deodorant. Spray deodorant. Socks. Dried nuts and mango slices and sunflower seeds.

She'd written everything down on the back of an old receipt. She'd written names that had agreed to all of this in faint grey pencil.

But had the people she'd rung remembered she wanted their donations? Did they still want to take part? Was anyone taking the time to ask the people at Friesly Grand Mosque about the homeless project, and what was going on with it, and whether the old lady who'd meant to set up a drop-off point for the donations had ever gotten round to doing it? And if she hadn't, well, who would?

The house was full of laughter. My mum's voice not the tired murmur I was so used to, but a loud and insistent bell ringing around the house.

She wandered around the relatives sitting on our leather sofas, nodding and smiling as they swapped stories about their tiny lives: the handbags they'd bought on discount, the root canals they'd put off, the schools they were sending their children off to. Mum encouraged them to try the *saag aloo* she'd transferred into a deep-set glass dish, the *pilau chaval* she heaped on to their plates.

'More *raita*, anyone?' she asked, when an aunty I hadn't seen since I was a baby stopped scratching at a bone stuck between her teeth to nod for more, when an uncle whose name I could've sworn I'd seen Nani roll her eyes at did the same.

Mum obliged in seconds.

She spooned the cucumber-and-tomato-infused yogurt on to their plates. She smiled at their split-second compliments about her hosting, laughed at the same time as everyone else when the conversation turned to the price of houses.

She checked the heat of the samosas and pakoras on the table. She disappeared into the kitchen and brought the smell of roti back with her, alongside a flat wicker tray which carried the steaming chapatis to hands that beckoned for *daal*, that pulled and prodded her into all four corners of the room.

'Oh good,' Mum said, as I watched my cousins nibble at their samosas, as their parents instructed them – with warning looks – to build up their appetite. 'You're back.'

'Did all of these people know Nani?' I asked, as she hurried me into the kitchen. Pulled open cabinets. Brought out glasses. A very large and long floral-patterned tray.

'Hmm?' Mum looked inside the plastic bag I was hugging to my chest. 'Yes.'

I almost missed the flicker of surprise passing over her face – an unspoken criticism that I'd only bought two cartons of juice for all of these people. But she inspected the expiration dates quickly and then got to pouring.

'How?'

She filled the glasses easily. The insides, dizzying with the colours of an autumn day. Cloudy. Crisp. Mum wiped any spills on the tray, inspecting the rims for any floating bits, any unpleasant debris.

'Mum, how did they know her?'

She placed the tray into my arms. 'Put this on the table inside.' She opened another kitchen cabinet. Glassware tinkled at the touch of her hands. 'Then go to the other room and get the extra wooden table for the men sitting next to the window.' She dropped napkins on to the tray. 'And these. They should be enough.'

I watched her prepare more glasses, her busy hands cleaning the glass with a tea towel I'd seen Nani use to do the same thing with my whole life. Had she taught Mum to do that? When? Had she been my age? Or older?

What stories did they share? Did Nani rub oil into Mum's

hair? Did Mum grow up with the sound of Nani's old sewing machine? Nani was the strongest swimmer of all the girls in the village. Her future husband – my nana – had held the winning accomplishment of going the longest of all the boys to not brush his teeth. Did Mum know if Nani had pulled him to his feet, forced him into a dimly lit room and set the brush going along his gums herself? Did Mum laugh at their strange love? Did she envy it later on in her life? It didn't punch. It didn't bite or go sour. Had Nani ever called her silly for her mistakes? Or had she seen the lesson learnt in her daughter's cries at my dad's shadow and prayed for better?

A burst of laughter came from inside the living room. A large piece of sunlight falling on to the kitchen floorboards, warm to see, far from our bare feet.

'Go!' Mum hissed at me, making the glasses sing in my awkward grip. 'Go!'

I did. But not without watching my mum steady the polite smile on her face, the dimples in her cheeks.

There wasn't much left in the Tupperware boxes by the end of the week. A few slices of bread and the dried ends in the cupboard. But when I looked in the very back of the fridge, when I pushed back the condiments and the iceberg lettuce, I could see a forgotten box half-foggy with condensation.

The label on the very top forced a smile out of me.

Aloo gobi. I made a sandwich. I wrapped it carefully. Then I found my Post-it note stack. And a pen. I put everything in my bag.

*

PC Chris wrestled with the gear stick in his hand, and the six-seater groaned as it pushed itself up one of Friesly's many hills.

'So,' he grunted, his small eyes showing up determined in the rear-view mirror. 'What have we learnt while Volunteering4Friesly?'

In the boot, the box holding the police leaflets tipped mercilessly on to its side. All of us inside of the vehicle groaned, imagining the mess awaiting us at the first street we'd eventually stop at.

'I'll tell you mine,' PC Chris said, flicking the indicator on. 'I've learnt to always make sure I'm prepared. For the best. For the worst. And to always make sure that I'm open to new experiences, because you never know what you'll get with them. Who you'll meet. How you'll grow.'

I stopped winding down my window, watched the world outside stir with no breeze. Nothing.

'Same,' I muttered.

Kemi rested her feet up on the dashboard in front of the passenger seat, her arms crossed over her chest. 'Same.'

Amir spoke from under the bill of his cap. It offered him the shade he needed to snooze. 'Same.'

The slam of PC Chris's arm on the back of his headrest as he reversed along a narrow alleyway and back into a parking space jolted us all upright.

'Come on, you lot,' he said sternly. 'Haven't you learnt anything from the Volunteering4Friesly programme? You know that we at Friesly Metropolitan Police are doing our best to tackle anti-social behaviour – like graffiti – before it develops into worse habits like criminal offences. It's all part of our Pursue, Prevent, Protect and Prepare strategy . . .'

A low scraping sound brought PC Chris's speech to an end. We all turned to see Amir making a show of scratching and searching the roof of the vehicle, the armrest, the seat belts, the seats.

PC Chris frowned. 'What are you doing?'

'Just looking for the wire.'

PC Chris raised an eyebrow. 'The wire.'

'Yeah, the one that's feeding you all these lines. It's PC Phillips on the other end, right?' I couldn't tell whether Amir was being sarcastic or serious. 'It's amazing. You sound exactly like her.'

'Hilarious,' PC Chris said. He unlocked the side doors for us to go and deliver the leaflets.

As always, Kemi was the first one out, jumping from the van with enthusiasm, followed by Amir, who headed to the boot to grab the leaflets, followed by me.

'Hey Amir, d'you ever think about it?' Kemi said, as the three of us prepared ourselves for more paper cuts, more stuffed letter boxes. And the touch of a too-warm sun on the back of our necks. I was already sweating. 'Anyone on this street could be Zakiya Bhatti. Or know her.'

'Yeah, well.' Amir handed us our leaflet bunches. 'If you magically recognize her, even though there's no pictures of her online, or any other articles except for the one about Zayd, tell her to reply to my messages already.'

I heard the sting in Amir's words. I saw the hurt on Kemi's face.

'It was worth a try,' I said.

Kemi chewed the inside of her cheek. 'I guess.'

Amir was first to set off delivering the leaflets. But it was Kemi who smiled at every neighbour who opened their door and questioned the multicoloured plasticky paper sheets they were being handed.

'We're Volunteering4Friesly,' she said brightly. 'This is what we do.' And then, in a low whisper: 'If you need anyone to help you cut your grass or babysit your kids, as well . . . Some of us do that, too.'

With her usual charm, she insisted on good rates for her services. She had a hands-on-waist confidence. Words came out of her mouth with precision. They didn't get stuck. They didn't tumble. She breathed into them and out they came, full of energy, full of life.

'What?' Kemi laughed at mine and Amir's questioning stares. 'I need to make money, OK? And we're not getting paid for these deliveries.'

'Oh yeah,' Amir said. 'I forgot you're not rich like those idiots you hang around with at school. Otherwise you'd be on that sports trip in France eating croissants with everyone else right now.'

'Sports residential,' Kemi corrected, writing her number on the back of one of the leaflets. She printed '*for help with errands, ring here (pay in cash only)*' in the same loopy hand-writing she'd inked on the glass of the bus shelter for me.

Then she hesitated, as if unsure of what she was about to say next. 'And they're not idiots, they're my best friends.'

Amir jogged up a neat driveway covered with ceramic flowerpots and a half-deflated kiddie pool. He called out from over a hedge.

'Who, Michael Taylor? Jasmin Gill? They think someone dropping their pasta in the cafeteria is the funniest thing in the world.'

I winced at the memory of my own early accidents. The chorus of rowdy groans which always started with Michael Taylor and Jasmin Gill hammering their hands on the edge of their lunch table and ended with Noor Bhatti and Tahmina Begum joining in, too, laughing and falling into one another.

Kemi frowned at us. 'So? That is funny, isn't it? There's always some idiot dropping their pasta all over the place. Of course you're gonna laugh at that.'

She pushed past the both of us, headed for the next house across the road. Dozens of cars were parked around it. Signs of a get-together showed behind the lace curtains, moving figures and a thumping beat. Kemi left the leaflets in the house's sunlit porch, her number inky and unignorable on the white backs.

'It's just that you guys don't know them very well. Jasmin and Michael are really cool. Trust me. I'm really good at reading people. I'm never wrong.'

Then she stopped talking. Kemi's mouth dropped open as the white door swung open and two people caught in an affectionate embrace stood on the other side. A tall Black boy with big glasses on his face. A Black girl with a dimpled smile, leaning into the boy's grasp on a fluffy black fleece.

'Nathan?' Kemi shrieked as the pair disentangled themselves. 'Precious?'

The boy Kemi had called Nathan stared at her. 'Kemi,' he said. 'Your sister's not with you, is she?'

Kemi shut the door, stumbling a little, as she backed away from the house. Then she just stood there, silent. Amir and I looked at each other, waiting for an explanation, a sunlit smile, a well-meaning word. But nothing came. Kemi simply walked up to a neighbouring house, put the leaflets through the door, and continued on to the next.

CHAPTER 15
KEMI

I really didn't want to talk about it.

Those two.

The sight of them.

Nathan and Precious. Precious and Nathan.

Their faces, their split-second expressions, burning into my memory. And if I closed my eyes, if I blinked, I saw them again. So close, so together, like two roots that got intertwined. In my memory, and in the moment. As teenagers, and young kids, in our playground, around the block, playing in the community allotment. That was when it wasn't just Nathan and Precious, of course. It was all of us, knocking into one another in the park, fighting over the swings. All of us. Including Ada.

Not Nathan and Precious.

Nathan and Ada. It had always been Nathan and Ada.

I busied myself with the zip on my windbreaker when it was time to head home after volunteering. I pulled it up. I pulled it down. Then I used the reflection of a police station window to fuss with my edges in the reflection. I made sure they were lying flat. Still pretty. Still set into patterns.

'Kemi,' said Eman, lingering with me by the police building, 'are you OK?'

I sighed and kicked a stray stone out of the way. 'Yeah.'

'Alright, well can you tell your face that?' Amir said. 'You look like it's the end of the world or something.'

I glared at him. His confidence, the easy manner with which he was trying to break me out of my misery.

I punched his arm to make him stop. Only lightly. But Amir flinched anyway. Then he put his fists up, just joking around. The both of us became locked in mock-spar mode while moss grew between the pavement slabs, while the blinds in the police station twitched suspiciously. Behind us, Eman mimicked the sound of a bell, a tiny little 'ding-ding-ding' leaving her lips. Me and Amir stopped, bemused smiles on our faces. We looked back at Eman, our necks golden in the sun, and bust out laughing. All three of us did. But only for a little while.

'I'm OK,' I said finally. 'Honest, I am.' I hesitated. 'I just didn't think my sister would've broken up with her first love just because she goes to university now.' I kicked another stone. 'And now Nathan's dating Precious, and no one told me anything.'

Eman and Amir leaned on the side of a low stone wall as I gave them all the details. It was like a waterfall of words.

I mean, Nathan had been like a brother to me for as long as I could remember. Ada had even once admitted to liking the idea of marrying him. And our dad, well, our dad had always told us that true loss was giving up on who you really were. So why was Ada being different now? Had a new place, had going to uni, changed her that much? Was that why she'd broken up with Nathan? And let him move on? Did she think she was better than him now? I thought so. I really did.

A silence followed this outburst. A heavy, short-lived thing. Not because Amir and Eman hadn't been listening, I think, but because neither of them knew what to say. So we just stayed there in the sun.

Me with my arms crossed over my chest.

Eman fussing with the lining of her sleeves, her eyes looking worried.

Amir beside us, letting the hot metal of his bike lock keys burn his hands as he muttered something about people and how shit they could be.

'Life, huh?' I laughed bitterly. 'Who would've imagined it would all turn out like this?' I looked at them. I mean, really looked at them. 'Or that us three would be standing here together?'

I pictured someone else seeing us outside the police station like that, our shoulders at different heights, our feet facing one another. The memory of the blue spray paint on our fingertips was still so bright in my head. The smell of soap for washing bus shelters. Bin bags. Police leaflets.

And how the bridge of Eman's nose wrinkled a bit when she was confused.

And how Amir threw his whole head back when he laughed.

'Not me,' Eman said. A secret smile spread across her face.

'Yeah,' Amir agreed. 'Me neither.'

*

'Ada?' I called into our tiny kitchen. The sound of my voice was loud against the quiet mugs that had been rinsed and left to dry on the sink, the quiet towel hanging in front of the little oven, the quiet back of my sister's neck.

Ada's limbs were always so long to me.

The frame of her body, gangly to some, graceful to others. I liked it the best when she stood completely tall, when she wasn't a victim of teenage self-consciousness, when she didn't fold into herself at the drop of someone else's insecurity, someone else's backhanded, distorted, ugly view of her beauty. Mum used to say the strongest plants grew because they were in the best spot to reach the sun. Ada used to say those strong plants usually got trampled on the most, were pulled to pieces most easily. Who would want to be destroyed like that?

Even at that moment, she was bent halfway down, hanging our washed clothes on the radiators, the backs of dining chairs and the window sills. Anywhere that got a good bit of warmth from the sun. Golds and yellows for daylight, not blues and blacks for shade. We didn't have a proper garden, just the community allotment. So we couldn't hang clothes on any washing line, obviously. And if we put the radiators on, well, no one would've been able to afford the bill, and we would've baked alive in that heatwave, and sometimes the radiators leaked and the landlord added the cost of any stains to our rent anyway.

'Yeah?' Ada said eventually, her brow low and furrowed as her fingers scraped at some soap still left on a T-shirt.

The two-second pause made me shy somehow.

Smaller than I'd ever felt before. That same little girl being tugged away from the finishing line, ready to cry again and again and again.

'So,' I said. 'Nathan's going out with Precious now.'

Ada's head bumped harshly against the wood of the chair she'd been placing a few sodden socks on. The noise made me jump, too.

Her eyes boggled behind her prescription glasses. 'Oh.'

I waited for her to explain it to me. I waited for her to look at me, shout *no way*, feel betrayed, irritated, sad. I mean, wasn't she going to tell me I was crazy? That she was still seeing him? That there were still butterflies cocooning in her stomach at the thought of him waiting for her every night at the bottom of our block's metal staircase?

That's how she used to describe it. Butterflies. That's how she described hanging out with him. Sharing the headphones I always tried to steal off her. Singing him songs she'd stolen from me and the person playing records upstairs.

I waited for her to say it again, talk my ear off, describe the nerves in her stomach when she saw her beautiful boyfriend.

I wanted her to tell me that the heat rushing to her cheeks wasn't shame that I knew they weren't together any more, but love, and embarrassment, because they were. I was wrong. They were.

'Well?' I rested my hands on my hips. 'Aren't you going to say something?'

Ada bit her lip. 'What's there to say, Kemi?'

I frowned at her, confused.

A weeks-old packet of strawberry laces I'd forgotten to put away rested on the kitchen counter. It was bright in the glow of the setting sun, and the sweets had melted all over the wooden top, making everything smell like the colour pink. Like old love. An expired Valentine's Day.

When the phone rang, Ada walked past the mess. I heard the smile in her voice as Aunty Sunbo enquired about something silly and mundane. How many chillies she needed for some recipe Mum had passed on, I think.

The chatter of my sister's words as she flipped through recipe books, as she nudged open drawers and cabinets, filled the kitchen. But I still felt like it was empty.

She was alone. And, somehow, so was I.

Everywhere turned into a ghost town on the week of the Barker Summer Festival.

An amplified microphone, a thumping dance beat, and as many fairground rides as the eye could see meant that all of the tourists – and a lot of the locals, too – were massed together in north Friesly. Riding on dodgems. The Ferris wheel. Setting up a good spot near the stage set up for performers. Chasing after friends in the fun house. Winning goldfish in plastic bags, and candyfloss, and giant stuffed animals. Taking a turn on the roller coaster. Once, twice, three times.

Dad took us when we were young. Ages ago. He won me and Ada matching hair clips from the hook-a-duck stand. They had flowers on them. They glittered in exactly the same way. But I didn't want to think about that too much on my morning run.

So I focused on the absence of a queue outside Varga's Antiques, the lack of old people dying to bargain with Marta and her wild dandelion hair. On Howard Li's pharmacy, showing up clean and bright without handprints on the glass front. On the car park outside Mahmood's Foods, empty except for dried leaves, torn crisp packets, old tissues, and Qasim Mahmood himself offering Danny *Dangar* a drinks carton, a box of mango juice. Danny *Dangar* didn't accept it. He slammed it hard on the ground, shaking. Then he and Qasim Mahmood stood staring at the thick orange puddle in front of them.

'Hey,' I huffed, as I glimpsed some movement at Clean Cutz's door. Eman wandered out of it smiling, looking down at a leather wallet and a glowing white slip of paper in her hands.

She took me in, all out of breath and in my running shorts. 'Hey.'

'*Hey!*' a chorus of voices shouted after a running boy with a razor slit in his eyebrow, a black delivery cap on his head. 'We're only breaking for ten minutes! Then you're helping us unload the shisha pipes back at Nishaan!'

Amir gave his pursuers a thumbs-up, which transformed into a muttered curse as soon as their backs were turned. Then he was standing before us, sweating and panting for dear life. 'Oi, you lot, let me chill with you for a second. Neelam Jalani's wedding to that rich guy on Monday is killing me.'

We ended up just sitting on the concrete wall outside Mahmood's Foods together. Three pairs of shoes hanging off the edge, wavering slightly in the sun.

'So you started reading from the Bible at the local church to earn some extra money,' Eman repeated carefully.

'Just to get paid five pounds in the end,' I finished, kicking that wall in my frustration. 'I swear, my mum's boyfriend is an idiot.' Bits of brick floated in the air, the smell of dried cement roasting in a very light breeze. 'I'm doing OK now though.' I patted my phone in my pocket. 'I get enough money from my errands hotline. People always want someone to mow their grass and babysit their kids for them.'

'Your errands hotline,' Eman said admiringly, while Amir rolled his eyes.

I didn't want to tell them that the money I got from those chores wasn't exactly big bucks either. Except for when I overcharged the people in north Friesly who'd heard about me. But most of those twenty-pound fees were spent on the bus there and back.

My weekends were beginning to involve more bus rides to north Friesly than I would've liked. Money talked though. It told me to keep working and cutting grass and babysitting. It told me that the reason why Jasmin and Michael hadn't responded to any of my texts recently was because they were busy getting ahead in life, spending their parents' money, financing their futures the way I should've been and wasn't.

'I've been getting my revenge on Emmanuel, too.' I smiled to myself, thinking of all the photos and videos I'd taken of him that deserved an audience.

If not Jasmin and Michael, if not even Ada, Nathan, Precious and Aron, then why not Amir and Eman? I scrolled through all the clips on my phone. That first photo in Say It

With Flowers, the reaction to the salt shower at dinner ... I showed them my most recent revenge: the mayonnaise I'd mixed in with Emmanuel's conditioner on one of the days he slept over and the way he'd looked when I'd snapped the photo at breakfast, sleepy and confused, one hand touching modestly at the grey and white of his hair.

My phone camera hadn't quite picked up my mum's wincing groans, smelling all that mayonnaise on his head. But I could remember them. I could remember the sad tilt of his head as my mum forced him out of his seat to wash it off, the laughter that I couldn't hold in at Ada walking in on Emmanuel's head in the sink, and at his drowning noises, and her serious downturned frown.

'I told them that I was only joking,' I said, while Amir howled in my ears, playing the old videos and zooming in on the new photo, 'so I didn't get in trouble for it.'

Amir handed the phone back to me, wiping at the tears in his eyes. 'Oh, I needed that. I really did.'

Eman looked over Amir's shoulder. 'Did they find it funny?'

'Who?' I asked.

Her leg kicked at the wall. 'Your family. Your mum and Ada. And Emmanuel. Did they find your mayonnaise joke funny?'

A dappled sunlit silence followed. I threw up my hands. 'Who cares what they find funny? What do they know? Emmanuel, as well. He's not even part of the family. Who cares what they think?'

Another silence followed. Only, this time, it felt dark like the shade on the other side of the pavement. Cold to the touch. Reedy as telephone pole wires.

Amir glanced between the irritated curl of my lip and Eman's downcast eyes. 'You lot are coming to the wedding, aren't you?' he said slowly. 'Neelam Jalani's wedding? Come, innit.' He touched his fist with mine and then with Eman's. 'We're boys now. You have to come.'

A headache bloomed behind the back of my eyes as Amir chattered on and on about the wedding, his sister, his cousin. But Eman's question and my own angry outburst were as loud as a whistle. Drowning everything out.

'Grammatically,' I said, searching for a gap in the noise, the too-loud pain, 'us lot being boys doesn't make sense.'

I jumped off the brick wall, anticipating Amir's explanation that it was about connection, a bond, an intimacy that went beyond conventional boundaries like gender. But I was trying to ignore the echo of my own voice, too. My shrieking banshee memory. Who cares what they thought? Mum. Ada. Emmanuel. Did I care? Deep down inside? No. I swatted the possibility away.

I nodded at Amir. And then at Eman. 'I'll accept the compliment though. And the invitation.'

We're boys now.

CHAPTER 16
AMIR

Uncle Nadeem's house was undergoing some sort of renovation. An extension on the south side or something.

So now there was lots of dust and dirt inside their place. Plastic tarps on the ground. The smell of mixed cement in the mornings. The sound of drills being switched on and hammers pounding on walls. The whole point of it was to create more space for the family, more room for Uzair to be annoying in, for Mikaeel and Shuaib to terrorize imaginary enemies in their boring video games, and for their logical answers to my funny jokes.

So of course Mum decided that while their house was getting fixed, there was plenty of room in our house for them in the meantime.

She turned the sofa that had seen so many of my *FIFA* victories into her own temporary sleeping space, sacrificing our space to chill in the living room, while Uncle Nadeem and Aunty Ayesha took over her room.

Mikaeel and Shuaib got Fiza's. They divided her bed into two sections with their pillows and pretended like it was some sort of secret mission while they were doing it, whispering into their hands, pretending they were walkie-talkies. Uzair had to move his mattress over from next door and put it on the floor in Fiza's room.

I had to move from the bottom bunk in mine and Zayd's room to the top bunk. Fiza was in the bottom now.

It was a bit much though. The amount of people we had over, the lack of privacy ... You had to wake up bare early if you actually wanted to enjoy going to the toilet.

Fiza slammed the door coming back into our room one morning.

'What's up with you?' I asked from the top bunk, one hand busy with texting the group chat about Uzair clogging up the sinkhole with his hair, one leg propped up and over the bunk-bed frame.

I heard my old mattress creak with her movements. 'They started laughing at me.'

'Who?'

'Mikaeel and Shuaib.'

Fiza climbed up the little wooden ladder on the side. 'Amir, do I look like a *churayl* when I've just woken up?'

I put my phone down. Inspected Fiza for witchiness. I saw her thick hair. The flat part she'd leaned on to sleep and the rest of it, standing up on end all electrocuted. And the dark rims around her eyes. When she smiled, like she was doing then, you saw the gap between her two front teeth, and a little bit of her pink tongue pushing its way forward, snake-like.

'No,' I lied.

Fiza turned to our shut door, and the boys who lay beyond it. 'Idiots. Who do they think they are?'

Downstairs, the adults in the house were too busy sorting breakfast – searching the fridge for enough eggs, ransacking the cupboards for bread, putting the kettle on boil, and doing it again when there wasn't enough tea to go around – to do Fiza's hair for her. But I knew where we kept the hair oil. I knew where the brush was.

She only shouted at me two times when we went downstairs and I made her sit between my legs on the still-half-bed living-room sofa. I set the brush going on her head. Told her to ignore the chaos whirling around us.

'Think of it as an experiment,' Mikaeel spoke into his hand – his fake walkie-talkie – while Shuaib came up from behind him and into the living room. 'What can a chicken eat?'

'Or not eat!' Shuaib fake-walkie-talkied back.

The two of them got to work trying to unlatch the sliding doors to the garden, a big box of chewing gum and the bag of chicken feed in their hands.

Fiza tried to scramble out from under my grip.

'Oi!' I shouted, making both annoying cousins jump out of their skin. I pointed the hairbrush at them. 'Don't even think about it.'

Mikaeel narrowed his eyes. 'It's for science.'

I narrowed my eyes back. '*Baloona*, is this your dad's house? "It's for science." Go and eat your breakfast.'

The two of them looked at each other, and then at us, before they dropped the chewing gum and chicken feed. They headed for the kitchen, grumbling along the way.

'Yeah!' Fiza yelled after their backs. 'And don't even think of trying something like that again!' Mikaeel and Shuaib turned around, confused. 'You heard me!' she fake-walkie-talkied slowly, deliberately, while looking them in the eye. 'Don't even think of trying something like that again.'

I couldn't help smirking at the way Shuaib stared, big-eyed and afraid, while Mikaeel pulled on his shirt sleeve, regained his attention, tried to urge him away from us. But I wanted to fight our cousins myself. I understood Fiza's constant lingering glances over to her beloved pets outside the window, her huffs and sighs when her spot on the sofa was taken up by two brothers who snickered at her sitting cross-legged on the carpet.

I mean, they'd only been staying with us for two days, and Uzair's trainers had already shoved mine off the rack in the hallway.

I even came back from volunteering once, daydreaming the whole day of a can of Coke I'd let chill in the fridge for two weeks, just to see him sipping it in the living room. He was watching his brothers through the lace curtains while Fiza instructed them on the correct distance to keep from her chickens. Especially Maximus. The confident rooster, the one with the big head, the golden legs, the red crown on his head, which she'd proclaimed her favourite.

But I couldn't say anything to Mum about it.

She, Uncle Nadeem and Aunty Ayesha were in intense Nishaan mode anyway, discussing Mohamed's increased wage in the sitting room, and worrying about Neelam Jalani's wedding.

The groom was a rich kid she'd met on her biomedical sciences course, and his family wanted shisha pipes in the main room and fresh baklava on the dessert table, a DJ deck around the guest tables, a flower arch, balloons, fireworks, a photo booth which gave out photostrips, and for the whole venue to smell like this really smoky brand of oud.

'Alright, Amir?' Uzair said, that day with the Coke can.

He was so annoying. I wanted to punch him in his face. I wanted to say: '*Fine. So you're helping me out and doing my deliveries for me. So you're keeping this police volunteering thing a secret. So what? What do you want me to do about it? Kiss your smelly feet?*'

Instead I just said: 'Alright?'

The carrier bag we'd got from Mahmood's Foods, all full of Fiza's snacks, was lying on the table. A notepad rested beside it. Doodly handwriting next to her homework – the first draft of a short story on someone who inspired her, which she insisted I edit already. But a red pen had already gone in and circled the major spelling mistakes.

'He's so quick at reading.' Fiza's voice came up from behind me, her hands pulling the sliding doors shut after Mikaeel and Shuaib came rushing back inside. 'Uzair said I haven't even made that many mistakes.'

Uzair smiled, clicking the red pen he'd been using. Once, twice.

Kasmey, he was asking for a fight. But I ignored him. Shuaib and Mikaeel ignored Uzair telling them to be careful getting water from the kitchen, too.

And I watched as Fiza kicked off her sliders and tucked her feet beneath her on the sofa, all eager at Uzair's shoulder, asking him what he thought of her ideas, the main character that inspired her, whether he was likeable enough or not.

'Well, he does things because he thinks they're the right thing to do,' Uzair said. 'That means he's realistic. Even if people don't agree with his actions, they'll understand his intentions. And a character being realistic is more important than him being likeable.'

'Right, right.' Fiza nodded. 'Of course.'

I busied myself with taking out the crisps and chocolate we'd spent so long buying together. Fiza definitely heard it, the loud rustling sounds I made even louder in my irritation. But she carried on chattering to Uzair, listening intently as he gave away his wisdom and underlined words that could be improved, circled punctuation that needed looking at.

Then she glared at me. *Stop being so mean to him.*

I glared back. *I'll do what I want.*

Fiza grabbed Uzair's pen and threw it at my head. The little traitor. I dodged it, obviously. I threw it back.

'Whoa, whoa,' Uzair said, one hand flying protectively to his hair. 'Relax, you guys.'

'Oi, you know you've got a house of your own, don't you?' I said to Uzair. 'Even if they're renovating it?'

He nodded.

'Well, why don't you piss off back to it then? Go on, chip! No one wants you here!'

Fiza glared at me. 'Amir.'

I didn't pay attention to her. I knew she was just happy to be getting extra help with her homework. From me, from him. It clearly didn't matter.

Uzair laughed. 'Leave him, Fiza. It's fine.'

He always did that when I said stuff like that. Laughed and

left me to it. But something about that, and the way Uzair's hand had just hovered near his stupid hair because of a flying pen, the offended way he'd stared up at me and Fiza – like he couldn't believe someone had actually tried to ruin his looks – really annoyed me.

I imagined someone else in his place. A lanky get, with a strong jaw and thick eyebrows. And a big nose. A big brother who would've just thrown a pen back at me if I'd said something rude. But my messages to Zakiya Bhatti were still unanswered. Even after Kemi and Eman had helped with formatting them. And I heard no one in that living room say:

Oi, man – Sharp teeth visible in his grin. The world's friendliest vampire. *You're taking it too far. Stop it.*

I would've listened to him though. I wouldn't have felt like there were too many people in the living room. No extra voice adding nothing to my sister's curious questions, no moving mouth that just didn't sound right when it suggested that I sit down if I didn't want to help out, play *FIFA* with my friends.

I sat down on the sofa, glaring at him. I kicked my backpack out of the way. Then I sighed and rooted around in it, looking for my phone, searching for a group chat full of Hassan's complaints about Neelam's groom, and, soon, mine about my annoying cousin.

But my hands touched cling film instead. A Post-it note. I frowned, pulling out a soft little bundle. A sandwich, wrapped tight, smelling strongly like *aloo gobi*.

'Amir!' Fiza yelled, her hands clamping quickly round her nose. 'How long has that been in there for?'

I ignored her. The Post-it note attached to the sandwich was pink, the message written on it in black ink.

I'm so sorry for what I said about your brother that day – Eman

The Sonic the Hedgehog doodle she'd drawn next to her note was detailed. Good-at-art-style good. Enough-to-make-Abshir-jealous good. I smiled to myself, sitting in the living room, ignoring everyone's moans and groans about the smell of gone-off *aloo gobi*.

CHAPTER 17
EMAN

I kept Nani's white receipt safe inside her wallet.

That little bit of paper which was only really covered in pencil scratchings, that almost-forgotten slip which only really betrayed my grandma's good intentions.

Half of what was written on that receipt was in our Mirpuri language, alif and *beh* characters I had to squint to make out. The other half was written in English. But I understood what she was trying to do through the list of ideal donations, the names and numbers which she'd gone through, one by one, and ticked off.

I recognized the height of her heart, the width of it. I knew her hope of gaining donations and helping the homeless who wandered our streets, begged for money at traffic lights, withstood the shame of standing at a rolled-up window, wanting someone to give them the value of eye contact if not their spare change.

The aunties knew it, too.

Wash 'n' Wear wasn't as busy as it usually was on the morning that I gathered my courage on the outside stoop and pushed the front door open.

'Hmm?' Balqis aunty squinted at me over a pile of leftover clothes, a line of silent washing machines. 'Eman?'

She folded up someone else's T-shirts and trousers, created a neat tower for them to return to, without anyone's assistance. On the far side of the launderette, Farida aunty checked the amount of change in the big glass jar we used for customers who only had notes, the launderette phone resting against her ear, with Azrah aunty at the other end, enquiring about a wedding suit we'd perhaps washed and dried and misplaced.

There it was again. The quiet that spread itself out, that made itself at home at everyone's expense.

And all because a plan to cook for myself and my mother had not been followed. And a few too-strong words had caused an eruption.

'*Assalamu alaykum*,' I said brightly to the aunties' moving backs, their buttoned-up cardigans.

The response was only slightly louder than my own echo. But I moved quickly. Like there was someone leading me. Like the wilderness I'd found myself trapped in was not quite so wild, not quite so green.

The bench in the middle of the room was usually Nani's spot. A pale wooden seat which offered a perfect view of the sunshine, the cobbles outside.

I took out Nani's wallet and my phone. I held the receipt in my hands, safe between my fingers, as I called the first name and number which Nani had been unable to get around to contacting.

'Hello?' My voice was a little shaky. I was so nervous.

But I only had to breathe through all of my words. I only had to imagine a warm and smiling woman next to me, resting her hands on the curve of her walking stick, urging me on with a nod of her head, a delicate dance to keep her thick googly glasses on the bridge of her nose.

Then the imaginary Nani beside me shifted into two other figures. Two fluffy space buns and warm brown eyes. A razor slit in an eyebrow and a cheeky grin. Shadows that always waited for my voice to join theirs. Who crafted a space in their conversations, and then pointed at it, as if to say: *Go on, Eman. This is your chance. We're listening.*

'Hello ...' I took a deep breath, my voice echoing in the quiet of the launderette. 'This is Eman Malik speaking, Maariyah Malik's granddaughter ... Yes, thank you. Well, I'm just calling to see if you'd still like to donate something to the homeless like my nani suggested a few weeks back? ... Yes, in collaboration with Friesly Grand Mosque ... OK. That's great! Thank you.'

Tomato soup and chickpea tins.

And maybe a multipack of mint toothpaste that had been on offer but which now, in hindsight, seemed excessive.

Perhaps there was a pack of toothbrushes that could be thrown in, if they were found in time, too.

I looked around, searching for a pencil, a pen, anything to update that tiny slip of paper with.

'Look in the wallet,' Farida aunty huffed, her voice carrying clearly from across the room now that it was done assuring Azrah aunty we hadn't seen Noor's sparkly *lehenga* ever since we'd wrapped it and left it for her to pick up.

I stopped patting down the pockets of my hoodie.

I felt Farida aunty and Balqis aunty watching me as I picked up that leather wallet again. I held it upside down over the bench. Shook it. Watched as pennies, a tiny pressed daffodil, bits of fluff, and – eventually – the shortest nub of a pencil came tumbling out.

I smiled at Farida aunty. 'Thank you.'

She was almost completely quiet, retreating back into the black of her jilbab and the very significant task of keeping that change jar organized, as I made my amendments to Nani's white slip of paper.

And then: 'You know,' Farida aunty said slowly, 'your grandma usually asked the person to confirm their full name first. So that she knew who she was talking to and no one got confused later on.'

'OK.' I nodded.

Balqis aunty moved her pile of folded clothes to the side of the bench as Farida aunty took one step, and then another, closer towards me. Still talking.

'Make sure you have them say how many tins they can bring, as well. How much is in a multipack? How many toothbrushes?'

I wrote that down, too. 'Right.'

'Maybe you could ask if people want to volunteer to build boxes of essentials for the homeless, too,' Balqis aunty suggested. 'So they have some food, some cleaning things, a blanket, gloves, all for one person.'

'Don't we need a drop-off space though?' I asked, to the old faces that now surrounded me, the old women who warmed my back. 'A place for everyone to leave their donations? A place for us to organize the boxes of essentials?'

'We'll –' Farida aunty and Balqis aunty both stopped and stared at one another, the fact that their words had matched up in an instant shocking them into silence.

Farida aunty cleared her throat, avoiding Balqis aunty's eyes. 'You go.'

'No, no.' Balqis aunty fidgeted with the ends of her *dupatta*, pretending to scratch at a non-existent stain. 'After you.'

I tried to hide the smile on my face watching this.

'Well, I was just going to say we'll figure it out,' Farida aunty said, crossing her arms over her chest, the ends of her jilbab sleeves long and dark and oddly elegant in the light.

Balqis aunty gasped. She threw her warm arms around Farida aunty's reedy waist. 'Farida, that's exactly what I was going to say!'

I couldn't help the laughter that escaped my mouth. The relief that rose high into the sweet launderette air as the silence escaped, fearful and furtive, out of the cracked open window.

'And if that doesn't work –' Farida aunty grimaced as she said this, though the ghost of a smile showed on her narrow face too – 'well, there's always the space we use for council meetings. The town hall's largest conference room.'

They suggested that Nani's condition could worsen at any point due to her age.

But it could also be fixed by a preventative operation, the doctors at Friesly General Infirmary said. Or, at least, they relayed this to Mum, who relayed this to the relatives still knocking on our front door, still settling in for living-room conversations that were only slightly about Nani at all.

But an operation to bring her back to us . . . That information shocked me out of my concentration on the precarious angle of a knife on a plate of apples and bananas. It fell. I caught it before it hit the just-vacuumed carpet. I set it back on the table.

Next to the cups of fresh orange juice, the plates of heated-up *biryani*.

'Eman,' my mum hissed warningly.

I threw my hands up, as if to say it was only an accident – which it was.

'An operation!' A cousin or an aunty from Nani's mother's side exhaled. '*Inshallah* it goes well. It's soon, isn't it? *Inshallah* you get to see her when it's done and she's back racing down the streets with her walking stick very soon. You must be missing her, hmm, Eman?' This cousin or aunty then jostled me good-naturedly. Had me spill a little of the mint sauce on to the table. 'I know your nani talked about you all the time. She loved you.'

My heart stammered at this confession.

'We miss her very much,' Mum said, with her hands on my shoulders. She steered me into the kitchen, insisting I find a cloth to clean up the mess on the table.

'Can we visit?' I asked while I had the chance. 'Can we visit Nani after her operation?'

'We'll talk about that later,' Mum said.

Someone was asking about where our cutlery was from though. From there the conversation turned to fine china, then bills to be paid, then home remedies for headaches, and then the weather. In the midst of all this, an uncle moaned about the chillies in the kebab recipe, insisting his own wife's cooking was better, and asked me to pour him some water.

'But you divorced her, didn't you?' I said, remembering Nani's stories about this uncle, the way she'd always wrinkled her nose at the mention of his name. 'For wanting to work as well as be a housewife? So you aren't allowed to miss her and her kebab recipe.'

'Eman!' Mum hissed, apologizing profusely, while the cleared throats and awkward murmurs around the room echoed the acknowledgement that I was my grandma's granddaughter after all.

I sat on the sofa trying to hide my smile at that, trying to ignore the heat of my mum's glare. Still, my hands rested politely on my knees, and I thought of teenage things that would have only been things – though important ones, the facts of my life – to Nani.

Like mine and Kemi's habit of racing to the same thin tree on our walks home together.

Or the way she begged me to let her do my eyeliner some day.

Like the strange beat of my heart, sometimes, when I looked around for Amir mid-laughter and found he was already looking at me.

Or the panic that rose in my throat after Kemi and I had accepted his invitation to Neelam Jalani's wedding on Monday and I realized, a little too late, my head swoony with the fact of our friendship, that I had nothing to wear.

But there was a suitcase under Nani's bed in our room. A double-strapped heaving monster of a suitcase which lingered with the smell of Pakistan, which carried the secrets of my grandma's first life. Jasmine flowers. Rickety alleys and boys leading cows through them. A view of a dam which stretched out as far as the eye could see.

'*Don't you know, Eman?*' Nani had pulled on the handle once in our old house when Mum and Dad were arguing, and I could hear the shrieks and sobs of a freshly stinging slap beginning to build in Mum's throat. '*I carry who I was when I was your age in here. Do you want to meet her?*'

We'd spent that dark morning turning over the plastic-wrapped packages of *shalwar kameez* her own mother had sewn for her in her youth.

Jewelled necklines, colours of white, and deep red, and soft pink.

We'd opened up the clasps on velvet-covered boxes of jewellery.

Nani had let her gold earrings, her bangles, her one intricate bracelet – which was lined with what looked like tiny glittering sequins – tell stories about village weddings she'd attended, birthday parties, and after-school dressing-up sessions just for fun, just to enjoy the silence that came with the end of her chores, a purple sky, dusk.

And her shoes? Nani's loafers were sensible and brown on her wrinkled feet.

Nani's *khousey* from her youth sparkled like stars, lay gentle within each other like spoons in a drawer, or like me and my grandma when we first moved to Friesly, and my nightmares were darker than the night, and my bed was shared with her.

I reached out and held them as soon as I saw them. The *khousey* still slept, beautiful, undisturbed like the first fall of winter snow. Too big for me.

Nani cupped my cheek, her eyes creasing into crescent moons. '*One day*,' she'd joked, while something glass-like or womanly crashed and fell to the floor downstairs, moments away from swearing us into secrecy, '*you'll fit into my history even better than me.*'

I wore her simplest wedding suit. White and clean and only slightly sparkling with gold. A snowish hijab to match.

And I stood outside Nishaan, my heart jumping like a rabbit as I stared down at the cobbles, my feet in Nani's *khousey*. They fit me now. Like a glove.

It shocked me more that the streets no longer smelled like blood though. Or like Nani's aloe vera, her little tub of Vaseline on her bedroom cabinet. Cracked-heel ointment. The coriander and mint she'd grown in the kitchen window. The cobbles just smelled like stone.

'Wow,' Kemi breathed, skipping any form of 'hello' to move her fingers over the delicate gauze of my *dupatta*.

I laughed off my embarrassment. That particular brand of shyness which came with the feeling of standing out, of drawing too much attention. Kemi's dress was sweet and striped. It came out at her waist, a skirt which fell cleanly to her knees.

'I like your dress,' I said.

Her hands continued to sweep over the pale golden fringe sewn to the edges of my *dupatta*. 'Yeah, yeah,' she joked. 'Don't pity me.'

I looked at her. I unwrapped the *dupatta* from where it hung modestly on my shoulder and threw it around her neck. Kemi beamed even brighter, with all of her teeth, and with Nani's *dupatta* glittering against her like that.

So did Amir when he saw the two of us there amid the din of so many moving bodies, the glitter of the delicate gold centrepieces on the tables, his sister's insistence he help her carry the starters to the guests trickling in like syrup, his friends yelling for photos behind him, and the glow of his own crisp *shalwar kameez*.

That was why it surprised me so much, the day after. When he sat in PC Chris's car with a face like thunder. And we all came so close to dying.

CHAPTER 18
KEMI

It was my third favourite feeling when people started calling up my hotline. The sound of money to be made.

My second favourite feeling is taking a shower before everyone else in the flat, changing into brand-new pyjamas, with crisp new bedsheets, and just lying there, clean as a pebble.

My first one is, obviously, when I'm on a running track, and I don't have to look back to know that there is so much distance between me and every other runner. It's just obvious. I can feel it in my movement, the whistle of the wind in my hair, the fact of my own stamina.

I loved it when I started seeing all of these notifications on my phone, though, asking if I was interested in babysitting, or cleaning a house, or weeding a garden, or mowing the grass.

At first, I thought the texts were Jasmin and Michael, finally getting back to me, finally filling me in on workout schedules and on eating to benefit your exercise, and sending along photos of France in all its beauty. But our group chat had fizzled to nothing but my own texts, my own photos of Emmanuel, and my videos of his being pranked. Double-ticked as having been delivered, but not opened. No read receipts.

It confused me a little.

I mean, my best friends had only been gone for a little over a month, but the lack of communication made it feel like an eternity. And they were supposed to be back soon. I had it on my phone calendar. The return of the three of us, typed in for Saturday.

I also had all of my new hotline jobs typed in. The rates for all of them, too:

BABYSIT @ HOWARD LI'S – 2 hours, £20
BABYSIT @ 224 WHERL CRESCENT – 2 hours, £10
CLEANING @ CHRIS + FADY'S FLAT – 3 hours, £30 (lots of mess)
MOW GRASS @ 16 FARLEY DRIVE – 1 hour, £10 (lots of grass)
GARDENING @ MARTA VARGA'S – 2 hours, £20 (lots of weeds)

And that didn't even include the jobs I'd confirmed in north Friesly! Sure, I had to take two buses in the swampish August heat to get to where the water ran clearer and sweeter than it did where we lived, but I could up my rates in north Friesly.

Those two buses usually took me up on a constant incline, to where the roads grew narrower and the country fields and patches of green and brown grass, full of grazing cows and dozing sheep, were infinite.

The houses in north Friesly were also spaced out and huge. These were big-bricked monstrosities that seemed to come out of the green moors, stretching out their driveways, where boats were kept strapped to the back of big Jeeps, and back gardens fooled a pet dog's estimate of exactly how big a back garden should be. Those houses were all wide windows, fresh paint on doors, and name plaques.

I didn't even know houses could have names until Jasmin invited me to hers for a party. Moorfield House, all crawling with ivy. It was a pale pink mansion masquerading as a cottage. It had lots of rooms. A kitchen that was separate from the living room. Spacious beds that didn't have to be shared with anyone. I thought that was mad. Jasmin's mattress could've fit me, her and Ada. But it was just for her.

'You should come over more,' she used to moan at me on the phone.

Looking back, the memory of me standing in her big house, staring at her big bed, in my best striped dress, my hair relaxed at my mum's request, made me feel weird.

'I'm not cool enough for you, am I?' Her voice always sounded so tinny and faraway on the phone. 'Because I don't live in south Friesly like you?'

'Jasmin,' I always laughed, 'that's not it.'

I mean, her birthday parties usually involved a mix of her secondary school friends – all of us who ran with her, who sat next to her in form time – and her primary school friends. Girls whose nail polish was always smooth and sleek, girls whose trainers always gleamed white. They spoke differently to me. Pronounced every word just right.

'What did you just say, Kemi?' one of them even said, turning to me at Jasmin's party, all curious about my choice of drink at the dining table.

'Hmm?' I started wondering if I'd messed up somehow. 'Sprite,' I said. 'I said I want some Sprite.'

The girl repeated the word, enunciating over my dropped 't', that casual hallmark of my south Friesly accent.

A fit of giggles seized everyone at the table. I remember looking around at all of these strangers, and at Jasmin, who wasn't a stranger. She laughed too. And pulled me along to the desserts table in her parents' living room, insisting to the numb expression on my face, the downturned frown of my eyebrows, that everyone was only joking. I knew that. I did. I smiled after a little while, even though I didn't really feel like it.

'I'll come over again soon,' I always promised Jasmin on the phone. 'I will.'

I guess I did that because I knew it was painful for her. Having her best friend reject all these invitations to hang out at hers. She'd always grumble about it at school.

She and Michael used to slacken their posture when they saw me coming in the mornings. They'd curve in their shoulders, and say this was how cool kids from south Friesly acted. Purposely not pronouncing the 't's in their sentences. Exaggerating a slang that sounded strange in their mouths: 'Wagwan' and 'is it', 'allow it' and 'bait'. *We're only joking*, Jasmin's bright smile always said, in the midst of this pantomime. So I'd joke back, tell them they were the worst roadmen in history, and join in their teasing as we approached our form room.

A secret part of me would always wonder what it was about me that screamed this slang, this language, this posture so loudly to them.

My sister, who attended one of the best universities in the country?

My mum's impressive knowledge of the Bible?

My grades, which were usually higher than theirs?

In PE, I caught my own reflection in the changing-room mirror. I thought that maybe I did slacken my posture a little bit. Maybe I did curve in my shoulders. But wasn't that because I was tall? And because our flat at home had lots of slanting ceilings that I was always banging my head on?

So who could blame me if the mansions masquerading as cottages in north Friesly had a strange effect on me?

The sky seemed bluer up in north Friesly, too. Like all this time I'd seen it, it'd been shoved inside a can no one had peeled open properly. So I'd only been seeing a corner, and mistaking it for the whole thing, never realizing there was more sky than that, never noticing there were four corners of blue instead of just one.

'You're late,' the old lady I saw every Sunday evening said, her arms leaning over her painted garden fence.

But she still handed me the cash for my cleaning, a few rolled-up fifties for all my weeks' work up front. That was just the way Aiza Bhatti was. Her twin sister's name, Azrah Bhatti. And her nieces, Noor Bhatti and Juveria Bhatti.

I knew who she was related to because Noor was in our form at school. She was alright. Smart when she wanted to be. Stupid when she wanted to be, too.

I knew I could charge Noor's aunty way more than I charged Howard Li, and Marta Varga, and everybody who lived close to where the river ran brown with mud, because

Aiza Bhatti spoke English without any accent, as though her ancestors had been born and raised on British soil like her prized roses.

I mean, her garden was basically a field. Her kitchen had a stable door in it even though she didn't own any horses. She wore a different pair of wellies every time I came around. Inside, Aiza Bhatti's house was stuffed full of antique furniture, and jewellery, and expensive oriental rugs she needed me to dust down. Her wrinkled mouth was full of endless stories about her beautiful family, every item in her home a testament to them.

'Be gentle,' she'd grumble from that stable door, overseeing my dusting with a security guard's scrutiny. 'That vase was a gift from my husband before he passed. He was a businessman, you know. He consulted with the top banking companies in the world. He travelled to the continent of Africa all the time . . .'

A gold bracelet, now with a broken clasp, came from the time she and her son had shopped at the artisanal fair in Lowbridge together. A large bleached photograph of a factory that hung on the wall was a keepsake from a family visit to the Barker Summer Festival many years back, when you could buy things of worth there, rather than stuffed toys and cruel bags of diseased goldfish.

And then, when I was in the middle of wiping down a wooden bookshelf: 'Careful, Kemi! That framed article you almost knocked over was written by my daughter. She used to work right here in Friesly, you know.'

'Really?' I said, only half listening.

'Yes, as a journalist. But then she got married. She left her hometown, gave up the family surname, even her job.' A proud dimple appeared on the old woman's face. 'But not her eye for injustice.'

Hearing that, I remember I stopped trying to scrub a stain off that bookshelf. I remember almost tripping over the tassels on a colourful 'Made in Sudan' rug. It knocked the wind right out of me.

'Zakiya,' I breathed.

Aiza stared at me. Blinked twice like I was stupid. 'Yes. Her name appears at the top of that article. I'm not surprised you can read, Kemi. You're a businesswoman, aren't you?'

The pieces fitted together in my head slowly, with the precision of someone completing a jigsaw puzzle.

'She doesn't live in Friesly any more ... She gave up her family surname when she got married. And the job too, right? She doesn't work as a journalist any more?'

'No.' Aiza sniffed. 'She works in management now, for a very expensive clothing brand. She's the best manager they ever had –'

I barely heard her. 'That's why she never opened Amir's messages on her press profile!' I said. 'It's not active any more!'

I couldn't believe it. I stared up at Aiza, rejoicing at my luck, and expecting her figure to still be there in the doorway. But there was nothing. A split second went by. There was no one.

I stood there, confused. 'Aiza? Where'd you go?'

Her disappearance scared me somehow. I half expected the entire house to fall down just then, the garden outside to roll up like a carpet, for me to open my eyes, claw myself into being awake, out of this coincidence, out of this dream. Empty-handed. But there were voices coming from down the hallway.

I set my rag and bottle of disinfectant down and followed the sound out to a hallway of dark polished wood decorated with intricate wall hangings.

'I'm sorry,' Aiza said, standing with her arms crossed over chest, a flash of her sister's dyed blonde hair peeking out from the space around her slim figure, 'I can't give you any more money, Azrah. Not when you haven't paid me back for the last time.'

'But I will, Aiza! I promise.' Azrah's voice was filled with desperation. 'It's just that Noor's suit for Neelam's wedding went missing, so I called in a favour with a friend to borrow her *lehenga*, but my friend didn't tell me she expected me to pay her for it –'

'So you didn't check properly? You saw a way for everyone to think of your daughter as beautiful and that's it? You didn't think to check anything?'

A painful, tense silence.

'I just want people to think well of my family.'

'That's always what it's about with you, isn't it, Azrah? What will people think? How will we look? What will they say? No. No more.'

'But, Aiza, we're supposed to be sisters!'

'Do you treat me like one? Or do you only think of yourself?'

I knew I shouldn't have been eavesdropping. I knew that wasn't what I was being paid to do. A spasm of embarrassment ran through me, a stranger in someone else's house, listening in on their secrets.

So I went back into the living room. I picked up the rag and the bottle of disinfectant and wiped down a photo of Azrah and Aiza as children in a steep south Friesly backstreet, their unlined faces staring into the camera, their tiny chubby hands clasped around each other's shoulder.

But I couldn't help wondering if Azrah and Aiza had ever watched quiz shows together and guessed one another's answers. I couldn't help thinking about whether they'd stayed up half the night refusing to sleep, humming one another's favourite songs, asking each other to guess the tune in the dark of the night.

I mopped the floor.

I poured the dirty water down the outside gutter.

Maybe Azrah and Aiza had even sat on a pair of metal swings in the cool evening air with their friends, mentally forcing the lights in other people's houses to switch off, confessing to one another – and the clouds, the watching moon, the listening stars – their secret superpowers. Like sisters do. Like sisters should.

What about friends, though? How did they act? As the secret of Zakiya's story filled the corners of my mind, I knew it deserved to fill the corners of Amir's mind, too.

Neelam Jalani's wedding was a blur of bright lights and colours to me.

The swirl of a kaleidoscope, shifting and whirling in the transformed space that Nishaan became for special occasions.

I mean, Ada, Mum and I had eaten there before. For all of our birthdays. Once Jasmin and I had gone in and ordered tea and sipped it like proper ladies, too.

After all, Nishaan was an eat-what-you-want, order-when-you-want Englistani extravaganza.

It was the most popular stop for brunch, as an after-school hang-out, for couples on secret dates, for family events, birthdays, and now weddings. It was where teenagers and the elderly, loners and large groups could coexist easily to the rhythm of a stuttering coffee machine, oil frying in the back, dozens of delicious orders for full English breakfasts, *parathas*, curries, *samosa chaat*, paninis, wraps, burgers, chips, Kashmiri tea that glowed pink, regular-coloured tea, ten different types of coffee and a fridge humming with fizzy drinks.

Things were obviously fancier for Neelam's wedding, though.

There were gleaming silk coverings on seats with red sashes tied to the backs in large bows. A stage was decked out with an ornate gilded chaise and so many roses and lilies you couldn't even count how many there were. Gold centrepieces winked from the middle of each table. Waiters carried metal trays that steamed with spiced potatoes, fish fritters and lamb chops for starters. There was roast chicken, lamb curry and chapatis for the main course. For afters, something Eman told me was called *gulab jamun*, which we had with ice cream, or a sweet carrot dish that I'd never tried before but which sang on my tongue.

I felt like I was close to a wedding I'd been to in Lagos, all fancy clothes, colours and the warmth of people. Far away from it, too.

'Watch, you can't hack it,' said Amir as he doused all of our plates with a green chutney, pouring a silver jug of it right on to our rice. The challenge of seeing exactly how much spice we could take glowed as bright as the ceiling lights from our spot upstairs on the balcony.

I rolled my eyes, my spoon at my mouth, while Eman and Fiza watched wide-eyed and Abshir, Ben and Hassan drummed on their legs in anticipation. 'I can,' I said. 'Easily.'

I swallowed the rice, smothered as it was in green chilli sauce. Then I pretended like my tongue wasn't completely on fire, like I didn't desperately need a refill from one of the big fizzy bottles Amir and Fiza had brought up the stairs and set by the railings of the mezzanine.

We dangled our legs over the balcony, plastic plates in hand, with a bird's-eye view of the stage and the waiters pirouetting like marbles through the revolving door of the kitchen in some distant playground game down below.

Up there, it smelled like spiced food and the boys' gummy-bear-scented vape pens – the latter an investment by Hassan after his parents and his sister strictly forbade him from even looking in the direction of the shisha pipes, the hookahs. The air crackled with everyone's laughter as they watched me give in, reach for my plastic cup and drain the leftover Coke in seconds.

There was a warmth in my chest that extended far out, like ripples in water. So I knew everyone else felt it, too. Even Amir, who squinted towards a lone figure on the other side of the balcony after a little while.

I knew I needed to tell him about Zakiya Bhatti.

I knew I had to let that information fill him with the same sky-bright feeling it had filled me.

CHAPTER 19
AMIR

I didn't see him at first.

The corner of the balcony he was standing in was poorly lit because of a sudden, unexpected bulb explosion. He didn't move from the darkness, or fix it either, no spare light bulb coming out of the pockets of his sherwani, none of his usual annoying problem-solving in evidence. He didn't even come up to us, no soft steps of his leather *khousey* in our direction, no familiar voice telling us to head back down the stairs, eat at a table, stop leaving crumbs all over the balcony carpet.

No, Uzair just stood there watching the wedding down below. A lone silhouette. I saw his hand reach up and wipe at his nose though. I wondered if he had a cold.

Downstairs, Neelam and her new husband Tariq posed on the stage for photographs, the distance between them on the chaise that me and Mohamed had positioned hours earlier just sweet enough to be romantic, just far enough apart to be *halal*.

I saw Uzair's shoulders sag with the weight of a sigh.

I wondered if he was upset that he'd never managed to do his cupcake business for weddings.

Or if he was reliving the pain of being whacked in the face with Neelam's football all those years back.

The blood that had leaked out all over his face, the gushing nostrils she'd so quickly shrieked over, the tissues in her pocket all over the grass as she'd tried to stem the red flow.

All in her usual blunt and big-boned way, of course. Until Neelam was laughing, and Uzair was laughing, and the rest of us just wanted them to stop staring at each other and get back to the game.

I looked at him, looking down at his first best friend marrying someone else. Or was he just mourning the end of his childhood? I don't know, man. Whatever he was thinking, it seemed painful. It seemed sad. Then a part of me whispered it was none of my business.

It was past midnight when the wedding celebrations finally died down. The early hours were especially warm and bright.

Like the night had forgotten it was supposed to get dark or something. Like even the clouds didn't want to darken up a pale, pale sky. And the moon was still easy to see.

'Happy birthday, Amir,' Fiza sang from where the two of us sat on the sofa in the living room, still in our party clothes, our heads swimming with the beat and volume of the Bollywood songs that had been playing on a loop for the past few hours.

I fist-bumped her. 'Thanks, Fiz-pop.'

We were both a little tired. A little buzzed. And my real birthday celebration was happening later on that day anyway.

'I'm not gonna give you a present because you already got it.'

I turned my head to my sister, confused. 'What you on about?'

Fiza pushed the ends of her fancy straightened hair behind her ears. 'Don't you remember? I didn't sit next to you on the balcony so that Eman could. Duh!'

She leaned in extra close on the sofa, smiling at me with the gap in her teeth showing, the sequinned headband she was wearing so close to falling into her eyes.

'I saw you, you know,' she said. 'You poured her drink for her. And when you gave it to her, you did it so your hands could touch.'

I flicked her forehead.

I'd tried to ignore how it felt when Eman's fingers brushed mine the way they had. I hadn't even intended it. I hadn't even meant to sit so close, pour the drink, none of that. But when she was sat right next to me, the shiny details of her clothes only a bit brighter than her eyes, and her fingers were fumbling over her plastic cup?

It was the simplest thing ever, pouring her drink for her.

And, also, not the simplest thing ever. My heart had never beat that fast pouring drinks for anyone. And I'd never got so quiet, so suddenly sweaty, hearing someone say thanks.

I cleared my throat, ignoring Fiza watching me so closely. 'Don't know what you're on about.'

But she was still giggling into my shoulder, leaning in and laughing and putting her socked feet all over my *shalwar* in her excitement.

Eman
Amir Ali

How can I tell you?
I could live in your quiet
For now, forever.

'Don't even think about it,' Fiza's voice suddenly snapped, her legs no longer climbing all over mine, all of her standing quickly to attention.

Mikaeel and Shuaib's socks slid to a dangerously sudden halt in front of the sliding doors leading outside. Within seconds, Uzair almost collided into their backs as he carried the plastic bag full of tea rusks in from the kitchen, his face suddenly inches from the floor, little crumbs mixed with cardamom crushed slightly in his hands.

The air in the room was steady like a red pen over a short-story homework task.

Mikaeel puffed up his chest. He tried to look dignified even though the waist-tie for his *shalwar* was loose. It trailed beneath his *kameez*, no longer keeping his pants up very effectively.

'We wanted to feed the chickens.'

Fiza pushed her headband up. 'Right now? They're asleep.'

'Well,' Mikaeel said, 'how do you know they experience time in the same way we do?'

The rest of us glanced at each other, waiting for a pause in their confrontation, a tumbleweed or something to roll past in this cowboy exchange.

'Oi, just show 'em the book you got on raising chickens,' I

said, because it was annoying me, all of this tense silence, all of these arguments over nothing.

The only interruption to all of it was the sound of Mum, Uncle Nadeem and Aunty Ayesha chattering about relatives and what they wore to the wedding, how much money an aunty or uncle had given to Neelam's family, if Azrah Bhatti had ordered her daughters' flashy clothes from Pakistan or Bradford, and if anyone had noticed Neelam's rich good-boy husband Tariq slipping out for a not-so-good cigarette break.

'You'll see!' Fiza yelled, encouraging Mikaeel and Shuaib to race after her as she headed up for that book, insisting that she was – as she liked reminding us all – always right.

'Wow.' Uzair sat down on the sofa next to me. 'That's the most hyper little girl in the world.'

I fiddled with the TV remote. Switched through a few channels. Realized quickly that there was nothing good to watch at 1 a.m.

'Watch her come down with a book that's bigger than your head.'

Uzair pretended to be offended. 'Oi, don't act like your head isn't bigger.'

'Yeah, yeah. Didn't your dad ever tell you it's *haram* to lie?'

And Uzair laughed. I mean, he always did. At anything I said. But it didn't bother me too much at that moment.

He crossed his arms over his chest. 'Well, we'll see when Fiza comes back down.'

I smiled. 'Get ready to be wrong.'

Uzair waggled his eyebrows at me, just joking around. And

then, mid-yawn: '*Ah-ha-huh*,' just like Zayd used to do, with that stupid singing-Elvis impression.

My smile died on my face.

Uzair looked at me, his eyes suddenly so big and so brown. 'Amir –'

But I didn't wait for what he said next. I just went upstairs – quickly, and without looking back – to my room.

My heart was going so fast. My head, full of Uzair doing that stupid impression.

All of him, standing up like some giant exclamation mark, taking up all the space in our house, and our history, and my head. How long had he been doing that impression? He wasn't Zayd. He could never be. He wasn't even there that first time Zayd did that impression.

Mid-spring, my brother in the passenger seat, fighting my mum over the radio. Strong jaw, big smile, all teeth and thick eyebrows. An Elvis Presley song on, and him not even finishing his impression properly because me and Fiza were already crying with laughter, and so was he, and Mum, and the noise the car was making as it struggled over a hill, all engine hisses and hums, sounded like laughing, too. That moment had nothing to do with Uzair.

I shut my eyes, sinking into the bottom bunk, my room dim in that strange early-morning light. I could still see the panels of that top bunk behind my eyes. Specifically, one of them. A felt-tip drawing on the polished grain.

'*That's you,*' *Zayd had said once when he'd reached up – halfway through trying to help me do a worksheet on quadratic equations – and drawn some ugly turtle-looking thing on the wood.*

Only because I'd got a new backpack for that school year. Scrimped and saved my Eid money for a Nike one that wasn't second-hand and full of holes at the bottom, or that didn't spell Nike wrong, the way that some of the knock-off backpacks Mum had given me before did. The only downside was it was a bit big for me. Zayd found that hilarious.

Little boy, massive backpack. Little turtle kid.

'No!' I'd laughed at that drawing. Drawn massive eyebrows on it. Given it sharp teeth. 'That's you!'

Zayd had stopped frowning at that maths worksheet, looked up, laughed and shoved me in the side.

Grinning that vampire-grin the whole time. Making me laugh even more.

We spent so much time doing that though. Laughing, smiling, grinning, joking. Not all the time. But so much that I felt it when I was lying there in that bottom bunk, no big brother next to me for homework help, not him hanging his stinky foot off the edge from his own bunk.

'Go plug in my phone charger, Amir. Go get some water from downstairs.'

No one howling with laughter when I swore at them.

'Shut up, man. I'm trying to sleep. Go do it yourself.'

No one in the half-darkness at all. Not with me. Not any more.

'Amir?' Fiza said, bringing the light of the landing with her. She stretched up to hit the bedroom switch. 'What's going on? Why aren't you downstairs?' I didn't have to lift my head to know she was standing in the doorway, holding a few books to her chest. The sparkly *lehenga* she'd worn for Neelam's wedding a little creased at the bottom from all her running around. The wavy bob of her head staticky from the heat, satiny from the headband.

Fiza's socks padded softly against the carpet. I felt her sit down.

'Amir, I'm worried about Maximus. I showed everyone the book, and apparently you can feed chickens at night, so we went out and scattered the food, but he's not eating. I'm really worried. I don't know what's wrong with him –'

'I don't care, Fiza.' My voice was muffled. I spoke into a pillow. 'I don't care about the stupid chicken.'

'But Amir –'

'Fiza!' I sat all the way up. Yelled in her face. 'I don't care, OK? I don't care!'

My sister flinched. Her breath hitched in her throat. Then she stood up and left. But not without leaving a slip of paper covered in red pen behind.

'Shit,' I said. The ocean roared inside my body as I picked up that paper, read over the first few sentences:

My brother Amir inspires me more than anyone else in the world. He's stupid, and funny, and sometimes he needs a reminder to cut his nails on time. But he cares about our family. He looks after me. I look at Amir and I forget I used to have two brothers because all I think of when I hear that word – brother – is his face.

I slipped on my sliders. I headed for the garden Fiza had exiled our cousins from, the mud still stencilled with chicken feet, the stone wall etched with our knifed-in initials, the grass going brown in patches. She sat scattering feed carefully, with too-small handfuls, with teary murmurs on her tongue.

I took the bag from her on the second try. The first time, she resisted. She held it away from me. The second time, I got closer. And I let her punch my chest. Again. And again. And again. Until she stopped crying. Until I was hugging her.

Then I helped her up. And we looked for the rooster in the garden together.

It was tiring being in PC Chris's car. Exhausting waking up when the sky above Friesly still glowed with streaks of candyfloss pink.

The glass of the shops we sped past reflected some of that colour, making everything blush.

The tall, winding spire of the old cathedral, the red-brick buildings where people slept and ate and lived. The chimneys that curled plumes of smoke on cooler days than that one. And the statue of the old man with the thick beard, the wide-brimmed hat, the pigeons cooing at his feet.

Sir William Barker.

Sir William Barker with a whole festival dedicated just to him and his memory.

We drove past the bus shelter I'd graffitied Zayd's name on. The glass, heat soaked and shining clear. No blue spray paint on it. Erased completely.

'Amir,' Kemi hissed from the passenger seat while PC Chris chatted his usual chat about the leaflets, and how well we'd been doing to make sure they were delivered without a lot of creases. 'Amir, is it your birthday today? Sixteen, innit? No wonder you're so quiet today. You must be getting mature.'

PC Chris laughed while taking a shortcut to avoid the festival traffic. There was bunting in the trees we passed. The wail of a fairground. 'A mature Amir Ali, huh? Imagine.'

I looked at him in the rear-view mirror. The small of his eyes. The light weight of the jokes he'd gotten used to swapping with us.

I couldn't think of a response that day though. I just felt tired. Like all of the bones in my body were heavy. Like I wanted to go to sleep.

'Amir,' Eman said, her eyes taking in the rise and fall of my chest, the stubborn line of my jaw. 'Are you OK?'

PC Chris flicked the indicator on, scanning the junction we were stuck at with tentative eyes, hesitant to move out even as the road began to clear. 'I wouldn't stress. Boys like him just want attention.'

'Wait, what do you mean?' Kemi said. 'Boys like what?'

I knew she'd felt it, too. The same strange tone I'd heard when he'd talked about my brother.

The unspoken clichés PC Chris believed to be true of Friesly boys and their cocky grins, their loud mouths, their empty pockets. They all knew about fast cars, too. They all knew the rush of firework sounds that weren't fireworks at all. The squeal of screeching wheels. *Rat-a-tat.* Scores to settle. Drugs.

'Well, y'know,' PC Chris said slowly. 'People say they want attention. Eyes on them. Reputations to maintain and all that. "I'm a hard gangbanger, don't mess with me." That sort of thing.'

I couldn't help myself. I started laughing. Even though it wasn't funny at all.

'Seriously?' Kemi said.

Eman frowned next to me. 'Amir's not like that.'

PC Chris's eyes showed up icy in the inside mirror. They darted between the three of us, and then to his hands on the steering wheel.

'It doesn't matter,' PC Chris huffed. 'Forget I said anything.'

'No.' Kemi sat up in the passenger seat. 'Keep going. You've clearly got lots to say here.'

An uncomfortable, awkward laugh. 'I'm warning you, Adebayo. Drop it.'

'But I want to know.' Kemi was in Sports Day mode. Fighting hard. 'I want to know what boys like Amir are interested in.'

I felt Eman watching me, worried.

But I was too busy staring at PC Chris, at the anxious squirming of his body while the traffic ahead of us was building up again.

The park, even from this distance, ringing with the sound of crowds celebrating Sir William Barker. The green of Friesly. The abandoned mills, the old history, the textbooks that celebrated our good old days. Were we past it now? Were the good old days gone? Because now we were good for nothing? Half-bad? Not good enough? Did that mean we weren't allowed to be celebrated, too?

'Chris,' I said finally, my voice hoarse with not speaking, 'keep going. Boys like me want attention, right? We're only interested in some things. Like what? What do you see when you look at us? Idiots? Criminals?'

I watched PC Chris jump at the sound of my voice, stamping haphazardly on the accelerator. 'Drop it!' he said. 'All of you, just drop it, alright? I'm trying to drive!'

The engine revved uncomfortably. And PC Chris must've misjudged what he was doing, must've forgotten to adjust gears, because the van shot off like a bullet, hurtling past the junction, the busy main road, the nearby greenery.

I remember us all yelling after that.

Top of our lungs, shooting past cars and vans which blurred into colours and shadows, which blurred too and became darker colours and shadows.

A pole emerged out of nowhere.

It hit us like a punch to the throat. Windscreen glass crashed down on us like words not left unspoken, like words finally said out loud.

CHAPTER 20
EMAN

It came back to me in flashes. Split-second fragments of memory, spilling from the pain in my skull.

I saw darkness.

Like the shadows in the green field of my grandma's childhood were swallowing me whole. Like there was no sunlight any more.

But then the darkness ended, and it was like morning again. A second morning.

My eyes opened, and everything was upside down, but the colours were there. Blue sky. Black seat belt. A silver pole, crushing the very front of PC Chris's car. A silver pole, causing smoke to rise from the bonnet, making the green of the surrounding moors taste smoky, starting a desperate ache in my lungs.

I saw birds on low-hanging branches looking in through the cracked windscreen, heads cocked, confused.

I heard the rush of cars on a nearby motorway. Traffic coasting along the dual carriageway, the sound of a breeze whistling in my ears. Darkness. Then light. Then darkness.

Like the beginning of creation in religious stories. Like

God himself, flicking a light switch on and off. Then came the emergency sirens. An ambulance? The police?

Kemi's voice slurred in her mouth. A flash of blood appeared on her forehead. 'Is everyone OK?'

I couldn't find my voice. '*Yeah*,' I wanted to say. '*Kemi, what happened? Do you know? Did you see? We're still alive, aren't we? Where did that pole come from?*'

PC Chris was talking. Amir was talking.

God flicked the light switch again.

A tear rolled down my face. *Nani, I'm tired. Nani, my arms feel heavy.*

'Katie was right.' PC Chris's voice, shaky from where he sat crushed in the driver's seat. 'Volunteering just doesn't work on kids like you ...' A sob. A groan of pain. 'You don't learn ... You don't learn anything.'

Amir, his throat as dry as a desert: 'We do.'

Their conversation ricocheted around my skull.

'Oh, what happens now? I've failed ... Volunteering4Friesly has failed. Kids like you don't learn, do you?'

'WE DO!' A stab of pain in Amir's voice. A bleeding wound for a boy. 'What do you know about us?' A hard tone, low and murmuring. 'You hate us ... You can't really know us if you hate us ... No excuses for us, for my brother, for Zayd ...'

'Zayd? Zayd Ali? Your brother?' Delirious muttering. 'I didn't know ... I read about him once ...'

A sob building in a throat. 'Zayd, if they knew you ... If they'd tried ... to understand ... you ...'

Something was wailing again. Something shrieked. It flashed. It had a voice, it had arms: 'Traffic accident by Junction

183, south Friesly. What does this look like? Three kids? One adult?'

I woke up in a hospital bed.

Not one just for overnight stays, I think. It was only a small bed, in a small room, with a pillow that felt hard to touch, an uncomfortable place to rest my head. An ache ran through my entire body from the force of waking up. But my ears worked. My eyes were fine. There was a scratch on my arm, a long strip of bandage over the blood.

And a woman on a chair next to the bed.

I knew her.

I knew the safety pin caught in the thick of her hijab. Her worried eyes. A mouth as poised, as prone to mistakes, as mine.

'You're OK!' Mum's eyes filled with tears. 'Alhamdulillah. Subhanallah.'

The words hadn't come back to me yet. My face hurt.

'Did I almost lose you too? Nani's operation is coming up. And you ...' Her bottom lip trembled. Her hands clasped mine. 'Don't leave me too, Eman.'

I stared at her. A series of film clips ran through my mind: patches and pieces of my mother's bruised face in our old house, and Nani's suitcase, and the drive to Friesly.

Episodes of *Hamari Zindagi*.

Shopping for jeans I didn't need. The patches on mine.

Then, Nani's fall and Mum smiling at our guests so easily. That professional smile. The dimples in her cheeks.

The words filled my mouth. 'Would it matter to you? If I left, too?'

Now my mum stared at me. Something flickered on her face. Surprise? Shock?

You don't know? You don't know I love you? Haven't I said so? Haven't I shown it?

'Yes,' she said shakily. 'It would matter, Eman. It would matter if you and Nani left me.'

She cried while holding my hands. It was the first time she had cried the whole summer. I looked around for a tissue. I ignored the burn in my arm as I wiped her face with the loose end of my hijab.

CHAPTER 21
CHRIS

You see the same sun wherever you grow up.

It rises and falls in the same way. It lights up trees in other people's back gardens, other people's places to play in when they're growing up. It's there when you crane your neck and look up at it. No matter how many times you're told to not do that. Stop hurting your eyes.

I should know. I lived in a lot of different places before I settled in north Friesly. I've stared up at a lot of setting suns, anticipating it, that familiar voice:

'*Stop messing around, Chris.*' My dad's voice climbs out into the present. '*When are you going to get a grip?*'

He always said stuff like that when I was little, and one of my eyes would be squinting at his silhouette coming home from work across the field near our house, while the other was blackened and blotted out from the sun. He always ruffled my hair when he said stuff like that though. No matter how angry his face looked, or how pissed off he sounded.

His empty hands were capable of fixing boilers for a living, of placing big bets at the bookies, of fiddling with the TV when we all ate frozen sausages and mash for dinner, and saving a secret love for me and my brother, Paul.

'*You know I've been waiting for you to come home for ages, don't you?*' I'd grin, chasing after him with a ripped-up wheat stalk in my hand.

I used to bunk off school, waiting for Dad.

I used to ignore teachers calling home, and the threat of Paul shouting at me later, and would go for a walk in the travellers' field near our house. I loved wandering up and down in there, pulling at straws of yellow wheat, my school jumper knotted around my waist, my mouth making clicking sounds at wild horses stamping their hooves by the sweetgrass.

I wanted them to come close to me.

I wanted to ride one, even though the travellers said that was dangerous and difficult, and I should go off home already for my tea.

They made more sense to me though, wild horses with knotted manes. Books and reading, I didn't understand. Maths either. It was alright but there was too much of it. In my head, I could ride a wild horse dangerous enough to hurt me. I could tame it so that it wasn't difficult any more. My dad would see it, too. Me, not hurt, not damaged by the danger of the situation but surviving it. And he'd be so shocked. He'd be so shocked by the fact of my fearlessness that he wouldn't even drink and cry about losing his job so often any more.

'*Chris!*' he'd yell. And he'd put his hands on his waist, suck in some of the fat around his stomach from growing older, and laugh: '*Now, how did you do something like that?*'

*

266

I didn't hear him say much like that, growing up. Instead, me and Paul got stuff like: '*Close the bloody doors, it's cold enough in here without you two acting like we've got central heating!*'

There were pleas for us to put our jumpers on in the winter, times when our dad would wink at us while crouching by the warm glow of the oven, his fingers wincing while putting hot potatoes in our coat pockets.

There was also: '*Paul, you're eighteen. All these bloody immigrants can get a job and you can't?*'

That was usually after his mates had come round, and the football was on, and all me and Paul ever heard from upstairs was the hiss of beer cans being cracked open and belly laughs which always made the next day's screaming matches between my dad and my brother extra painful to my ears.

'*Chris,*' he said once, the day after, '*come and help us put your suitcase in the car. My mate in Yorkshire's got a better place for us than this dump.*'

'*Why?*'

I was confused because I thought we had a good deal already. We had an all-boys' house where only us lot knew how to get the lumpy sofa just right to sit on, and Paul had lots of friends he snuck out to see at night, and no one was even bothered that I'd stopped going to school completely.

'*Where are we going?*'

My dad looked at me, a hard glint in his eye. '*Somewhere that still feels like England.*'

Then he told me again to help him with the suitcase.

I remember him and Paul arguing about what was good for us on the ride up to our next house in Hent, Dad getting red in the face from shouting, Paul even redder because he hated anyone shouting at him in the first place.

We lived in three more houses after that. Two in Bramracken with Dad's friends, one in Hent which was more of a flat than a house.

There were two new girlfriends for Dad in those countryside towns who didn't stick, either. But there was one who did.

Donna.

Dad met her through his mate. He fixed up her boiler because she mentioned it was broken, and she made him cups of tea while he worked, and they talked about how it was getting harder and harder to say things like Merry Christmas when it was Christmas because everyone was getting offended over nothing these days.

Donna had a lot of family in north Friesly. So we moved to north Friesly. And still a part of me missed when we used to live in the first house with the travellers' field next door to us and all of those horses.

'Bloody hell,' Dad said when Donna showed us the sights in our new place, which was a house, not a flat or a sofa bed. It was surrounded by all the rolling green hills, the massive moors.

'Makes you feel tiny, doesn't it?' she teased.

'Yeah,' I breathed.

I liked Donna a lot.

She had hair that was bouncy and blonde compared to our family's darker looks. She had a way of laughing that made the spidery ends of her eyelashes close shut, and that made Dad laugh too, asking where her eyes went, if she could see anything, when she was happy.

I remember putting my hands on my waist the same way Dad did, watching people climb up and down a hiking route like little determined ants.

Growing up, I didn't think Dad was racist.

I think he just found people funny sometimes. Like the Pakistani family that were hiking in the moors that day, with their food in plastic boxes, their too-bright scarves. He waggled his eyebrows at us, watching them go by. Then he blew his nose. He said the air always smelled a little spicy around people like that. Donna told him to stop it, smiling wryly when he yelled at them, asking if they had soap where they came from.

A wind rushed past us on the moors, lifting the shirt around Dad's belly, making Donna laugh, and Dad laugh, and me laugh. Behind us, Paul rolled his eyes. But he was smiling too. I could tell.

There weren't a lot of different races at my school in north Friesly either.

At least, not compared to all these people with darker skin and bright clothes in south Friesly.

That was where Dad did most of his plumbing, for Donna's friends, and Donna went round on the outskirts, cutting people's hair in their houses by appointment. I went along with them on weekends, too, as I got bored when Paul started up an apprenticeship at a local garage.

But there were still some people who smelled different to me and Paul at my school in north Friesly. Not that I went around sniffing them or anything like that.

Mostly, I kept to myself. People thought I was thick because I didn't ever want to read out loud. And I didn't want to explain that the reason why I couldn't be bothered with fractions or decimals was because I'd missed those lessons at my other school to go for a walk with some horses in a field.

So I just nodded at kids who seemed alright, shrugged my shoulders at teachers' questions, and earned some weird sort of respect for that.

I tried to joke about it once though. The different smells people had.

'You've got soap, haven't you?' I said when a kid called Adam Shah kicked a football over to me in PE. 'Where you lot come from?'

I liked Adam Shah. He was rubbish at reading, too. Earlier that day, he'd given me a ruler to stop me from getting detention. It was a broken one from the ground, but it was still a ruler.

'Yeah,' Adam said. 'We've got toothpaste here in England. Why, when's the last time you brushed your teeth?'

I laughed because everyone else playing football with us laughed. I thought it was a good answer, as well. I told Paul the story on our walk home, said I thought Dad would find it funny, too.

Paul played around with the earring he'd had put in that day. 'Change it a bit when you tell it to Dad, alright? Make it so you said the comeback. You embarrassed the Paki.'

I frowned. Adam had just told me he was born in England like us. 'But he's not a —'

'He is,' Paul said. 'You said it yourself, Chris. He smells weird, doesn't he? He's a Paki. Dad'll say he is.'

We had beans on toast for tea, and potato smileys that Donna fried fresh in the hot oil. And I made sure to tell Dad the edited version of the story when he came home. It had been a difficult day for him. He kept losing out on customers. There were a lot of rival plumbers in south Friesly, a lot of 'them' that kept embarrassing him.

He laughed a lot hearing my story though. He ruffled my hair.

On Monday, I gave Adam Shah his ruler back.

'That saved me from detention, that did,' I said.

Adam had a lazy smile. 'You brushed your teeth this morning, didn't ya?' he said. 'Come on –' he started packing his stuff up, super quick, even though we'd just got to school – 'the police are raiding a house on my street. D'you wanna see?'

My grades weren't the best, but they were better than they had been. So I ignored the guilt building in my stomach, and I went with him. We watched the backstreets of north Friesly, the police in their cars parked by someone's house, the majesty of their very tall horses, the authority of everything those police officers did . . . So confident. So fearless.

I didn't want to admit it. I couldn't. At least, not out loud. But Adam really didn't smell that different to me. Adam was my best mate until me and Dad passed him and his dad one Friday evening in the north Friesly shopping centre. He was wearing baggy clothes and a weird round hat, looking at discounted joggers in a sports shop. So was his dad. They didn't look English in their baggy clothes, their weird hats. But I knew they were. Sort of. They could speak it, couldn't they? Adam's dad bought us ice cream from the van once. He wasn't so bad.

So Adam nodded at me, grinning. And I grinned back. Dad pulled my arm, quick as a slap, and just as harsh. He jerked us out of the shopping centre.

He shouted loud enough for them to hear it. 'God, they're everywhere, aren't they?'

We had the same conversation over and over again on the drive home. Didn't I know? They weren't like us. They smelled different. They caused trouble. They asked for attention. They stole jobs.

The next day, Adam walked right past me in the PE changing rooms. In football, we were on the same team, but he didn't pass me the ball. I knew not to pass it to him either.

An accident. This is what I told Katie Phillips and our superiors over at Friesly Metropolitan Police it had been.

My cohort participating in the Volunteering4Friesly summer programme had been involved in a traffic accident which hadn't been anyone in particular's fault. How could it have been? Surely they recognized how dangerous it was to drive in Friesly, what with the steep hills, the constant need for clutch control, the frequency of traffic accidents at Junction 183, south Friesly, the weak road surfaces, the heavy traffic, the speeding drivers . . .

'Still,' Katie advised our superiors during this midday meeting, 'the Volunteering4Friesly programme has been a monumental success. My charges have truly benefited from it. They recognize their community and have been sharing images and videos of their volunteering on social media. They have the spirit of Friesly. We should celebrate that.'

Everyone in this meeting, this mesh of black and blue uniforms, overlooked the bandage wound around my head, the fact that I didn't speak very much, and the grimaces that accompanied my movements when I did speak. Then again, I'd never said much in front of them, had I?

I'd always agreed with everything instead. That everyone we arrested was a criminal, a thug. A gangbanger. A drug dealer. In it for the drugs, the women, the bling-bling. Katie had the loud mouth they liked. So they agreed with her.

A celebration of the programme's success would take place at the final council meeting of the summer. In less than a week's time. A celebration was called for, as to them, this was the first Friesly accident in a long time that had not involved drugs.

Distantly, I heard the pain in Amir's voice. I'd read an article in a newspaper a long time ago.

I hesitated.

Then: 'What about Zayd Ali?' I said. 'That one didn't involve drugs either, did it? It was never confirmed what went on there.'

PC Phillips stared at me. Her eyes were brown but they were cold.

'I read about what happened to that boy,' I said. I thought of a raid on a house I'd watched a long time ago. 'I joined the police because I admired their confidence –'

A voice boomed from behind a desk: 'And injuring yourself and everyone under your care has done that, has it? Demonstrated your confidence?'

'Wow, Chris!' Katie leaned forward, hissed harshly, cruelly, in my ear, 'You're the best.'

I thought of blaming my outburst on the pain in my head, the ache seizing every muscle in my body.

I remembered the crowd of bodies around the coffee machine during my first few months at the station. The wildness of their limbs, untameable. The jealousy that burned in the pit of my stomach as I watched the other police officers embrace Katie, speak with her, laugh with her while I lingered behind, while I spilled milk, while I stood alone.

I'd tried, hadn't I? Back then? To get close, to stand in their circle, to joke around. Black and blue uniform. A sea of black and blue.

My bandaged head spasmed with another burst of pain. Katie continued talking. All confidence. Taming the difficulty of any situation. Not hurt, not damaged, but surviving it.

But what about me?

Where was the evidence of my fearlessness?

CHAPTER 22
KEMI

My sister met me in the reception at Friesly General Infirmary.

There was a plaster that was attached really closely to my hairline, pulling awkwardly at the curls, and an ache in my body – a tiredness I was desperate to be rid off – but my sister was having me be discharged. So tiredness would have to wait.

'Let me guess,' Ada said, before I could even open my mouth. 'You didn't mean to get into an accident. And you didn't mean to get involved with all of this police stuff in the first place. It just happened.'

Her voice was hard. It made the spot where my forehead had recoiled off the car dashboard throb.

'Huh?' I said in the glow of a confused streetlight. It was on early. Too early. The sky wasn't even dark yet.

Ada nudged me in the direction of our block. I followed blindly. Used her braids, the sight of her back, as place markers, as familiar locations. They were, weren't they? The pattern of her hair as comfortable as the mess of overgrown hedges on the street corners we turned. Her arms and legs like corner-shop windows, like a stomped-on kerb near our flat. Her eyes bright as the metal staircase leading upstairs, across the concrete pathway, to our front door.

'It's always something with you, isn't it, Kemi?' The roads we were crossing echoed with the sound of distant roller-coaster rides at the Barker Summer Festival, the smell of just-lit fireworks. 'There always has to be something.'

I felt dizzy. That was how it felt to kick my legs up when we were swinging in the dark and staring at the night, at the faintest stars, and aeroplane lights. Me and Ada. Us, and Nathan, and Aron, and Precious. Nathan and Precious.

I waited for the green man to light our way, help us along the steep incline to the block, past pavement slabs and cracks I'd avoided with Eman for weeks. Ada continued, even when her breathing got all deep and ragged.

'I shouldn't be surprised though, should I? You're just like that. You can't think of anyone but yourself.'

'What about you?' I said in my dazed state. 'You're selfish, too. You don't even care that Nathan and Precious are dating. You think you're better than them.'

My sister stumbled a bit. Her back, my precious place marker, turned around. A street corner disappeared before my eyes. Then I realized she was crying.

'Kemi, I didn't even know they were dating! Nathan broke up with me before I came back to Friesly for the holidays, but I didn't know he was seeing anyone! Definitely not Precious. I thought – I thought Precious and I were friends . . .'

I was so tired. It didn't make sense. But it did, too. Under the thick layer of fog in my head, it did.

'So you weren't the one that broke up with him.'

Ada shook her head.

'And Nathan didn't tell you why he broke up with you.'

Ada shook her head.

'And the only reason you didn't want to hang out with them is because you felt betrayed.' I reached out for her, my sobbing older sister. 'Ada, I didn't think –'

She jerked away from me. Like in a dream, when objects fall away from your hands and rush right past your eyes.

'That's your problem, isn't it, Kemi? You don't think. Unless it's about you, and how you feel, you just don't think.'

I wished I was on someone's shoulders. I wished I could still see all of Friesly, all of the corners and roads I called home.

'Do you think Mum doesn't know? Hm?' Ada carried on, eyes wild and weepy. 'That you don't like Emmanuel? That you won't give him a chance, because you think she can't be happy with anyone but Dad? Don't you think that hurts her? Hmm? All your stupid little pranks?' Ada's chin was wobbling. 'And how I'm gonna go back to uni and she won't even be able to talk to me about all of this? Do you ever think about how you make her feel?'

My heart beat fast in my chest. My mind filled with Dad's face, and his smile, and the warm way he talked, and laughed, and joked.

His wedding portrait and me in the hallway. His giant hands keeping me up, giving me the best view, and the way he'd taught me to double-knot my shoelaces.

'Dad would've never wanted her with someone like Emmanuel,' I said.

'Kemi –' Ada's voice carried like our neighbour's favourite record, drifting so easily, weightless yet heavy, a lead balloon – 'you don't know what he would've wanted.'

'I know this whole sports residential thing in France was supposed to be, like, really hard –' Michael leaned back on his palms in Fowley Park, inspecting the grass he'd just ripped out of the ground like he wasn't fresh off the bus back to Friesly at all – 'but I'm telling you, Kemi, it was proper easy. Right, Jas? Tell her.'

Jasmin stretched her legs out in a patch of sunlight, serene as usual, long-haired and long-limbed and smiling.

The both of them so chatty it was like there'd never been a lull in our group chat, there'd never been a sudden and surprising silence. I wanted to ask them about it. But their return to Friesly only involved a nostalgia I couldn't fit in with, a trip I hadn't been able to afford. And still couldn't.

The calluses on my hands were polished like street cobbles.

They ached like a dead father's love.

Where did it go, that love? When someone went away forever?

'It looks like you went on one yourself,' Michael had said on getting off the bus. He'd gestured to the plaster on my forehead. 'Y'know, a trip? Get it?'

Beside us, Jasmin had stopped fussing with the strap of her large away bag to burst out laughing. That was always the pattern, wasn't it? A joke that seized all of us. A tickle erupting in all of our throats. But there wasn't one in mine. My throat just felt dry.

'I think you would've loved it though,' Jas carried on, nudging my Reeboks with her Nikes. 'All those runners who thought they were so good kept getting beat by us. I know you couldn't help it, but you should've, like, found a way to come or something. It could've been me, you and Michael just winning all the time.'

Michael laughed, his blond hair glowing white in the sun. 'Yeah, you should've come up with the money or something. You should've, like, knocked on the PE office at school and begged them to let you go.'

'Begged them?' I tried to joke. 'You want me to have gone on my hands and knees and begged them?'

'Don't make it weird, Kemi.' Jasmin fussed with the extra hair tie she always kept on her wrist. Her hair was long and brown and straight down her back. 'It just would've been fun if you came too is all.'

They launched into some story about a short runner from some school in Hent who'd tried really hard to keep up with Michael's long strides in a long-distance cross-country run. A whole summer of being goaded by him and Jasmin about his height had made him so determined he would win if he could just match Michael's pace, if he could just make his stamina last longer than his short legs.

Obviously, it didn't work.

Obviously, the guy ended up collapsing halfway through, because of heatstroke and dehydration, and he'd needed to be taken to the big hospital in Paris.

Not before he'd thrown up over himself, though.

Not before he'd exhausted himself so bad, and developed a case of shin splints.

They both found this story really funny. The smell of sick on a hot day. This short guy, and his shut eyes, lying on the grass, sobbing like a wounded animal. They started howling about how he'd stacked it, and then Jasmin and Michael fell over each other in this semicircle we'd made on the grass in Fowley Park, a mess of hair, and smiles, and my confusion.

I looked at the pile of grass Michael had pulled out of the ground. The green strands with nowhere to go. 'Was he OK in the end? That guy?'

Michael and Jasmin looked at each other, still baring their teeth, their mouths pulled up and showing dimples.

'I think so.' Jasmin shrugged.

Michael was silent a little while longer. His light eyes showed up even lighter in our bit of sunbeam. Watching me. Then he laughed again.

'Come on, Kemi,' he said. 'That's not the important bit. I'll show you. I'll show you the important bit.'

He got up, dusted down his trackies, tried to sort out his sticky-uppy hair, and re-enacted the exact moment when that short runner's body had given up on him. Always with the same dog-like grin on his face. A way-too-convincing drop in his gangly legs. And a laugh-track from Jasmin when all of him was covered in grass stains and dirt.

Michael was always like this, wasn't he? Jasmin, too. The both of them always clowning around. Always looking for a joke. Once they got started, there was no stopping them. And I was always in the middle, arms draped casually around their shoulders, clown number three.

That was us for as long as I could remember. So why wasn't it us now? The change was strange and unignorable – like when a piece of food gets stuck in your throat, like when you feel your body is rejecting something.

'Hey, look who it is!' Michael whipped his head around at someone shuffling their way down the park's pathway. Bow-legged. Whispering. 'My favourite homeless guy!'

Jasmin nudged me in the side, giggling so hard I could tell she expected me to join in.

Well, I always had, hadn't I? Laughed when she laughed? At jokes about other girls in the PE changing rooms? Deodorant someone clearly couldn't afford. Smelly hair that wasn't as long and soft as hers. Blank faces that never knew the answers to the questions she and I answered in class.

'My man!' Michael yelled. 'How's it going? I haven't seen you in ages! Wait, wait. Say that thing you always say. I missed it. I missed hearing it.'

He put his hand to his ear, waiting. Still as a statue and waiting, as Danny *Dangar* kept shuffling down the path, his carrier bags in his hands, his eyes down and determined, whispering the same word he always whispered: 'Please ... Please ...'

'There it is!' Michael clapped his hands together.

He jumped at the sound, Danny *Dangar*. He jumped that bright golden morning, his hands trembling, his eyes even more downcast than before. His hands dropping the plastic bags he carried everywhere.

Michael and Jasmin found this hilarious. They cackled over Danny *Dangar* crouching down and scrambling after the stuff that had fallen out of his bags. The empty crisp packets, the pieces of paper, the dried twigs and leaves, the pennies, and a shiny lunchbox someone who knew him much better than I did had packed for him.

There was a pain in my body. It went beyond the plaster pulling at my hairline, the tiredness I still hadn't shrugged off.

'Sorry,' I said as I crossed the green to where Danny *Dangar* sat on the path, and bent down, both of us squatting like frogs. Obstacles for anyone who wanted to walk down that path.

'Here –' I handed him his pennies, his leaves, his precious things – 'here you go.'

He just took what I gave him. Quickly. Eyes still down. Eyes ignoring me while the ones behind me stared, their laughter gone, their voices dull and mumbling.

I walked to the stoop outside Clean Cutz with new exhaustion once Michael and Jasmin had said their goodbyes.

I knew they were confused. I'd felt it in the way they'd looked at me before they'd left, their bodies angled away, not towards me, their shoes stomping up towards the bus shelter to north Friesly before I could even tell them about all the times I'd taken the two buses up there, for mowing, or cleaning, or babysitting.

Still, I couldn't blame them. I felt confused too. So I dropped my head in my hands on the stoop outside Clean Cutz and I tried to puzzle it out. I tried to puzzle out the questions without any answers blooming inside my brain.

'D'you need something?' a familiar voice called from behind me, bringing a burst of morning radio, of buzzing hair clippers, with it. 'You're shaking your leg. Your dad used to say you only did that when you were thinking really hard. But I know you only need to use the toilet. D'you need the toilet, Kemi?'

'No, Uncle Jafari.' I spoke into my knees. 'I don't.'

And he burst out laughing, sitting down to share that sun-dappled stoop with me. That sometimes happened, in the golden hour when his smoking break and my rest-after-running coincided.

Usually, we'd annoy each other for as long as we could. We'd interrupt the rush of the cars down the roads, the thumping radio systems, with him rolling his eyes and saying I had no respect for him, and me saying he had to earn it, not expect it, and him saying how could a little girl like me talk like that? To him? To an old man like him?

Complete with old-man sound effects, of course. Groaning, and moaning, and complaints about his bad back.

Just so I'd feel sorry for him.

Just so I'd laugh so much at his bad acting that I'd stop roasting him for it.

Things were different that golden hour, though. Uncle Jafari's face studied mine for a moment. Dark eyes, narrow and serious. His long fingers rolling a cigarette in front of him.

'Alright, c'mon.' He scooched closer to me on the hard stone, eyes still on the tobacco. 'Start talking. What's wrong?'

'Nothing. Stop asking stupid questions. Don't you have hair you should be cutting right now?'

He licked the cigarette paper to seal it. 'Alright, Miss Attitude. Don't you have Bibles to be reading from? Words to mispronounce?'

I looked at him. His face, with the easy grin, the crow's feet at the corners of his eyes. I snatched that perfect rolled-up cigarette from his fingers and threw it in with all the already-smoked ends on the ground. Uncle Jafari stared at it for a second. He scooched away from me slowly, nimble as a cartoon character, before he picked it up and lit the end.

'Wow.' He gave me a sideways glance as he blew the smoke away from me. 'You really are your father's kid, huh? He used to try binning all my cigarettes, too.'

I knew it, as well. Uncle Jafari used to tell stories about my dad hating his habit all the time. But it hurt somehow, hearing him say that.

'I don't know.' I spoke into my knees again. 'Am I?'

We sat together. Just two people in front of a battered barber's shop door, warm against the hardened wood, warmer still because of Uncle Jafari's cigarette.

Cars kept going by. Customers coming back from Mahmood's Foods with heavy bags and sweaty backs. The sound of chatter surrounding us.

Uncle Jafari tapped the front of my Reeboks with the side of his own dusty brogues.

'What's wrong?' he said.

And I looked at him. His listening old-man eyes. Same ones I'd seen my whole life. At birthday parties, at family events. Even after my dad had died, and no one had listened to our relatives asking if he even needed to still be invited, he wasn't really family, was he? Not by blood.

I kept my gaze on the ground. 'I just – I don't think I'm a nice person. I know I'm supposed to be. Y'know – like – like the star Dad said I was. Lighting up everyone's lives.' I looked at Uncle Jafari. 'But what if I'm not nice? What if I haven't been? And I only bring darkness everywhere I go?'

'Hey.' Uncle Jafari rested a hand on my shoulder. 'Don't say that.'

'But it's true, isn't it?' I was crying now. 'It's true. I'm not a nice person, and we can't afford the same things other people can, and maybe it's karma. It's karma because I'm not nice.'

Uncle Jafari let out a big sigh as he patted my back. 'You're smart, aren't you, Kemi? You get good grades at school. I know you do. You know what words like photosyntho mean –'

'Photosynthesis.' I sobbed. 'You mean photosynthesis.'

Uncle Jafari laughed his hyena laugh. 'See? See? But listen, Kemi. Don't you know that someone who isn't nice wouldn't care about whether they were or weren't? Hmm? We wouldn't be having this conversation if you really were a big giant meanie.'

'So?' I sobbed.

'So,' he repeated dramatically, 'use your brain, stupid. You care too much to really be a big giant meanie who'll be a failure someday.' He looked up at the sky. At the birds, cawing across the deep bright blue. 'Yemi, your girl's too much like you. She has your soul. Tell her, will you? Tell her to breathe. And then, to keep caring. Tell her it's a good thing when she feels like she's done something wrong.' Uncle Jafari looked back at me, smiling, as if he knew what I still needed to tell Amir. 'Because she'll always remember how it feels when she's done something right.'

I held my breath as I walked towards Say It With Flowers.

Up past the succulents and spider plants in the ceramic pots outside, past the plastic foliage hanging low to obscure the white and loopy sign.

I didn't have time to register the surprise on my mum's face, or Ada's raised eyebrows, seeing me come in.

I just went around the newly arranged funeral wreaths, the plastic-wrapped large-leafed bouquets, and pulled up a chair next to the curve of Emmanuel's back. He was taking advantage of a day off to help cut the stems on a bunch of bright white tulips, his clumsy hands covered in gardening gloves, his lips twisted with concentration.

I cleared my throat. Sweat built on my palms. 'Are there any spare clippers?'

Emmanuel's eyes boggled behind his glasses. But he didn't hesitate. 'Let me see.'

In the midst of his fussing around the shop, and the awkward silence of my arrival, Ada slid a pair of metal clippers across the worktable.

I looked at her. Her touch sparked electricity. 'Thanks.'

Emmanuel caught the glance between us. 'Here.' He smiled at me, those clumsy hands growing careful as they guided mine around the stems. 'It's like this, see?'

I didn't see the ice thaw around me, the temperature rise higher, as Mum and Ada exchanged their own glances with each other. But I felt it, warm like a hug, as the shop filled with chatter, slowly, then all at once.

So that when I accidentally chopped off a tulip head, Ada burst out laughing. And so did Mum. And Emmanuel. And – eventually – me.

CHAPTER 23
AMIR

Hearts can't speak. They just pump blood around your body.

But if mine could, I think it would call me stupid. And I get that. I understand it. Teachers, strangers, members of my own family have called me that before. I've always shouted at them for it: 'What's stupid about me? Tell me. Tell me if you're hard.'

I didn't want to do that to Mum though. She looked at me, with my bandaged-up hand from where it had been sprained during the accident, her eyes still and strong as water. They'd looked like that ever since PC Phillips had told her about the graffiti, about the volunteering, and I knew she was thinking it.

'Ma.' I chased after her, shoes skidding on the smooth floor of Friesly General Infirmary. 'Ma, I did it for Zayd. It was all for Zayd.'

'*If they knew you . . .*' The memory of my own voice, hurtling like the hills as PC Chris's car billowed smoke, was so loud in my ears. '*If they'd tried . . . to understand . . . you . . .*'

I searched my pockets for the newspaper article, pulled it out from where it had stuck itself inside my hoodie. 'See? Remember this? Ma, look –'

My head bobbed low, even lower, as an accidental rip split the article in two. A cry of pain escaping my throat as it dropped to the hospital floor.

It had felt so heavy in my hand earlier that day. Precious. So much so that I'd jumped when Kemi had called me while I was reading it over and I'd felt my heart stutter hearing her talk about Zakiya Bhatti:

'She doesn't work as a journalist any more, Amir.' The hospital machines were harmonizing with Kemi's words. 'That's why she never saw your messages. It was nothing to do with your spelling! She just probably doesn't even have access to her press profile any more. But I have her number. Her mum gave it to me. You can ask her about the eyewitness. You can finally find out the truth.'

My hands had shaken throughout all of that phone call. The idea of calling Zakiya, unbelievable. Insane. But now I had her number saved in my phone. The fact made me jittery. I was practically trembling, staring at the shreds of the article on the floor, no Kemi in my ears, no shadows in front of me except my mum's.

Her back was straight. Her trainers, tapping anxiously against the floor.

'You need to stop this, Amir,' she said, her voice crisp as she helped me pick up the pieces. 'The lying, the dangerous behaviour ... It's not fair. You haven't even been able to tell your mum truthfully what you've been doing all summer. How could you lie to me like that?'

Her eyes were a flood. I put Zakiya Bhatti's torn article in front of them.

'I tried to show you this, remember?' I said. 'Ages ago? It's about Zayd and how he didn't do anything wrong. My friend found the person who wrote it. We can call her. So that . . . So that . . .'

My heart was hammering around in my chest so much, I couldn't focus properly.

'Ma,' I exhaled, pushing out the words, 'I just want people to remember him like we do. People think he wasn't good. People think he was a drug dealer –'

'So what?'

It felt like all of me was being ripped into two, as well. I stared at my mum.

'What?'

'Amir –' she trapped my face with her palms, smiling despite her tears – 'we knew him, didn't we? How he laughed at his own jokes? His smelly socks? His bedhead in the mornings and how he got you and Fiza hooked on movies because he loved you, and swapped seats on the sofa with the both of you because he never wanted to leave either of you out? So why does it matter what other people think?'

A raindrop rolled down the side of my face. 'Because they're not remembering him right.' I clasped her hands with mine. Ignored the pain in my hand as I pushed them away. 'And I thought you'd want to remember him right, Ma.'

I meant to turn around, to walk away. But I got frozen, looking at her. Drowning. An ache in my limbs and a worse one in my chest.

The sounds of the hospital got even louder. Beeping machines, trolleys rattling, lift buttons being pushed and lighting up ahead of us. Conversations about charts needing to be checked over. Blood pressure rates. Medicine dosages. Nurses and doctors, rotas and responsibilities.

'What was Zayd's favourite food?' Mum asked me.

'What does that have to do with anything?'

'Just answer the question, Amir. What was Zayd's favourite food?'

I frowned, trying to remember.

Dishes he was too lazy to clean, piled high in the kitchen sink.

Paprika and chilli stuck to a pan.

A colander to drain the washed meat.

'A spicy chicken panini. With chips he used to put in the microwave to heat up. And Coke.'

'What's our bestseller in the restaurant?'

The menu flashed in my head. The 'bestseller' sticker, always under sandwiches. It emphasized a chicken panini, with chips and a choice of drink – Coca-Cola being the complementary suggestion.

'Do you know what *Nishaan* means, Amir? Why I chose that name? *Symbol. Signifier. Mark.* Of him. Of Zayd.'

I covered my eyes with the palms of my hands. My words catching in my throat, wet with water.

'I'm s-sorry. I thought n-no one was thinking of him. I thought it was j-just m-me and I didn't have an o-older brother any more. I th-thought I w-was alone.'

The sobs went through my entire body. My bones rattled with the force of them, shaking my shoulders, all of me, from the inside. Mum came closer. She was shorter than me, but she leaned up, placed her hand on the back of my head and held me into her. The tree. The tree hugs so good.

'I'm sorry too.' Her voice was a whisper. 'I'm sorry too.'

She sat by me when I called Zakiya's number in our living room later on. She and Fiza helped me keep breathing as the phone connected and a woman's voice told us she'd been expecting our call.

Uzair's banged-up Ford Fiesta looked dull in the shadow of the hospital building.

Its paint still chipped. Its owner no longer stacking the seats with brown-bag deliveries. And the scent diffusers wound around the dashboard mirror, new and especially pine-fresh.

I knew that because I got a big gust of the smell when he came to pick me up after my sprain had been checked over again, and Mum had had to go back to the restaurant for a till-related emergency, and no one else was free to come and get me.

I didn't say anything about it though. I didn't argue when Uzair told me to put my seat belt on. I didn't fuss with the radio station either, but kept my hands to myself.

'How's the hand?' Uzair said, checking both ways as he eased out of the hospital car park.

I held the soft cast up. 'It hurts. But they've given me painkillers for it.'

We came to the car park exit gate, the machine that took Uzair's slip. 'Paracetamol, innit.'

I smiled into my hands. In our family, everything could be fixed with paracetamol. A headache, a pain in your ears, a swollen lip from an allergy . . .

'Once,' Uzair said, after merging on to the ring road in the direction of home, 'me and your brother were playing cricket out on the street. And about halfway through, we got bored. I mean, it was barely a cricket match because you had parents' evening, and your mum had taken Fiza with her, so everyone was out, and you can't play with two people, can you? So me and Zayd put down our bats in the middle of the street, and we said, OK, why don't we do a new game? Me and you, let's race to the end of the street. You know where that old *bayji* lives? With all the flowers in her garden? Zayd said let's race to the end of the street, and whoever wins, they can tell the loser to go in her garden and pick her blackberries. That's what the winner gets to eat. The old *bayji*'s blackberries.'

I didn't realize I was smiling at him telling this story. I don't think he realized he was smiling, either.

'So me and him, we get ready for the race. We're what, ten years old? We get ready, and we say go, and we're running. We're running all the way to where that old *bayji* lives. And I know I'm faster than him, I know he's lazy. He used to swear down he had asthma every time he lost, but, *kasmey*, Amir, he was just lazy when he ran. So I win. And I tell him go on then, get me the blackberries. And he looks like he's gonna die, he pulls this face like he's gonna die. "I've got asthma, Uzzy", he says. "No, you don't, and you lost, so go and get the blackberries", I say. And he goes in that *bayji*'s garden. He creeps in, closes the gate, goes around her big hedges, the flowers she's put around her grass, in the borders, and he squats down with his skinny knees and he picks the blackberries. He's got his shirt out – like this, like the shirt is a basket or something. "How much do you want?" he shouts at me, smiling, all casual and that, and I'm thinking, *Why is he shouting, man, we're gonna get in trouble.* But he shouts it again at me – "Uzzy, how much do you want?" – except this time, the old *bayji* comes up behind him. And she has this broomstick in her hands. It's proper thin, all the end bits are spiky and dry. She must've been brushing her conservatory or something with it. I don't know. Anyway, she whacks him with it, with the spiky bits. She goes, "Are you stealing my blackberries?"' and she whacks him with it, proper hard, on his bum. And Zayd drops the blackberries, and because he's only little, he stands up and goes, "Ow! My bum bum!"'

Uzair couldn't stop laughing as he told me that's when he knew Zayd definitely didn't have asthma. No one who ran as fast as Zayd did getting away from that spiky brush, holding his aching bum bum, could've had asthma.

'And when we got home –' Uzair wiped the tears from his eyes, laughing over his words – 'he goes, "Let me get the paracetamol." Do you know what he did with it, Amir?'

I was laughing over my words, too. 'What?'

'He thought, well, I know where to put it because it's my bum bum that hurts . . .'

Uzair's Ford Fiesta continued to echo with the sounds of my groans, the chaos of that memory, as we sped down the black tarmac, closer and closer to Sir William Barker's statue, grinning all the way.

The quiet that came after, too. It still vibrated a little. It still pulled up all the hairs on the back of our necks.

'Do you do stuff like that with your brothers?'

Uzair glanced at me. 'Mikaeel and Shuaib?' His smile fell a little. 'Nah. Nah, they don't really like to play with their old brother. They're ten.' He flicked the indicator on. Took a shortcut down a backstreet. 'I'm ancient.'

I thought of the two of them, always together, always whispering into their hands, fake walkie-talkies, or watching science documentaries together, and the way they were in our garden, following after Fiza, yet matching one another's steps all the way.

That was what twins were like, wasn't it? Telepathy, they called it. So it was never a big deal when Mikaeel ate the peas Shuaib had left out of his vegetable samosas, or that Shuaib knew when Mikaeel had forgotten to grab a full roll of toilet paper and left it out on the landing for him.

Did it happen with cousins too?

Who were the same age? Who'd once dropped their cricket bats, and pushed off the edge of a kerb together, racing hard – with all their might – for the promise of summer fruit? I'd never thought about it before.

I watched the silhouette of Uzair's face. The boy-band hair, the thick eyebrows, the straight lion-like nose.

'You're not that old,' I joked.

Uzair's lips curved into their cat-like smile. 'Oh, I could beat you and Fiza in a race any day.' He ignored me rolling my eyes as I scoffed to myself. 'I've got game too, you know. Anyway, d'you want that little hijabi that came to Neelam's wedding to fancy you back? I'll tell you what you should do. Girls love me.'

I couldn't help myself. 'Yeah, that's why Neelam married someone else, innit?' I said.

Uzair gasped, pretending to lose control of the steering wheel. 'You've only sprained one hand, haven't ya? Give us the other one! Give us it!'

I fought him away, pretending I still hated him. But I knew – when we reached our street, and the *bayji* from all those years ago still stood sweeping her garden out front, and we exchanged knowing smiles – that I couldn't. I didn't.

'Hello?' Zakiya Bhatti had sounded younger than expected on the phone. 'Is that Amir Ali? You know, I've been expecting your call.'

The two torn parts of the article written by Zakiya Bhatti – now Zakiya Akhtar – stared up at me, Mum and Fiza's patient faces from the living-room table.

'Your friend said you've been wanting to get in touch with me for a while. It's about my first and last article, isn't it? About Zayd Ali? And the eyewitness who saw his death?'

Zakiya told me that even if she did work in management now, she'd continue to want people to know there had always been an eyewitness who'd never wavered from his testimony. An eyewitness who'd uncovered a truth which I knew to be real no matter what others thought, or said, or did. That truth was:

Zayd Ali came into Mahmood's Foods to buy breakfast groceries.

Zayd Ali left Mahmood's Foods with nothing but breakfast groceries.

*

295

'You better have the exact change for those,' Qasim Mahmood grumbled, eyeing the group of little kids who stood indecisively around the ice-cream freezer with his usual irritation.

He didn't say anything after those kids had paid for their ice creams. Calippo Shots and Cornettos, melting in the heat as soon as they stepped out of the shop and on to the tarmac.

But he recognized the grins on their faces when they saw Danny *Dangar* come sloping around the corner. The taunting thrust of their shoulders, the way they started walking a little too close to where he was walking.

Qasim Mahmood rapped angrily at the glass of the automatic doors. And the kids turned around. They knew to stop it, whatever they were doing. They knew to bin their wrappers in the right place, too, as soon as they saw Uncs' watching face.

I let Fiza drag me around in the cool air conditioning, picking up more crisp packets, more Coca-Cola cans, and Mr. Bubble ice lollies from the freezer, while he muttered quietly to himself at the counter.

After all, I'd promised her she could have whatever she wanted.

And usually I would've said something about how heavy our basket was getting, already full of junk that was just going to rot her teeth. But Qasim Mahmood sat thumbing his prayer beads so close to us. He barely glanced at us as we dropped our basket in front of him, though. He didn't seem even slightly concerned about me not shouting at my little sister about her sugar addiction, my silence – my strange nervousness – as I faced him.

Fiza took clear advantage of it though.

She added a few extra Snickers to the haul with a grin on her face. I thought I saw Qasim Mahmood smile, too. Watching her. Just for a second. But I must've imagined it, because pretty soon he was scanning our stuff with the usual dull glare pulling his eyebrows down, the usual grunt as he double-knotted our bag for us.

'You know you have to eat all this stuff before we get home, right?' I said, hauling the bag off the loading part of the till, exaggerating my groan as I did so. My sprained hand was pretty bad anyway.

Fiza rolled her eyes at me. 'You say that like it's gonna be hard.'

I teased her about her tiny mouth and her giant stomach, and she teased me about my giant mouth and my giant ego, and then we both saw Qasim Mahmood's reflection in the sliding doors.

Old man with his rolled-up sleeves. Pen in his *kameez* pocket. Old man with his always-watching eyes and his prayer beads held tight in his grip.

'Amir,' he said, before the sunlight outside swallowed me and Fiza whole.

I turned back to face him.

Qasim Mahmood hesitated, lips smacking over nothing. 'You're doing alright, aren't you? After your accident?'

He spoke into his large wrinkled hands. But then he lifted his head. Slowly. Until we were both looking at each other. Our eyes, different shades of the same brown.

'Yeah,' I said, over the lump in my throat.

I hesitated as I faced the retired champion boxer. A southpaw. One of the best of his time. Then I stepped forward. I threw my arms around him.

'Hmm!' Qasim Mahmood said from the force of the hug.

He stiffened even more when Fiza's arms joined in too.

But I saw his hand move to pat the chain of our joined limbs. I saw it in the reflection of the sliding doors. Three pieces of a puzzle locked together.

Four, if you count Zayd. I do. I did. I always will.

CHAPTER 24
EMAN

Friesly Metropolitan Police insisted on having a celebration for the participants and the perceived success of the Volunteering4Friesly programme.

After all, we had reached the very end of the summer schedule with nothing but pride for our own efforts, hadn't we?

The youth of this town reformed, renewed, even rescued from the pitfalls of anti-social behaviour. The graffiti. The disrespect.

PC Phillips considered it a success.

So PC Chris had to as well. Even if, to him, that success didn't include an injured arm, mild concussion, a sprained hand, or the destruction of his favourite six-seater. Or far too many people – locals, tourists, police officers – climbing up the twenty stone steps of the town-hall building in search of the largest conference room.

It was just our luck to have to suffer through this, he'd said, with a roll of his eyes, to Kemi, Amir and me in a small spare room in Friesly General Infirmary. We'd agreed with him about that.

Also, to participate because he'd admitted to the injustices involved in his job, and his own stupid views, too.

'I'm sorry,' PC Chris had muttered slowly, while we all ached with our injuries, and with the force of something new. 'I've never been as brave as I've wanted. I've never been brave enough to disagree with others. Even when I know they're wrong.' He'd looked at us like he was seeing us for the first time. 'But I'd like to be.'

My head still ached from the force of the accident. But I believed that he meant that. I don't know why. There was just something about the look on his face.

'I expect you've all practised for the presentation?' said PC Phillips, interrupting our chattering in the town hall's largest conference room.

Kemi feigned ignorance, like we hadn't already discussed exactly what we could say we'd learnt from our volunteering. 'Presentation . . . ?'

PC Phillips' face turned three different shades of red. 'You –'

'Relax, Katie!' PC Chris came up from behind us. 'They're just joking with you.'

His haircut didn't look so bad in this light. The dot-to-dot acne on his face fading, less red than it had been when we'd first seen him.

Kemi, Amir and I fought the urge to laugh as PC Chris gave us a warning look, and PC Phillips headed off towards the north Friesly kids on the other side of the room.

It suddenly occurred to me that I'd never learnt their names.

But the girl with the ginger hair, the blond boy with the glasses and the taller girl who often wore a pair of blue denim dungarees were all scanning revision cards. The cards were small, rectangular and white, but even from across the room, I could see they were covered with tiny neat handwriting.

The front-facing chairs filled quickly with our neighbours, and with shop owners, and with their families and friends.

Howard Li from the pharmacy, his wife and his children in the front row.

Marta Varga at the very back, her dandelion hair so easy to see.

Kemi's mum, who worked at the flower shop. Her sisters, Aunty Sunbo and Aunty Ifeoma, crossing their arms on the chairs beside her. Ada in the front row.

Qasim Mahmood.

Baasim's mum and dad, Iqra's mum and dad, Awais' dad, Juveria and Noor's mum and dad . . .

The aunties, only arguing about small things, and beaming when they saw me. They threw their thumbs up. I beamed back. And I was glad when the chair at the end of their row was left empty. Just by coincidence. But someone else had usually sat there, hadn't they? With their walking stick nestled under their wrinkled hands, their googly glasses picking up on all of the errors at our town's council meeting?

Meet me at the hospital after your meeting, Mum had texted that morning. The result of Nani's operation – the doctors' desperate attempts to fix the bleeding in her brain – would be known very soon.

OK, I'd texted back.

It shocked me, the extra vibration of my phone afterwards. A kiss. I smiled. I sent one back.

I really hoped Nani would be able to take her place in that chair again soon.

The very front row was left empty. For the local MP, and the mayor, and the council members. I pictured the mayor, and the thick red robe she wore for these sorts of occasions, and the heavy gold chain that glinted expensively around her throat.

'I can do this, can't I?' I said. I watched Kemi's eyes go big at the size of our audience. Amir used the hem of his hoodie to waft a breeze over himself. 'I can talk in front of all of these people, can't I?'

'Well,' PC Chris said uncertainly, like he wasn't sure if it was appropriate for him to say this or not, 'you've survived a lot worse.'

'It has always been incredibly important to us that those that share our hometown know exactly how much we appreciate their community, whether they live in the rural and tame north of Friesly or the industrial and wild south of Friesly.'

The girl in the dungarees paused for laughter here.

She got a little bit of it, too. From her peers – the blond boy in the glasses and the girl with ginger hair, who smiled their tame north Friesly smiles towards the very front row. And from the front row itself, whose members seemed to carry themselves in the same tame way, ears pricking confidently and calmly while the volunteers from north Friesly carried on.

'It has been a privilege to participate in the Volunteering4Friesly scheme. We have learnt exactly what it means to be a part of this community – in words and in actions.'

But hadn't Nani always told me and Mum about the people in the front row? How they sat so comfortably while the lines at the Job Centre grew longer and the youth centre shut down?

Then there was the metallic taste in our water supply.

The empty buildings on our side of town.

The state of the falling-apart cemetery by the river.

While the north hosted the Barker Summer Festival. While the north invested in tourism and grew stable within the sight of guided tours and the green of the moors.

Nani's wallet was a welcome weight in my pocket, the receipt with all the confirmed donations sweet as the peach pits I used to carry in my dress after Nani had halved the fruits for me.

'Friesly deserves to have people who care. Friesly deserves to have people who will do the hard work of picking up litter on the streets, not speeding down them. Cleaning the graffiti off the glass of a bus shelter, not doing the graffiti in the first place . . .'

Kemi, Amir and I glanced at each other, fast as a sleep twitch. Then we turned to PC Chris. He shook his head, waving his hand dismissively. *Leave it. Leave it alone.*

I pictured Nani sitting down in our kitchen, exhausted from the walk home from these meetings, after already being exhausted from waiting for a gap to speak in. She had a plan for a collaboration with Friesly Grand Mosque, an idea to share, a way to prove there was a sense of community in this town. If someone would listen, that is. I could make sure they would. I planned to.

Outside, rain began to fall. It felt so strange to hear. New and needed after so many months of wishing for it. An August downpour.

It was the only sound that was louder than the girl in the dungarees, the murmuring agreement of the front row in the town hall's biggest conference room.

But then there was another noise.

A tinkling sound, like bric-a-brac rattling around in boxes.

And then, the sound of skin meeting wood, of hands pushing easily against the weight of those doors, a surge of faces wandering in with cardboard boxes stacked high with toothpaste and toothbrushes, tuna cans and soup, socks, jumpers, gloves, leave-in conditioner, shampoo . . .

'This is the place to leave the donations for the homeless, isn't it?' a woman I'd spoken to on the phone earlier that day said. 'I'm not getting that wrong, am I?'

I didn't notice the uncomfortable silence in the room until I was the one breaking it.

'This is the place!' I said, ignoring the way PC Phillips was glaring at me. 'You can leave them at the back of the room. We'll figure out a way to make the care packages from all of your donations later. Thank you!'

Our donating neighbours moved quickly, depositing box after box, taking up so much of the room within the town hall's largest conference room that after a little while, PC Chris had to take the girl with the dungarees' microphone from her and ask everyone to stand up and move their chairs forward.

'I'm sorry, but what on earth is going on here?' the MP said, circling in on PC Phillips' rigid back, her stuttering, stammering mouth.

'Yes,' a councilwoman chimed in. 'This is supposed to be a celebration of the Volunteering4Friesly scheme, isn't it?'

Their frowns, together with the murmuring conversations that broke out in the front-facing rows, only worsened PC Phillips' state of anxiety.

I didn't pay attention to any of it though.

There were still a lot of people coming up the town hall's twenty stone steps with their donations. There were a lot of faces who needed confirmation from me, Kemi, Amir and the aunties that this was indeed the right place to leave them.

'I ... They ... Chris!' PC Phillips flushed ten different shades of red this time. She grabbed on to PC Chris's shoulder with real vigour, ignoring the gasps coming from the audience.

'Didn't I tell you to control your kids? Look at them! Look at this chaos! I know they're responsible –'

The mayor of Friesly rose from her seat with all the charm and poise that Nani had always rolled her eyes at.

'They are, are they?' she said softly. 'Those three individuals are responsible for this?' The mayor of Friesly clapped her hands together. 'How wonderful! A true example of community spirit organized by ...' The mayor rested a quizzical finger on her bottom lip. 'By?'

'Eman Malik,' PC Chris said, smiling at my reddening face.

'And my grandma!' I said. 'Maariyah Malik.'

Then I looked around, to where the aunties sat asking one another if they'd heard what the mayor said, and to where Kemi and Amir were trying not to laugh, and to where PC Chris was trying to avoid PC Phillips' deadly gaze.

'And my friends. Kemi and Amir.'

'That's all very nice, Eman,' PC Phillips said, cutting across the floor to nudge the girl in the dungarees towards the microphone stand, 'but I believe we were in the middle of something very important.'

I wanted to say this was important too. I was about to. But a series of noises at the big oak doors forced all of our attention away again. A faint *rap-rap-rap* sound coming from outside. A *knock-knock-knock*ing.

Like someone had been left out in the rain, and was desperate to come inside, and couldn't open those heavy oak doors all by themselves.

Well, everyone who'd confirmed they'd donate to Nani's homelessness project had already shown up, hadn't they?

Kemi, Amir and I glanced at each other.

Behind us, PC Chris looked just as confused as the shifting back row did, his eyebrows furrowed, his mouth a little open.

'Just ignore it,' PC Phillips said, the lines around her mouth deepening in displeasure. 'Carry on with your speech.'

'Um . . .' The girl faltered, clearly flustered by PC Phillips' impatient tone. She rifled through her notes. 'W-where was I?'

But the *rap-rap-rap* continued. And then I heard it: the quietest 'Please . . . Please . . .'

'It's Danny *Dangar*,' I said to Kemi and Amir, thinking of his slippers all sodden with the downpour, his carrier bags, his tired loping legs. 'It's Danny, out on his own in the rain. We can't just leave him out in the rain, can we?'

Then I realized I must've spoken louder than I'd intended to, because suddenly the girl in the dungarees, and PC Phillips, and the mayor, and everyone was looking at me.

'The local drug addict,' someone in the front row murmured, and the communal 'Ah' in response resulted only in the mayor urging the girl in the dungarees to carry on. She nodded, hesitant, still fussing with her notes.

But the *rap-rap-rap* kept going. The 'please ... please ...' continued as Danny *Dangar* paced back and forth at the very top of the twenty stone steps.

Suddenly, all of the people in the front-facing rows were turning around. The people sitting on the floor, the ones leaning back, with their ankles crossed over one another, were too. The itch to move, to do something to help, spread far and wide within the town hall's largest conference room.

It was there in Kemi and Amir's twitching limbs. In the aunties' restless movements. In Howard Li's confident walk. In Marta Varga's whirling body. In the way PC Chris's black boots strode over the wooden floorboards. And it was visible in Kemi's family. And in Amir's family. In Qasim Mahmood. In Baasim's mum and dad, Iqra's mum and dad, Awais' dad, Juveria and Noor's mum and dad.

And in the girl in the dungarees, the boy with the glasses, the one with the ginger hair.

The girl in the dungarees nodded at me, catching my eye

despite PC Phillips' protestations. 'Community, right?' she said. 'We look out for each other.'

I nodded back. 'We do.'

All of us listening to the sound of Danny *Dangar*'s shuffling. All of us desperate to let him in.

There was always someone who moved quicker than everyone else, wasn't there? In the history of my family, in the record of a small village in Mirpur, Pakistan. I imagined she was there, urging me along with the familiar tapping of her walking stick, her odd-one-out leg, as I went to open the big oak doors. Behind me stood a crowd of people desperate to do the same.

I smiled to myself. I watched as several people stood up to let Danny *Dangar* have his seat. It occurred to me in that moment that I carried Nani everywhere with me. It occurred to me that she was everywhere I was.

But I still ran to her side after the ceremony in the town hall's largest conference room was over.

I knew I had to tell Nani about what had happened. The mayor, our community, Danny *Dangar* . . . I knew I had to explain to her what had come back to me, in whispers and smiles and snatches of conversation on my way out of the town hall. I was my grandmother's granddaughter. And she'd always moved fast, hadn't she? My nani? Despite her shorter leg? So I could, too. With my slow ones, my washing machine number twelve soul.

The dream was far behind me now. The fear of it. The shadow that came with feeling left behind. I remembered it well though. I guess because Kemi and Amir's trainers were a lot quieter than the sound of loud Pakistani chappals, smacking against some villagers' cracked heels. And the streetlamps switching on around the place I knew like the back of my hand gave off a brighter light than any weak oil lamp. And any background beautiful *athaan* came from some rushing car's radio. But I still cried, mid-run, when I heard them. I still cried, moving so fast against the pavement, the road, to the hospital.

I was my grandmother's granddaughter. I could cross a patch of green, a bad dream, a hopeless feeling, like she always had.

'Nani,' I sang, with the drag of my lungs, the rhythm of my legs. 'Nani.'

GLOSSARY

Alhamdulillah: An Islamic term from the original Arabic that translates as 'praise be to God'.

Alif, beh, ain, ghain: Figures of the Arabic alphabet that are used to recite from the Holy Qur'an.

Aloo gobi: A dish with origins in Pakistan and India that is made with potatoes, cauliflower and turmeric.

Angrazey: An informal term popular with Urdu, Punjabi, Hindi and Mirpuri speakers that loosely translates as 'English'.

Apa: An Islamic term from the original Arabic that translates as 'teacher'.

Assalamu alaykum: An Islamic expression of greeting from the original Arabic that translates as 'may peace be upon you'.

Astaghfirullah: An Islamic term from the original Arabic that translates as 'I seek forgiveness from God' or 'I turn to Him in repentance'.

Athaan: The Islamic call to prayer that is played five times a day to beckon worshippers.

Atta: A term with origins in Pakistan and India that refers to grain flour.

Baji: A term with origins in Pakistan and India that loosely translates as 'sister'.

Baloona: A term with origins in Pakistan and India that loosely translates as 'whirlwind'.

Bayji: A term with origins in Pakistan and India that loosely translates as 'grandma' or 'elderly woman'.

Besharam: A term with origins in Pakistan and India that loosely translates as 'shameless' or 'bad mannered'.

Chaat: A dish with origins in Pakistan and India that is made with yogurt, savoury snacks, onions, chickpeas and various garnishes.

Challo: A term with origins in Pakistan and India that loosely translates as 'let's go' or 'oh well', depending on the context of the conversation.

Channa: A dish with origins in Pakistan and India that predominantly consists of chickpeas.

Chappals: A term with origins in Pakistan and India that refers to a type of shoe.

Chaval: A dish with origins in Pakistan and India that is made with rice, potatoes and occasionally meat.

Choori dar: A style of Pakistani fashion consisting of a long dress and tight-fitting trousers.

Churayl: A term with origins in Pakistan and India tat translates as 'witch'.

Daal: A dish with origins in Pakistan and India that is made with lentils and spices.

Dangar: A pejorative term with origins in Pakistan and India that calls to mind a donkey, service animals or cattle.

Desi: Of South Asian origin or descent.

Desi nashta: An informal term with origins in Pakistan and India that translates as 'South Asian breakfast'.

Dupatta: A term with origins in Pakistan and India that refers to a scarf worn loosely over the head and neck.

Fajr: The Islamic term for the morning prayer.

Falooda: A sweet drink delicacy with origins in Pakistan and India, made with rose syrup, vermicelli, sweet basil seeds, milk and ice cream.

Gori: A term with origins in Pakistan and India that translates as 'white woman' or 'fair-skinned woman'.

Gosht: A term with origins in Pakistan and India that refers to the cooking of meat including beef, lamb, mutton, chicken or goat.

Gulab jamun: A sweet delicacy with origins in Pakistan and India, made by deep-frying dough and boiling in a sugar syrup.

Halal: The Islamic term for 'permissible' or 'allowed'.

Halwa puri: A traditional Pakistani and Indian breakfast that features semolina pudding (or halwa) and a soft fried dough (or puri).

Haram: The Islamic term for 'impermissible' or 'forbidden'.

Inshallah: An Islamic term from the original Arabic that translates as 'God willing'.

Jahannum: The Islamic term for hell.

Jannah: The Islamic term for heaven.

Jalebi: A sweet delicacy with origins in Pakistan and India, made of cornflour and fried in oil.

Janglee: A term with origins in Pakistan and India that refers to a wild person or uncivilized individual.

Jilbab: The Islamic term for a full-length outer garment, covering the head and hands, worn in public by some Muslim women.

Jinn: From Islamic folklore and mythology, an intelligent spirit of lower rank than the angels, able to appear o and possess humans.

Jollof rice: A dish with origins in Nigeria and other countries in West Africa that is made with rice, tomatoes, onions and peppers, and can include meat within it.

Karak chai: Strong, spicy tea originating in Pakistan and India.

Kasmey: A term with origins in Pakistan that loosely translates as 'I swear'.

Kava: A herbal tea with origins in Pakistan and India.

Khala: A term with origins in Pakistan and India that translates as 'aunty'.

Khousey: A term with origins in Pakistan and India that refers to a style of shoe resembling slippers, usually handmade, and embroidered with ceramic beads.

Kutha: A term with origins in Pakistan and India that translates as 'dog'.

Lehenga: A term with origins in Pakistan and India that refers to an ankle-length skirt and blouse ensemble that is heavily embroidered and worn for formal occasions.

Maghrib: The Islamic term for the evening prayer.

Mano: A popular term with origins in Pakistan that translates as 'cat'.

Mashallah: An Islamic term from the original Arabic that translates as 'what God has willed', used to praise and admire.

Mithai: A sweet delicacy with origins in Pakistan and India, made of flour, milk and sugar.

Nishaan: A term with origins in Pakistan and India that loosely translates as 'symbol', 'signifier' or 'mark'.

Paapu: A term with origins in Pakistan and India that loosely translates as 'older brother'.

Pagal: A term with origins in Pakistan and India that loosely translates as 'crazy' or 'insane'.

Pakorey: Spiced fritters originating in Pakistan and India.

Paratha: A flatbread with origins in Pakistan and India that is made with flour and butter.

Pindiya: A dish with origins in Pakistan and India that is made with okra.

Puff-puff: A sweet delicacy with origins in Nigeria and other countries in West Africa, which is made with butter, eggs and flour and fried in oil.

Puri: A small round cake of unleavened wheat flour deep fried in ghee or oil.

Raita: A cold side-dish consisting of yogurt and finely chopped vegetables.

Saag aloo: A dish with origins in Pakistan and India that is made with spinach and potato.

Sabzi: A catch-all term with origins in Pakistan and India for any vegetable dish.

Salaam: The Islamic term for greeting a fellow Muslim with a handshake while uttering 'Peace be upon you'.

Salan: A dish with origins in Pakistan and India that is made with chicken, garam masala, ginger, tomatoes and onions.

Shaitan: The Islamic term for the devil.

Shalwar kameez: A term with origins in Pakistan and India that refers to traditional dress of *shalwar* (pyjama-like trousers) and *kameez* (a long shirt or tunic).

Sherwani: A term with origins in Pakistan and India that refers to a formal knee-length coat buttoning to the neck, typically worn by men.

Soorna: A term with origins in the Mirpuri community that refers to pigs or pig-like creatures.

Subhanallah: An Islamic term from the original Arabic that translates as 'Glory to God' or 'God is perfect'.

Sunnah: An Islamic term for the manners and habits of the Prophet (Peace be upon him).

Tarka: A cooking term used in Pakistani and Indian cuisine in order to temper spices in oil.

Tava: A circular griddle used in South Asia, especially for cooking rotis.

Topi: A hat or cap typically worn by practising Muslims.

Wudhu: The Islamic term for the process of washing the body before engaging in prayer.

Yara: A term with origins in Pakistan and India which loosely translates as 'friend'.

ACKNOWLEDGEMENTS

It's true what they say: a writer never forgets a single supportive comment made towards them on the subject of their work. I certainly never have. It took me eight years to write this novel, to truly understand the secrets and winding streets of Friesly. I am grateful beyond words to my village of family, friends, and loved ones who encouraged me to finish the story. Now I'll do my best to put down some words to capture the kindnesses and debt I feel towards this village.

I am thankful to my agent, Claire Wilson, who saw the potential in Eman, Amir, and Kemi and took a chance on me to write them well. I am also thankful to the team at Penguin who rallied around Friesly with such warmth: Sara Jafari, Natalie Doherty, Michael Bedo, Shreeta Shah, and Catherine Alport.

I would not be the person that I am today without the support of my family: I cannot ever repay my mama, Samina Ansar, who bought me my first books, let me take my laptop into the garden, and found me shady spots to sit in whenever I needed them. Equally, I cannot ever repay my baba, Major

Ansar Hamid, who asked about the progress of my writing every week, and never questioned my bedroom light still being on in the night. I am blessed to have siblings that recognize my passions: Ayesha, you are my first best friend, who read all of my first poems and stories and told me I was good enough to write even more. I aim to make you proud every day. Rabiah, you are my second best friend, who reminded and continue to remind me to take breaks and be luxurious. You created mood boards with such care and affection. Thank you for your love. Ahmed, you are my third best friend, who made me laugh, continue to make me laugh and understand when I am being intensely, extremely, very serious about intense, extreme, very serious things. I could never be as chaotic with anyone as I am with you.

My bayji, baji, nana, and nani remind me every day that service to others is the rent we pay for existing on this earth. Mirpur and Azad Kashmir are not secrets to be ashamed of but facts of my heritage to be truly proud of. My nephew Zakariya also reminds me every day to have more fun, be more destructive, love others a little harder. This is the virtue of youth.

Still, it was nauseatingly awkward and always a little embarrassing to be as sensitive and headstrong as I was when I was a teenager. Thank you to my English teachers, Donna Welford and Stephanie Lamping, who encouraged my opinions and let me stand up to read my work during our English lessons. You taught me so much – but especially to value who I am. I am extremely lucky to have learnt the value of an English teacher through both of your examples.

It was also nauseatingly awkward and always a little embarrassing to continue to be as sensitive and headstrong as

I was when I attended university. Thank you to my supervisors at Murray Edwards College, Cambridge: Raphael Lyne, Leo Mellor, and Jenny Bavidge.

I am indebted to the editors who decided to commission my freelance writing at *NME*, *BuzzFeed UK*, *gal-dem*, *Rookie*, and beyond. I am particularly indebted to the community at *Buzzfeed UK*, back in 2017: Ailbhe Malone, Tolani Shoneye, Aisha Gani, Victoria Sanusi, and Ikran Dahir. With special thanks to Chelsey Pippin-Mizzi, who took me under her wing and introduced me to the literary world with such kindness. Thank you also to the folks behind the At Sea writing residency in Margate: Ryan Bowman and Alice Bowman. With special thanks to the staff and students at Mercia School, whose kindness and support shaped so much of the final rewrites of this novel.

I am so extremely blessed to be witness to the whims and personalities of so many generous, hilarious individuals – and deeply privileged to be able to call them my friends. To those who read early drafts and offered me their opinion, thank you. To those who texted me and met with me exactly when I needed your kind company and laughter, thank you. It means a lot to be able to rely on your support: Jessica Sandoval, Kim Choong, Sabina Begum, Nimrah Malik, Arenike Adebajo, Tasnia Begum, Phoebe Thomson, Raisa Islam, Charlotte Petter, Mehj Ahmed, Francesca Castelo, Milly Winston-Jacques, Maddie Smith, Harriet Lowes-Belk, and Saiqua Parveen. Thank you also to Moharem El Gihani for the steadfast support and writerly curiosity over the years. I truly appreciate it.

Thank you to my students. I love teaching you. And to those I no longer teach – who wonder if I remember you, if I miss our lessons together, if I reminisce about our chats at breakfast, or breaktime, or lunch – I do. You taught me more than you know.

Alhamdulillah. Any goodness seen within this text or my abilities is a reflection of His strength and His abilities. All praise is to Him.